He would have to make his own way. Maybe there was some cattle ranch up the way that needed an able-bodied hand. Or a newly established town that could use help with building a schoolhouse or a church.

Even in his drunken state, he was already doubting the wisdom of his hasty decision. He knew the army pay he'd managed to save wasn't going to last long. And while hiding out in Mexico for a time was possible, making it his home wasn't an option worthy of consideration.

Once again, he'd made himself a fine mess. He'd done it often enough as Cal Breckenridge, and now was about to do the same as Will Darby.

He rode on until dark, swaying in the saddle. His empty tequila bottle had been tossed into the Rio Grande some miles back.

Making camp on the sandy bank of the river, he managed to remove the saddle from his horse and tether him to a scrub mesquite. Without even bothering to remove his boots, Will stretched out on the saddle blanket and was immediately lost in a drunken sleep, his restless dreams mixed with bloody war battles and boyhood memories of happy times spent with his brother, Clay. They were still young, chasing fireflies near the house, laughing as they ran.

Then the dreams turned into a real nightmare. Someone was kicking at him and cursing. When he opened his eyes, he saw the huge form of a man dressed in buckskins pointing a pistol at his face. Two others stood nearby, toothless grins on their tobacco-stained faces.

"Get to your feet," the man with the pistol said, "and show us where your money is. I'd advise you do it quick."

RALPH COMPTON

REUNION IN HELL

A Ralph Compton Western by
CARLTON STOWERS

BERKLEY
New York

BERKLEY
An imprint of Penguin Random House LLC
penguinrandomhouse.com

Copyright © 2020 by The Estate of Ralph Compton
Penguin Random House supports copyright. Copyright fuels creativity, encourages
diverse voices, promotes free speech, and creates a vibrant culture. Thank you for buying
an authorized edition of this book and for complying with copyright laws by not
reproducing, scanning, or distributing any part of it in any form without permission.
You are supporting writers and allowing Penguin Random House to continue to
publish books for every reader.

BERKLEY and the BERKLEY & B colophon are registered trademarks of
Penguin Random House LLC.

ISBN: 9780593100691

First Edition: April 2020

Printed in the United States of America
1 3 5 7 9 10 8 6 4 2

Cover art by Dennis Lyall
Cover design by Steve Meditz
Book design by George Towne

THE IMMORTAL COWBOY

This is respectfully dedicated to the "American Cowboy." His was the saga sparked by the turmoil that followed the Civil War, and the passing of more than a century has by no means diminished the flame.

———◆———

True, the old days and the old ways are but treasured memories, and the old trails have grown dim with the ravages of time, but the spirit of the cowboy lives on.

———◆———

In my travels—to Texas, Oklahoma, Kansas, Nebraska, Colorado, Wyoming, New Mexico, and Arizona—I always find something that reminds me of the Old West. While I am walking these plains and mountains for the first time, there is this feeling that a part of me is eternal, that I have known these old trails before. I believe it is the undying spirit of the frontier calling me, through the mind's eye, to step back into time. What is the appeal of the Old West of the American frontier?

———◆———

It has been epitomized by some as the dark and bloody period in American history. Its heroes—Crockett, Bowie, Hickok, Earp—have been reviled and criticized. Yet the Old West lives on, larger than life.

———◆———

It has become a symbol of freedom, when there was always another mountain to climb and another river to cross; when a dispute between two men was settled not with expensive lawyers, but with fists, knives, or guns. Barbaric? Maybe. But some things never change. When the cowboy rode into the pages of American history, he left behind a legacy that lives within the hearts of us all.

—*Ralph Compton*

PROLOGUE

May 1865

A MONTH HAD passed since Confederate general
Robert E. Lee surrendered, officially bringing an
end to the bloody war between North and South. As
word of the Union Army's victory spread, the disappointment that initially swept through the ranks of the
Confederacy was gradually turning to thoughts of going home, families, and peacetime.

The war and its cruelties were over; young men on
both sides could lay down their arms and cease being
soldiers.

In some cases, however, military units remained on
active duty despite the surrender and declarations of a
truce. An example could be found deep in South
Texas, where three hundred Confederate troops remained camped near the banks of the Rio Grande.
Their responsibility, as it had been in wartime, was to

protect the transportation of cotton to the seaport of Los Brazos de Santiago, near Brownsville.

Just to the north, most of the sixty-five hundred Union troops had been withdrawn, but Colonel Theodore Barrett remained in charge of five hundred soldiers who were also assigned to observe activities at the port.

For the ambitious Colonel Barrett, it was a tortuous, frustrating assignment. At age thirty, he had been an officer for three years but had yet to see combat. The attack on the Confederate encampment would be his last chance to achieve battlefield glory that might pave the way to a postwar promotion and a place in military history.

His planning left much to be desired. An attack that originated on the coastline and moved inland was initially successful, as a few prisoners and some supplies were captured. But by the end of the day, a hundred Confederate cavalrymen had driven the Union soldiers back.

Both sides summoned reinforcements in preparation for another day of battle.

In the Confederates' camp, disgruntled soldiers sat in their tents, some drinking coffee, some from bottles of tequila purchased from Mexican soldiers across the river in Matamoros. Among them were brothers from Aberdene, a small community in East Texas. They had joined when a recruiter had visited the family farm.

The two young men, quickly assigned to the Texas Cavalry Battalion, were as different as family members could be.

Clay, the elder by two years, was a man of quiet inner strength and self-reliance. As a soldier, he followed orders without hesitation or question.

Cal, on the other hand, was headstrong, often reckless, and outspoken. He was among the soldiers drinking tequila.

"I'm of a mind to saddle my horse and take leave of this godforsaken place," he said. "We're told the war's over, that we've done lost and surrendered. Yet here we are in another battle. My question is, why? And what for?"

He took another drink. "What is likely to happen tomorrow when we resume our shooting is that I'll be killing some of those Yankee no-goods—or one of them will manage to aim well enough to see me shot dead. It's my observation that neither option carries much logic. The . . . war . . . is . . . *over*!"

Clay sat cross-legged, drawing circles in the dirt as his brother spoke. He knew what Cal had in mind and that trying to convince him otherwise was futile. Before daylight, his brother would be miles away from what remained of the fighting.

By dawn, as preparations were underway for the second day of battle, the younger Breckenridge had saddled his horse, crossed the Rio Grande into Mexico, and was traveling east. As he'd written in the note he'd left for his brother, he had no particular destination in mind.

He wrote:

All I'm of a mind to do now is to put me a good amount of distance from soldiering. I've took all the orders I can stand. I hope you will stay safe and return home soon. Pa will welcome you and the help you can be to him on the farm. Give him my love though I doubt he'll much care.

> *Your brother,*
> *Cal*

P.S. I'd have wrote this better if I'd had more time and wasn't so drunk.

* * *

NOTHING THE UNION soldiers attempted during the second day worked. An attack from the right flank failed. So did a frontal assault. The Confederates had borrowed artillery from the French and Mexican armies in Matamoros and prepared to make their stand on the edge of a place called Palmito Ranch.

By late in the afternoon, Colonel Barrett's troops were caught in a trap laid by the Confederate cavalry near the Rio Grande. Barrett ordered his forces to retreat after setting up a skirmish line of men to slow the approach of the mounted Confederates.

For those ordered to form a line and aim their rifles on the fast-approaching enemy, it was a suicide mission. And one quickly abandoned. As the Confederate horsemen came closer, the Union soldiers left their assigned position and ran before a single shot was fired.

As Clay Breckenridge approached, however, his attention was drawn to a single Union soldier who stood his ground. Their eyes met for an instant, and Clay thought he saw a faint look of resignation on the enemy soldier's face as he lifted his rifle and prepared to shoot. It was as if he had accepted the fact of his own death even before Breckenridge aimed his pistol.

The shot struck the Union soldier high in the chest. His rifle dropped to his side as he slumped to his knees, then pitched forward into the sand. Death came quickly.

It was not the first life Breckenridge had taken during battle, but it was the last—and the one that would remain with him. It would define his entire war experience, with all of its dark questions, haunting regrets, and troubling memories.

Referring to the two days of fighting as the Battle of Palmito Ranch, the *Galveston News* reported that it was probably the final confrontation of the Civil War. The reason for the post-surrender Union attack remained a mystery. Several soldiers on both sides had been wounded, but there was only one casualty reported.

"One Union soldier, Private John Jefferson Williams of the 34th Indiana Infantry, was killed," the story read. "He is likely to be the last battle fatality of the Civil War."

The article made no mention that it was Clay Breckenridge who had fired the shot that killed Private Williams, which suited him fine. It was not a moment in history he was proud to have been a part of.

PART ONE

—— ◇ ——

CLAY'S STORY

CHAPTER ONE

CLAY BRECKENRIDGE STOOD on his front porch, drinking coffee as he looked out on the fog that had swept across the bottoms overnight. The morning plowing he had planned would have to wait until he and his team of mules would be better able to see their way. He reached down and stroked the hindquarters of his dog, Sarge. "Appears we're gonna be getting a late start," he said.

It wasn't that he felt any great urgency. The East Texas farm, which his family had staked claim to when he and his brother were just youngsters, was small. The plowing for spring planting amounted to only twenty acres of grain and corn to feed his livestock and a garden spot for raising vegetables. The rest was open grassland interrupted by a large stand of pecan trees that were home to wild turkeys and squirrels. Along the southern boundary was a shallow spring-fed creek that provided ample watering for his mules, a small herd of cattle, a few goats, and his horse.

A quiet and picturesque spot, it had been Clay's home all of his life, except for the time he left to fight for the Confederate Army. After the war ended, he immediately returned to help his aging father with the farm. And when Ed Breckenridge followed his wife in death, the elder son dutifully assumed responsibility for maintaining the farm.

Sarge was still wagging his tail when he lifted his ears to acknowledge a distant sound that was, at first, too faint for his master to hear. Only as it got closer could Clay determine that it was likely an approaching horse, moving slowly and with strained effort.

Though there had been no problems with renegade bands of Comanches recently, Clay hurried into the cabin to get his rifle. "Might be somebody's just lost his way," he said, "or a horse that broke loose and can't figure where he's at."

Sarge responded with a low growl.

Minutes later Breckenridge detected a dark shadow just beyond the yard. Moving in the direction of the barn, it appeared to float through the bank of fog. Clay grabbed his rifle and a lantern and hurried toward it, Sarge trotting at his side.

Inside the barn stood a horse that Clay immediately recognized. It was nibbling at a bundle of hay while favoring a badly swollen front leg. Tied atop its saddle was a body.

For several seconds Clay stood motionless, staring at the dead man, bloated and discolored, a pattern of dried blood indicating that he had been shot in the back.

Breckenridge finally set his rifle and lantern aside and slowly began to loosen the ropes that held the rider in place. After he pulled the rigid corpse from the saddle, the weary horse shook his mane and limped away.

Looking down at the body that he had placed on a bed of hay, Clay suddenly felt his legs give way and his breathing turn to rapid bursts. He covered the dead man with a saddle blanket, then sat beside him and gently stroked his matted hair. Sarge nuzzled his master and softly whined.

This was not the way Clay had hoped his younger brother would return home.

CHAPTER TWO

I T WAS NEARING midday when Clay arrived in Aberdene and pulled his wagon to a stop in front of the marshal's office. Behind him, Cal Breckenridge's body lay beneath a blanket. Sarge had ridden along, standing sentry on the journey into town.

Dodge Rankin, a short, portly man with a salt-and-pepper beard and a warm smile for any and all who did not violate the law, had served as marshal for over a decade. Tamping his pipe against the hitching rail, he acknowledged the arrival of his visitor. "Your timing's perfect," he said. "I just got back from Ralph Giddens' place, where some of his cattle got rustled during the night. Indians from up in the Territory, be my guess. Been some time since I've seen you."

The somber look from Clay made it obvious to the marshal that small talk was not in order. Stepping from the board sidewalk, he approached the wagon bed and lifted the blanket to view the swollen face of the young man, who was barely recognizable.

"This who I'm thinking it is?" Rankin said.

Clay nodded.

"Best come into my office, where we can talk. I'll send someone to fetch Doc Franklin so he can begin tending to the necessary matters."

Inside, Clay was recounting the morning's events when the doctor arrived, short of breath, his round face flushed. Darwin Franklin was Aberdene's only doctor, undertaker, and veterinarian. On any given day, he might deliver a baby, treat a cow whose milk had mysteriously turned sour, or help a grieving resident select a coffin.

"I'm sorry for you misery, Mr. Breckenridge," the doctor said. "Rest assured I'll fix him up properly. Have you given any thought to funeral plans?"

"No," Clay replied. "No funeral." In truth, he could not think of anyone who might attend. Too, his brother had never cared for preaching and hymn singing. "Once you've tended him and seen to a sturdy coffin, I'll be putting him to rest back on the farm, alongside our folks." Then, as an afterthought: "Soon as possible I'd appreciate you coming out to check on his horse that arrived lame and in some degree of pain. I'd prefer to avoid putting him down if at all possible."

"I can be there early tomorrow morning," Dr. Franklin said. "Meanwhile, it might be of use for you to start putting some warm rags on the horse's leg to reduce the swelling."

Rankin watched the doctor leave before returning the conversation to the death of Cal Breckenridge. "I can't recall seeing young Cal since you boys were getting ready to go off and fight against the Union," he said. "You seen or heard from him much lately?"

Clay shook his head.

"Got any thoughts on who might be responsible for this?"

Though Clay didn't immediately answer, the marshal was already certain that the list of suspects might well be lengthy. A close friend of the boys' father from the time his children were young, Rankin knew many of the troubles Cal had caused his old friend. Ed Breckenridge had occasionally shared his worries with the marshal when they were fishing together and drinking persimmon beer. The father could never understand what caused the anger and rebellion that so darkened the soul of one son while the other was kindhearted and loving.

There was a troubling meanness in Cal. He picked fights, drunk or sober, and had no friends aside from his older brother. He wasn't above stealing now and then, rarely pulled his weight at chore time, and showed little respect for his elders.

When he joined the Confederate Army along with Clay, Ed allowed himself hope that the discipline of military service might provide the maturity his son so badly needed. Instead, his heart was broken when he learned that Cal had deserted.

Thereafter, Ed Breckenridge never again spoke his younger son's name.

"Bein' as we don't know from which direction his horse might have come or how far he traveled," the marshal said, "it's likely to be difficult determining responsibility for your brother's killing. But you've got my God-honest word I'll be asking questions. And if you think of anyone I might need to speak to, just let me know."

Clay stared at the floor as the marshal spoke. "Somebody will pay for what's been done," he said, his voice barely a whisper yet filled with a resolve Marshal Rankin had never before heard from the man seated across from him.

* * *

A GRAVE HAD been dug in the grove near the creek by the time the hearse arrived. Clay was in the barn, applying heat packs to the leg of his brother's horse when Dr. Franklin called out.

Joining him on the trip to the farm was Jonesy Pate.

"Just so you know," Pate said, "I invited myself to ride along after Doc here told me what has taken place. Figured you fellas might could use a hand with the lifting and burying." A rancher and Breckenridge's nearest neighbor, he and Clay had been friends since boyhood days. He'd been in town, having breakfast in the hotel dining room, when he'd overheard the doctor talking about Cal's death.

Silently and with little ceremony, the men lifted the wooden casket from the hearse and lowered it into the grave. While Clay and Jonesy shoveled dirt, the doctor headed to the barn to examine the lame horse.

Once the burial was complete, Jonesy leaned against a tree trunk, studying his friend. Clay had read no scripture nor said a prayer once his brother had been laid to rest.

"What are you thinking?" Jonesy asked. "You've been mighty quiet."

As they walked toward the barn, Clay reached into his pocket and withdrew a folded two-dollar note he'd removed from his brother's body before taking it to town. He handed it to Jonesy, who unfolded and read the message scrawled on it.

Will Darby was a no-good coward. . . .

"Who do you reckon Will Darby might be?" Jonesy asked.

"My brother. It's a name he took after he left the Confederates. He wrote me about it sometime back so I'd know the name he was using and his whereabouts. I wrote him a letter, telling him of Pa's failing health and urging him to pay a visit. But he never showed."

"Got any notion what this note's about?"

Clay shook his head. "Only that somebody had a powerful grudge against him and appears to want the world to know about it."

"You tell Marshal Rankin about it?"

"I got no reason to think the note was for the marshal's benefit."

Doc Franklin was rubbing liniment onto the horse's leg when they entered the barn. "The heat you've been applying has helped with the swelling enough so that we can put on a splint," he said. "I'm guessing he done damage to ligaments, most likely stepping in a gopher hole.

"I think there's a good chance the leg will heal to a point that he'll be able to walk without a problem, but should you choose to keep him, he'll not be of much use for anything except eating and keeping the mares company."

Clay stepped forward and stroked the animal's neck. "Then I reckon that's the future he's got to look ahead to," he said. "My brother thought highly of this horse. Raised him from a colt. And I figure the horse loved him back. When the need came, it was him who brought my brother home."

After the doctor left, Clay and Jonesy sat on a bench outside the barn, silently facing the warm sunlight as it peeked through the limbs of the distant pecan trees.

It was Clay who finally spoke. "I'm wondering," he said, "if you might consider doing me a favor."

"Whatever you need."

"I might be away for a spell and was wondering if

you could spare one of your hands to come over and see to things here on the farm—keep doctoring Cal's horse, feed the stock, keep my dog company, things of that nature. I've got calf money set aside, so I can afford to pay a fair wage."

"I expect I could spare old Ruben. He's a hard worker and honest, just not much at cowboying anymore, truth be known. When do you think you'll be needing him?"

"Soon," Clay said. "Maybe a couple of days from now."

"Then I'll bring him over day after tomorrow so you can tell him what it is you'll be wanting him to see to," Jonesy said as he rose to leave.

Clay walked with him to where he'd tethered his horse. As his friend climbed into the saddle, he buried his hands into his hip pockets.

"You know," he said, "my brother wasn't near as bad as most folks believe."

CHAPTER THREE

Smoke had just begun to lazily curl from the cabin's chimney when Jonesy Pate and Ruben arrived at the Breckenridge farm. Ruben was leading a pack-horse.

"We're wasting daylight," Jonesy called out as Clay stepped from the barn and pulled his hat tight against his head. "I got no idea where it is we're going or how long you figure it's gonna take us to get there, but until we get on our way—"

"We?" Clay turned his puzzled look from Jonesy to the packhorse. He saw bedrolls, a couple of rifles, saddle-bags no doubt filled with foodstuff, and a couple of canteens.

"Don't want you getting lost or lonesome," Jonesy said, "so I made up my mind to go with you." He'd known from the first time Breckenridge spoke of his brother's death that he was determined to find who-ever killed Cal. And apparently he had some idea of where to look. Pate had doubts that it was a mission his friend would be able to accomplish alone. Despite his military service, Clay was a farmer, not a fighter. "No need for arguing. You get on with telling Ruben here what it is you'll be needing him to do in your absence. Then we can be on our way."

Resigned, Clay smiled. "I'll be grateful for your company."

"Want to inform me what direction we'll be heading?" Jonesy dismounted and began petting Sarge.

"West. Out to a place called Tascosa," Clay replied. "Least that's where I'm of a mind to start asking questions. When I last heard from Cal, his letter came from there. It's a resting stop for cattle drivers and buffalo hunters. My impression is it ain't exactly a peaceful place to visit. What we'll do is just follow the Red River the better part of the way. In time we'll be up on the high plains. Somewhere up there is Tascosa."

As he spoke, Ruben stood nearby like a soldier awaiting orders. Clay waved him toward the barn. Inside, he first took the old cowhand to the stall where Cal's horse waited.

"*Es* a beautiful horse," Ruben said.

Clay showed him the salve he was to rub on the bay's injured leg. "He's improved considerably, so I'm thinking maybe you can lead him out into the pasture of a morning so he can graze for an hour or two every day. Sunshine and fresh air will do him good."

As he showed his spread to Ruben, it was obvious that Breckenridge was proud of his place. The barn and the pens housing pigs, goats, and laying hens were stoutly built. Tools were stored in an orderly fashion. There was no disrepair or neglect to be seen. "About all that'll need doing is to keep the animals fed and watered," Clay said. "As for your own needs, there's venison and beef in the smokehouse. In a bin out back of the cabin, there's sweet potatoes buried in straw, and the chickens lay eggs regular. In the kitchen you'll find necessaries like coffee, flour, and corn meal. In the cupboard is a half-full bottle of whiskey you're welcome to sip on if you're of a mind."

"*Muy bueno.* Your home is very nice. I will watch over it with much care."

Clay shook his hand. "If its suits you," he said, "we'll do our financial settling up when I get back. In the event you don't see me again, go to the bank in town and ask for Hector Wayne. He'll see you are paid what's owed you."

He began to walk toward the cabin, then stopped after a few steps. "One more thing. Of a night, Sarge is used to sleeping at the foot of the bed. And he's pretty set in his ways."

Ruben nodded. "We will be good friends," he said.

When Clay emerged from the cabin he had a saddlebag slung over one shoulder and at his hip was his old holster with CSA embossed on it. It was the first time Jonesy had ever seen his friend wearing a sidearm.

THEY TRAVELED ALONG the southern bank of the river for the first two days, the weather mild and the sky blue and cloudless. Then came a late-afternoon spring storm that turned the horizon black and forced them to quickly seek shelter from the approaching wind and rain.

They had just managed to urge their nervous horses under a hillside outcrop when the storm began. Loud peals of thunder and jagged bolts of lightning alternated as the storm's intensity grew.

While Breckenridge unsaddled the horses, Pate had managed to gather enough dry mesquite to build a fire. He set a pan outside their shelter, letting it fill with rainwater so he could brew coffee.

In time the storm calmed to a gentle rainfall, and Jonesy began to remove his clothes. "I'm past due my bath taking," he explained to his surprised companion as he stepped from the shelter of the rock overhang. "Bathing in the clean rain is a far sight better than in that muddy river," he said. Wearing only his hat, boots, and long johns, he danced in the rain, lifting his face to let the cool drops fall into his mouth.

For the first time in longer than he could remember, Clay laughed so hard, tears filled his eyes.

Jonesy was still doing his rain jig when there was a rustle in a stand of nearby bushes and a young boy suddenly stepped into the clearing. He looked to be fifteen, maybe sixteen, and was soaked and shivering. He stared silently at the near-naked man.

"I guess you ain't never before seen a growed man dancing in the rain," Jonesy said as he moved toward the youngster. "What is it that brings you out in such weather?"

The youngster pointed in the direction of the river. "Our wagon got washed away," he said.

Clay had hurried from his shelter as soon as he'd seen the boy and placed a blanket across his shoulders. "Come get by the fire and dry yourself," he said. "You got a name?"

"Lonnie."

With little prodding, the boy explained that his parents had left Kansas en route to a friend's ranch in far West Texas where jobs awaited. "Pa and me was gonna learn to do cowboying, and Ma was going to tend to the cooking and cleaning," he said.

"When we come to the river, Pa got all excited, saying Texas was just on the other side. We seen that the storm was coming, but the water looked shallow, and we thought we could get across before the rain came."

What his father hadn't considered was that the rain

was already coming down hard upriver, causing it to quickly rise and flow ahead of the storm.

"We were in the middle of the river when the water came in a rush," Lonnie said. "It happened so fast, there wasn't nothing to do but jump out of the wagon and swim for the bank. Ma, she never learned to swim, so last I saw of her, she was being washed downstream. Pa yelled for me to swim toward this side since it looked a bit closer. He was going after Ma, but I never seen nothing but his hat floating past."

Clay and Jonesy exchanged glances as the boy explained what had occurred.

"We're about to lose daylight," Jonesy said. "Come morning, we'll saddle up and see if we can locate your people. Meanwhile, let's get you something to eat."

The campfire was still aglow and the rain had stopped by the time the exhausted youngster, dry and fed, fell asleep.

THE MEN FOUND the wreckage of the wagon almost a mile downstream. The ribs that had held the canvas cover in place were bare, skeleton-like, and two of the wheels were a hundred yards away, tangled in a dam of brush and tree limbs. Near the bank, when the water was again shallow, was a dead horse.

The bodies of Lonnie's parents lay on a sandbar that had resurfaced in the middle of the river following the storm. Both were bruised and torn by the rocks and brush they had repeatedly collided with while being hurled through the flooding. The man's arms were wrapped around his wife's waist.

"He tried to save her," Clay observed. "He did all he could. His boy'll be needing to know that."

Jonesy nodded in agreement. "What is it we should do now?"

"I'll stay here and try and make the bodies as presentable as possible while you ride back and fetch the boy," Clay said. "He can say his goodbyes, and then we'll find a proper burying place."

Though both were already searching for answers to long-range questions, neither mentioned it. Only when Jonesy had ridden away did Clay whisper to himself, "One step at a time."

L ONNIE WAS SILENT as he rode behind Pate to where his parents' bodies had been found. He then sat motionless on a rock pile, watching as the men dug side-by-side graves in a shaded area where wild grapevines wound through tree limbs. Only when dirt had filled the burial sites and Clay and Jonesy began gathering smooth river stones to cover the graves and ward off predators did the youngster participate. Once the task was completed, Jonesy walked to a nearby hillside where spring wildflowers had begun to bloom and picked small bouquets to place on the graves.

"This is a mighty nice place you picked, Mr. Clay," the boy said.

As he spoke, there was a rustle in the nearby brush and a mare, her coat caked with mud, appeared. Part of the team pulling the ill-fated wagon, she had managed to break away and reach safety. The horse slowly walked toward the boy.

"Her name's Maizy," Lonnie said as he gently brushed mud from her mane. "I gave her that name when Pa brought her home. When there was no plowing to get done or town trip in the wagon, I rode her to school." A hint of a smile appeared as he spoke.

"You got anything in mind to say to your folks before we take our leave?" Breckenridge asked.

Lonnie shook his head. "I done said it in my head,

private." He then led Maizy to stand by the tree stump so he could use it to climb onto her back. "I'll wait until we get back to the camp before I start cleaning her up."

Clay and Jonesy watched the youngster ride bare-back along the riverbank. Once the boy had put enough distance between them, Clay addressed their problem. "I'm thinking he has a right to speak his mind on the matter," he said, "but we've got to decide on what we're to do about him. Impression he's given is that the folks they were headed to work for ain't relations, just friends. If he's got kin, he ain't bothered to mention them."

THEY DISCUSSED THE matter after dinner. Maizy's coat shined after Lonnie had found a rocky basin of clean rainwater to bathe away the river mud. He'd borrowed Jonesy's knife and dug caked dirt and pebbles from the horse's hooves.

"It ain't our intent to leave you on your own," Jonesy said. "We're wondering if you've given any thoughts to what you might be wanting to do."

Lonnie shrugged. "I reckon I could try going on to the ranch where we was heading and see if they'd hire me on," he said, "but I don't rightly know the location. All I knew was we was heading somewhere out in West Texas. Even if I did know where it is, I expect it would be far out of your way. I wouldn't mind to ride along with you folks for a spell. I won't be no trouble. I can cook pretty good. And I'll tend the horses."

When there was no response the boy was quiet for a minute, then said, "You ever hear of a place called Eagle Flat? It's a little town located somewhere on the Red River."

Neither Clay nor Jonesy had ever heard of the place.

"Ma made mention of it several times as we was

traveling. She said she had a cousin who had married a cattleman and was living there. I think she must have been in poor health. Ma, she was wondering if we might have time to stop in for a visit, but Pa said it was too far west of our route."

"Our plan is to continue heading in that direction," Clay said. "I reckon you could come along until we can find this Eagle Flat and your ma's cousin." He glanced toward Maizy. "Unfortunately, we ain't got another saddle."

Lonnie grinned. "I ain't never rode with a saddle anyway."

CHAPTER FOUR

E VEN FOR THE travel weary, Eagle Flat offered little
to get excited about. A week into their trip, it suddenly appeared on the treeless high-grass plains. Just
a mile south of the river, it gave the impression of having been constructed hurriedly and with scant fore-
thought. It was little more than a way-stop for cattle
herders headed north.

At one end of town were the livery and a corral. Out
front, the tools of the local blacksmith were displayed.
Down its single street were a saloon, a general store,
and a tent with a sign in front that promised groceries
were sold inside. Next to it was a smaller sign pointing
to another tent where barbering, baths, and laundry
were available.

For Clay, Jonesy, and Lonnie, the most welcome sight
was Sally's Café, located opposite the grocery.

"I'll eat anything they got that don't have the taste
of woodsmoke to it," Jonesy said.

It was early in the afternoon when the three entered

the small clapboard building and saw that all four of its tables were empty. "All's left is the venison stew, boiled cabbage, some beans, and a half pan of corn bread," the cook said, "and I might scare up some blackberry cobbler and coffee to go with it. You fellas are welcome to take a seat. Don't recollect seeing you in here before. Name's Sally. I'm owner, cook, and dishwasher. Occasionally, I sweep the floor if it needs it."

The response was a momentary silence. Jonesy removed his hat and dusted it against his leg. Clay did the same while young Lonnie stood motionless, hands buried in the pockets of his britches.

Clearly, none were expecting Sally to be a man. He stood six feet, was broad shouldered, had a flaming-red beard, and a booming laugh he burst into at the surprised looks on the faces of his customers.

"Real name's Salvador Santos, only Meskin living in Eagle Flat," he said. "Picked up the nickname when I was doing cooking during the war and it just stuck." He pointed at Clay's Confederate holster. "I see we fought on the same side."

A FTER SERVING LONNIE a second helping of the cobbler and refilling everyone's coffee cup, Sally removed his apron and pulled up a chair. "Don't look like you're herding cattle," he said, "and you folks don't seem crazy enough to be thinking about settling here."

"We're looking for somebody," Clay said.

"Who might that be?"

"Truthfully, we ain't sure since we got no name. All we know is it's a rancher and his wife. The wife might be a relation of the boy here."

Sally shook his head. "That ain't much to go on, is it? Most everyone who lives here permanent owns a small cattle ranch—everybody trying to improve his lot on the stake he claimed. I reckon there's a couple of dozen folks around here fitting your description."

"Looks like we'll be visiting a good many strangers, then," Jonesy said, shaking his head.

Sally promised to see if any of his customers could be of help.

B ACK IN THE muddy street, Jonesy rubbed his stomach. "Now that we've got our bellies full," he said, "I'm thinking our mounts might enjoy a visit to the livery for some oats and a bed of clean straw to rest on for the night. They might even allow us to bed down with them."

"I'd like that," Lonnie said.

From inside the semidark of the stable, owner Sam Dunham called out as they approached. "Thank the Lord Almighty," he said. "My prayer's done been answered. Please tell me you're the handsome, rich strangers who have come to buy this woebegone place and take it off my hands."

Clay and Jonesy laughed. "Afraid not," Breckenridge said. "Best we can do is payment for a night's lodging for us and our animals."

"Aw, I figured as much," Durham said. "Just so you know, I also do blacksmithing and doctor animals. In my spare time, I'd probably consider robbing the bank if we had us one." From an oversized chaw that caused one side of his mouth to bulge, he spit an amber-colored stream of tobacco.

Jonesy leaned toward Clay and whispered, "Is it just me, or don't it seem folks here ain't quite got their wagons fully loaded?"

"I gotta say they've been right interesting so far."

The livery owner, despite being on a first-name basis with every rancher in the area, was no more help than Sally after they described the nameless people they were hoping to find. Maybe, he suggested, someone visiting the saloon later might be able to provide them some information.

"Aside from when there's a cattle drive coming through, most everybody who comes in for a drink or two is either a local rancher or somebody who works for one," he said. "Wouldn't even surprise me if the man you're looking for is there."

Sally was sitting at the makeshift bar when they arrived and waved them over. "I see you fellas are taking in all the sights of our fair town," he said. "Based on the limited information you passed along, I asked a few folks about it but learned nothing useful."

"How many ranchers you say are in these parts?"

Sally had been giving it more thought. "Since we spoke earlier," he said, "I've been attempting to count up in my head. My best guess is twelve or fourteen. There's some that come and go. See, what we've had here since folks started settling this country are those with small claims and small herds. Of course, everybody's hoping to get bigger in time, but it ain't happened yet."

The community of Eagle Flat, in fact, had enjoyed more prosperity than most of the outlying ranches. A city council had recently been formed, and there were plans to soon start building a hotel. There was even talk of a school and a church and the need for a town marshal.

The growth came from the decision on the part of more and more cattle drivers to bypass the larger northward trails like the Chisholm and bring their smaller herds through the less congested grasslands. Eagle Flat was an ideal place to stop for food, drink, and supplies before heading across the Red River.

Two men who had been seated at one of the tables in

back of the saloon approached just as Sally was com-
pleting his description of the community's promising
future. Both walked unsteadily, attempting to focus
glares on Clay and Jonesy.

Before Sally could make introductions, the elder of
the two spoke. "We were wondering what your business might be here," he said. "Ain't no cattle being
moved through at present. That kind of visitor aside,
we don't get too many strangers passing through."

Sally again tried to introduce Clay and Jonesy but
was cut short. "Don't reckon you boys got any knowledge about the rustling that occurred last night," the
owner said.

Jonesy stood. "If you're suggesting we're here to steal
cattle," he said, "you cannot only rest assured that ain't
the case, but be aware I strongly resent your thinking.
Seems to me you've had way too much whiskey."

The accuser swung wildly at Jonesy before Clay
quickly grabbed him and pinned him, facedown, against
the bar. Clay was surprised at the swiftness with which
he'd removed his pistol from its holster. "Don't know
where your homes might be," he said, "but I think it's
time you go looking for 'em. Go on. Git."

As the two drunken ranchers were escorted from
the saloon, a group of card players left their table to
approach. "It ain't our nature to be unfriendly to folks,"
one said. "We're hoping you'll overlook the disrespect
showed and allow us to buy you a drink. The fella who
confronted you is going through a rough spell. I've
known him ever since he settled in these parts, and tonight's the first time I've ever seen him drunk. He was
the one whose cattle got stolen last night. And that
come only days after his wife passed. He was in town
today to arrange her burying."

Clay and Jonesy looked at each other. "This fellow,

he come out this way from back in East Texas?" said Clay.

"That's my best recollection."

"And his name?"

"Abraham Silverton."

"And the name of his deceased wife?"

"Her name was Charlene. A mighty nice lady."

Clay nodded. "You think there's any chance of our going out to speak with him sober without us getting our heads shot off?"

Sally stepped forward. "I'm acquainted with Abe," he said. "Let me get my breakfast folks fed in the morning. Then I'll take you out to his place. I assure you, there'll be no shooting."

THEY HAD SOME reservation as they made the morning ride to see Abe Silverton, but all tension vanished immediately when he appeared in the doorway to his barn.

"You boys step down and let me try apologizing for my drunken behavior," he said. He was rubbing the bruise on his forehead. "Guess I rightfully deserve this knot on my head."

Clay and Jonesy smiled while Sally nodded approvingly. Lonnie wasn't sure what the rancher was talking about and sat silently on his horse. It was Clay who brought him into the conversation. Pointing in the boy's direction, he said, "This youngster is our reason for being here."

Abe nodded toward Lonnie. "Welcome to Silverton Ranch," he said. "What's left of it."

The visitors dismounted and shook hands with Silverton. "We've been told of the misfortune you've recently experienced," Clay said. "We're particularly sorry about the passing of your wife. It was her we were hoping to speak with."

When Silverton gave them a puzzled look, they explained about the recent flood and Lonnie's recollection that his mother had mentioned a cousin living out this way.

"And your ma's name?"

Lonnie spoke for the first time. "She was called Loretta."

Silverton nodded. "Name Loretta's familiar," he said. "I recollect my wife speaking of knowing her when they were young girls playing with dolls and such. Even after my wife's folks moved away from . . . I can't recollect the name of the little town. . . ."

"Lawrence," Lonnie suggested.

"That's it, Lawrence. Strange name for a town if you ask me. Anyway, as I understand it, they continued to see one another from time to time, at family get-togethers, funerals, weddings, things of that nature. After we settled out this way, I recollect my Charlene saying she was going to mail your ma a letter to advise her where she was."

"Ma was wanting to come for a visit," Lonnie explained.

"I'm right sorry she wasn't able to make it," Silverton said.

"What we were hoping to discuss with her was the possibility of there being any more kin she might be aware of," Jonesy said.

Abe shook his head. "None I ever heard of. I reckon that puts you folks in something of a fix."

As he spoke, one of his hands emerged from the barn, leading a horse pulling a wagon loaded with tools, cedar posts, and a roll of barbed wire.

"Got to do some repairing down in the back pasture where my cows was taken. Thieves made off with twenty or thirty head."

Aware there were no answers to their problem on the Silverton ranch, Breckenridge and Pate said their farewells and prepared to leave.

"You folks still got a lot of traveling ahead?" Silverton said.

"Headed up onto the high plains," Breckenridge replied.

Silverton looked at Lonnie. "Give us a minute before you head back to town." He waved Lonnie to follow him to the barn. Shortly, the youngster emerged, smiling, as he sat in a saddle atop Maizy.

"It was my wife's," Silverton said. "I expect she'd be pleased knowing it's being put to good use."

CHAPTER FIVE

THOUGH THE SUN was not yet up, the aroma of brewing coffee and frying pork already wafted from Sally's Café. Having settled their account at the livery, Clay, Jonesy, and Lonnie tied their horses to the hitching posts out front. They were planning on breakfast and an early getaway.

While Lonnie had been inside the livery the previous evening, cleaning his saddle with an oil rag Sam Dunham loaned him, Clay and Jonesy sat outside, enjoying the warmth of the spring night and discussing what they should do about their young friend.

"Ain't like we're eaten up with good options," Pate said.

Breckenridge agreed. They couldn't simply ride away, leaving Lonnie to fend for himself. On the other hand, there was no way to assure his safety if they allowed him to accompany them on the potentially dangerous mission they had in mind.

"He's got a good head on his shoulders and will do

as he's told," Clay said. "We'll just have to do all we can to see the boy's protected from harm."

"All things considered," Jonesy said, "I enjoy the youngster's company."

"Me, too."

S ALLY WAITED UNTIL they had almost completed their meal before he took a seat at their table. He placed a bandanna wrapped around a dozen still-warm biscuits in front of Pate. "Don't want you folks getting hungry on the trail," he said. "I hope once you're done with your traveling and headed back home you'll remember to stop here at Eagle Flat for a visit."

He then reached over and ruffled Lonnie's unruly red hair. "Boy, you be sure and watch out for bad men and rattlesnakes," he said.

T HE DAY WARMED quickly once the sun was up, and they rode in single file along the bank of the river. Clay, bringing up the rear, watched Lonnie thoughtfully, trying with little success to put himself in the boy's situation.

His thoughts drifted to the time when he was Lonnie's age. Life growing up on the farm had been good for him and his younger brother. Their parents had expected them to do their part of the work but also realized the importance of boyhood fun. On summer days, Clay and Cal fished and swam in the creek that wound through the Breckenridge place. They hunted squirrel and rabbit and turkeys and felt a special pride when their mother would prepare a meal from what they brought home.

It seemed there was always a pie or cobbler cooling on the windowsill above the kitchen sink.

Even when Cal became increasingly rebellious, getting into fights at school, arguing with their father, and talking of running away from home, the good times outweighed the bad. At Lonnie's age, Clay had felt safe, loved, and happy.

His reflection was interrupted when he heard Jonesy call out, "Whoa. What do we have here?"

The answer to his question was easy. At the mouth of a ravine was what had obviously been a campsite. There were several cold firepits, and debris was scattered about. The ground beneath a nearby stand of trees where horses had been tethered was stomped bare and hard. There were burned-out torches and a stench of rotted food.

Pate and Breckenridge dismounted and slowly walked the abandoned encampment. "Had to been at least a half dozen of them," Pate said, "and they weren't Indians."

"A gang of night rustlers be my guess," Clay said. "If I was a betting man, I'd wager the folks who was camping here are the same ones who stole Abe Silverton's cows the other night."

Jonesy nodded in agreement.

"You know," said Clay, "that morning I went into town to speak with Marshal Rankin about Cal, he'd just got back from looking into a cattle rustling. Reckon it could be the same folks?"

He had heard tales of such thievery while in the service. Not all men fighting for the pride and honor of the South were upstanding, law-abiding citizens. Around late-night campfires, some would brag of stealing cattle. To hear them talk, it was a simple, low-risk crime.

"Most ranchers, particularly the small ones, don't bother having hands ride fences of a night," one slightly drunk private had explained. "So you pick yourselves a moonless evening, bust a hole in the fence, and drive twenty or thirty head out. Long before first light, you're across the Red River into Indian Territory. There, you meet up with some trail driver who ain't particular whose cattle he's moving. Before he gets to where the herd's gonna be sold, he cuts out those that was stole and sells them separate, earning himself a nice profit. Sometimes, Indians living on reservations in the Territory will meet you just as you cross the river and buy every cow with government money they've been given. They'll take them back to the tribes and sell them off for food. Everybody's happy as a pig in slop — except for the rancher whose stock got stolen in the first place."

After Clay shared his story, Jonesy felt good about having his own hands patrol the fence line of his place. "You figure that's what happened with Silverton's cattle?"

"Wouldn't surprise me."

Clay didn't mention his concern that his brother had always seemed unusually interested in the campfire rustling stories before his decision to desert.

As the days and miles passed, Lonnie was increasingly inclined to join into conversations, even occasionally instigating them. He continued to avoid talking of his parents but expressed great interest in his new surroundings and the purpose of the trip they were taking. Clay and Jonesy were glad to explain the geography, the animal and plant life, but remained elusive about where they were headed and why.

The youngster also had a knack for cooking. When they stopped to rest the horses at midday, he would take one of the rifles and hunt squirrels or rabbits to fry in lard for the evening meal. In the mornings, he had coffee brewing and biscuits warming even before the others were awake. He also saw to it that the horses were well cared for.

* * *

ONE EARLY MORNING, Lonnie saw a lazy trail of
white smoke rising above a distant tree line. "Might
be folks living nearby," he said, "but I ain't seen no
fences."

"Lot of this country is still open range," Jonesy explained. "Settlers can't afford fencing or just ain't inclined, being as they're so isolated. I'd suggest we detour
in that direction and see if those folks might have some
hay or grain we can purchase for our horses."

As they approached the adobe-and-cedar-log house,
chickens scattered and a dog rushed out to greet them.
His bark was friendly.

"Hello the house," Clay called out.

An elderly man with a tangled beard and shoulder-
length hair appeared on the front porch. He was
frail, dressed in overalls, and pointing a shotgun in
their direction. The dog had been far more welcoming.

"State your cause for being on my property," he said.

"We're traveling west and wondered if you might be
willing to part with some feed for our horses," Clay
said. "They're getting a tad weary of nothing but prai-
rie grass and bush berries."

"Won't be free."

"We'd expect to pay a fair price."

"Then climb on down." He leaned his shotgun against
the outside wall as his wife appeared in the doorway.

"I've got leftover pear pie you boys are welcome to,"
she said.

The interior of the house was clean but spare: just
two rooms and little furniture—a kitchen with a stove,
a table, and two wooden chairs; the other room was
filled by a rock fireplace and a bed. The only thing
adorning the wall was a small mirror.

As his wife placed a plate of pie and a glass of milk

in front of Lonnie, Nester Callaway was apologizing to his guests. "We're not normally lacking in hospitality," he said, "but these have been hard times of late. Causes a fella to have suspicions of everybody."

Two nights earlier, rustlers had also visited his place. "They made off with the whole herd, even the new calves. Wasn't but ten cows and a breeding bull, but they were all we had." He explained that he and his wife had come to Texas from southern Missouri where he'd worked as a sharecropper. They had staked their small claim in this isolated region and used their savings to buy a few head of cattle.

"All I got left now is two stubborn mules and a milk cow. My days of being a cattleman are past. Now either I farm us a living or we go back to planting cotton in Missouri."

The tired look of defeat on their host's face distressed Breckenridge and Pate. "Your story is similar to others we've been hearing during our traveling," Jonesy said.

"How far from the river is your place?" Clay asked.

"A shade over a mile," Callaway said. "I wanted to be close enough for hauling water and far enough away in case of flooding."

"Shallow enough to drive cattle across?"

"No more than knee-deep, bank to bank." Callaway changed the subject. "You folks didn't stop in to hear about my woes," he said. "Let me go out to the barn and see about some feed for your horses."

The men followed him, then lagged behind. "Just how quickly is it we're needing to get to Tascosa?" Jonesy asked Clay when Callaway was out of earshot.

"We got no deadline. Why?"

"There's probably not much chance, but I'm wondering if we might be able to find this old fella's cattle. Maybe put a stop to this thieving that's going on along the river."

"You saying we ought to take on a bunch of outlaw rustlers?"

"Don't seem anybody else is of a mind to. We brought them rifles for a purpose other than squirrel hunting, didn't we?"

CHAPTER SIX

I WOULDN'T WANT you fellows harmed on my account," Callaway said. "What would be your plan?"

"We don't rightly have one," Jonesy said, "aside from seeing if we can find where they forded the river and track where they headed once they got across. If they ain't already sold your cows, maybe we can figure a way to steal them back. We'll be gone only a few days, so if we could leave the boy here to help you with chores and look after our packhorse, we'd be obliged. He'll not mind sleeping in the barn."

"My wife and me will be right happy for his company."

Locating where Callaway's cattle had been driven across the Red River wasn't difficult. Breckenridge and Pate had followed the trail of the herd from the pasture northward to the sandy bank, then picked it up on the north side. The flat, grassy landscape on the Texas side quickly changed to rolling hills and brushy valleys in Indian Territory. Soon, the thick vegetation made tracking more difficult.

Throughout the day, Clay and Jonesy depended on occasional broken branches or trampled patches of grass to point the way.

"They won't drive the stock too far north before selling them off," Pate said, breaking a lengthy silence. "Somewhere up this way, they've likely got a meet-up spot where they conduct their business."

"I'm wondering how long they have to wait for a buyer to come and take the cattle off their hands," Clay said.

"My bet is they got themselves a pretty well-organized operation. Somebody driving cattle up the Chisholm has a standing deal with these thieves. Old man Callaway's stock will get mixed in with a larger herd and later cut out when they get up north to a sale."

The big question—what would their plan be once they caught up with the rustlers and Callaway's cattle?— still lacked a satisfactory answer. "All I can guess right now," Jonesy had said, "is that there's likely to be some shooting."

Midmorning of their second day out, they crested a rise and saw riders in the distance. "Without glasses," Clay said, "it's hard to be sure, but it looks like there's four of them. Don't seem to be in too big a hurry."

"Most likely the folks coming to get the stolen cattle. Think we can follow them without getting seen?"

"We can sure give it a try. But if they do see us," Jonesy said, "I got a story I can tell about us heading north to avoid the Texas law."

"What is it we're supposed to have done?"

"Got near caught trying to rob us a bank. Funny thing is, we didn't get no money for our troubles. The local sheriff and his men, they come before we got our robbing completed. I figure if we tell it that way, nobody's gonna think we got money they can be thinking about stealing."

"And what if they're not inclined to believe that hogwash?"

"That'll be when the shooting starts."

They followed at a safe distance until late in the day when the riders disappeared into the mouth of a box canyon. "That's got to be where the cattle are being kept," Clay said. "It's unlikely they'll be moving them tonight, so once it's dark, we can sneak up to the top side of the canyon and see what we're up against."

They waited until the half-moon was high, casting long shadows across the landscape. Leaving their horses behind, Clay and Jonesy quietly made their way up to the canyon rim. From their vantage point, they could see men huddled around two small campfires. Near one were the four men they had been trailing much of the day.

Seated around the other fire were four others. Each had a blanket across his shoulders. They talked loudly and with considerable animation, well on their way to getting drunk.

"They seem in high spirits," said Jonesy.

"Probably because they'll soon be shed of the cows they stole and headed home."

At the back of the canyon, behind a makeshift fence that was nothing more than ropes strung from one tree to another, the cattle had settled in for the night. So, too, had the men's horses, tethered nearby.

"Whatever our plan's going to be," Jonesy said, "we'd best come up with it pretty soon. And while we're at it, let's hope they are a cowardly bunch."

Clay nodded in agreement as he silently backed away from the canyon's edge. "Our presence will be a bigger surprise if we wait till they're sleeping," he said.

* * *

THE RUSTLERS HAD posted one guard at the mouth of the canyon. As Breckenridge and Pate crept near, they could see he was leaning against a boulder. They could also hear his loud snoring. Clay placed the cool barrel of his pistol against the man's ear while Jonesy ripped away his bandanna and forced it into his mouth.

As they tied the wide-eyed sentry to a nearby tree, Jonesy whispered into the rustler's ear. "If standing guard is your main job," he said, "I'd suggest you begin looking for another line of work—in the event we decide not to come back and shoot you dead."

Breckenridge cocked his pistol and moved its barrel to the man's forehead. "I got questions that need answering with just a nod or shaking of the head," he said. "No noise.

"Are the men you were sitting with earlier the ones who stole the cattle?" The man nodded. "Ones who just arrived, are they here to buy the stock and take them away?" Another nod. "These folks friendly with each other?" The man indicated they weren't just before Breckenridge slammed his pistol against the side of his head, knocking him unconscious.

After sneaking to the campsite, Breckenridge shoved the barrel of his rifle against the bottom of a sleeping man's foot.

"What the . . . ?"

"Just stay put where you are," Clay said as he cocked his sidearm. Around him, the others were stirring. Pate was less subtle with his method of waking the others. He stood among them and fired several shots into the air.

Dazed and drunk, two tried to get to their feet but quickly fell to their knees. One, suddenly sick to his stomach, began retching as Jonesy collected their weapons.

"The way nobody gets himself shot," Clay shouted,

"is to do as you're told so we can finish our business here as quickly as possible." Turning toward the bewildered wranglers, he said, "Though we got no reservations about shooting you boys or knocking you in the head, it ain't you we've got our problem with. If I was you, I'd get my horses saddled and take my leave fast as possible. Head back to where you come from and make up whatever story necessary to satisfy your boss."

As the men staggered in the direction of their nearby horses, Jonesy gave Clay an approving nod. "That nicely evens up the odds," he said.

Clay stuck the barrel of his pistol into the stomach of one of the rustlers. "I'll need you to fetch a rope and tightly hog-tie your partners," he said. "Then I'll do the same to you. I want everybody layin' facedown, breathing dirt."

The rustler gritted his teeth. "Not doin' it," he said.

"Your choice," Clay said, then shot him in the leg.

With that, the hostility of the rustlers disappeared. They were all now sober, awake, and scared. "You boys are crazy," one shouted.

"You ain't seen nothing yet," Jonesy said.

After everyone was tied up, he rebuilt one of the dying campfires, adding dried logs until a roaring blaze lit the canyon. That done, he made the rounds of where everyone had been sleeping, collecting their boots. Soon the ripe odor of burning leather filtered through the night.

As the bewildered wranglers rode away, he gathered their firearms in a duffel bag, removed the hobbles from their horses, and slapped their hindquarters. "They won't likely stray too far," Pate said, "but rounding them up in sock feet and with a shot leg won't be real easy."

"How long you think they'll stay tied up?"

"Long enough for us to get the cattle close to the

river," Pate said. He smiled at Clay. "Not bad work, considering we never had us a plan," he said.

E XCEPT FOR A few calves that occasionally strayed, driving the small herd was easy. It was near dusk by the time they had crossed the river and were nearing Callaway's property.

"Might not be a bad idea for you to ride on ahead and tell him we're coming," Jonesy said. "That way he'll be less likely to start shooting at us."

Lonnie was the first to be aware of Breckenridge's approach. Each evening after dinner he'd sat on the front porch, waiting for his friends to return. As soon as he recognized the approaching rider, he ran in his direction.

"Alert Mr. Callaway we're bringing his livestock," Clay told the smiling youngster.

While they were gone, Lonnie and Callaway had enlarged the corral to accommodate whatever cattle were returned. "From now on, I'll drive them from the pasture up this way of an evening for feeding and safekeeping," Callaway said. "Maybe having them closer to the house after dark will discourage someone from trying to steal them again."

Mrs. Callaway stepped onto the front porch to welcome Clay and Jonesy back and announce that she'd just put on a fresh pot of coffee. "Is there cause to worry that the rustlers might return?" she asked.

"I reckon not," said Pate. "At least not until they can find themselves proper new footwear and figure where at the bottom of the Red River their firearms might be."

When Breckenridge described Pate's burning of the rustlers' boots, Lonnie laughed for the first time since they had known him.

* * *

Long after the men had the cattle down for the night and the horses tended, they sat at the kitchen table, drinking coffee and eating biscuits as Jonesy provided details of the trip north.

"And there wasn't a single person got killed?" Callaway said, shaking his head in amazement.

"Truth of the matter is," said Jonesy, "as outlaws go, these boys weren't much, really. I ain't suggesting we convinced them to come to Jesus, but I expect they'll not be bothering cattlemen in this neck of the woods for a spell."

"I just want you fellows to know how much I appreciate what you've done," Nester said. "When is it you plan to be on your way west?"

"Tomorrow morning," Breckenridge said.

"Not before my wife cooks breakfast. She's planning on it."

Lonnie rose and started clearing the table. "I've got us blankets laid out in the barn," he told Clay and Jonesy.

With Clay carrying a lantern, the three men made their way toward a welcome night's sleep. "Boy, we missed you being around," Jonesy said as he laid an arm across Lonnie's shoulders. "But it sounds like you made Mr. Callaway a right good hand in our absence."

They were at the doorway to the barn when Lonnie responded, "I know you're tired and wishing to sleep," he said, "but I was wondering if we might have a brief conversation."

Clay nodded. "What's on your mind?"

"As you're no doubt aware, having been in his presence, Mr. Callaway is not in good health. He tires easily and has trouble with his breathing at times. I've been trying to help where I could, though he's not ever asked for it.

"What I've been thinking is this: Unless there's something I can contribute to your business up on the high plains, maybe it would be a better idea for me to stay here and help Mr. Callaway while you're gone. I've done suggested it to Mrs. Callaway, and she says I'd be welcome. I think he'd be warm to the idea as well. Then, when you're done with your business and headed back this way, maybe we can do some talking and you can give me some ideas as to what I'll be needing to do with myself."

"Sounds like you've thought out a fine plan," Jonesy said. "Let's discuss it with Nester in the morning."

MRS. CALLAWAY WAS up before dawn, laying in a fire and cooking. By the time her husband and Lonnie had turned the cattle out of the corral and headed them toward the pasture, Breckenridge and Pate were ready to leave. From the cabin came the mixed smells of eggs, fresh bread, and redeye gravy. She had prepared so much food that there wasn't room enough for all of it on the table. Bowls and platters covered the top of her stove.

As they ate, they discussed the idea of Lonnie remaining to lend a hand for a while. "He'll be welcome and well cared for," Nester said.

"And fed properly," Mrs. Callaway added.

She and her husband stood on the porch to allow the visitors to say their goodbyes to Lonnie.

"Can't promise how quickly we'll be back," Clay said, "so don't fret if you don't see us for a bit. Just keep us in your thoughts, and we'll do the same for you folks."

Jonesy reached into his saddlebag and pulled out a pistol. "When I was drowning all them outlaws' sidearms in the river," he said, "I decided I'd keep this Colt dry. Thought maybe it was time you had one to call your own."

Lonnie's eyes danced as he took the pistol, turning it over and over in his hands before placing it in the waistband of his britches.

CHAPTER SEVEN

A FTER TWO DAYS' hard riding, Breckenridge and Pate reached the Texas High Plains. On the third day, Tascosa came into view. They had left the basin of the Red River and traveled west across the flat and wind-swept countryside. They passed a few sheep ranches, and their horses occasionally shied as tumbleweeds blew across their path. The late-day sky as far as the riders could see was filled with red dust.

"Don't look like the Good Lord wasted much time creating this part of the world," Jonesy observed.

The scenery didn't improve much as they reached the outskirts of town. There were a half dozen adobe structures crowded together, all facing the lone street that ran through the makeshift community. The only wooden structure was a stable with several rows of tents behind it. Like Eagle Flat, Tascosa seemed to have a single purpose. Cattle drivers, looking for a less congested route north to Dodge City, had begun com-ing this way. The need for a resting place where chuck wagons could be restocked, tired horses could be fed and shod, and cowboys could find whiskey, hot baths, and poker games had given birth to the village.

As Breckenridge and Pate slowly rode through the town, such as it was, they saw no church or school, and no evidence of a jail or any law-enforcement presence.

"Looks like it's wide-open and every man for himself," Clay said.

"And this is where you believe your brother was living?"

"Just a guess, but I think it best if we get ourselves the lay of the land before we begin asking any questions."

There was no evidence of a café, but they found that the saloon served a limited menu. "Seems as good a place as any to get ourselves better known," Jonesy said.

As they entered, they scanned the room filled with boisterous cowboys and a few buffalo hunters badly in need of shaves and baths. There was no room at the bar, and most of the tables were occupied. The place smelled of stale beer, boiled cabbage, and cigar smoke.

Jonesy leaned toward Clay and whispered, "If I didn't know better, I'd guess there's been a jailbreak and everybody's chose to hide out here."

From behind the bar, a female voice welcomed them. Her auburn hair was pulled back, held in place by a red ribbon. She was tall, slim, and tanned, maybe thirty years old. "You boys just find yourselves a chair, and I'll tend your needs shortly."

When two men left a small corner table to join a poker game across the room, Clay and Jonesy took a seat and continued to survey their surroundings.

"Howdy, strangers," the woman said as she appeared at their table. "If you're hungry, we've got steak and beans and corn bread. If drinking's your pleasure, we got whiskey and beer, both homemade."

"We'll eat and wash it down with your beer," Clay said.

The woman nodded and smiled. "Name's Madge," she said. "This is my place. You're welcome so long as you don't start no fighting, spit tobacco on my floor, or cheat at cards."

Jonesy laughed. "Fair enough, I'd say." After she'd left, he glanced across at Clay. "What do you think chances are that all three of those rules get broken on a regular basis?"

One fight, in fact, broke out at the bar even before their meal arrived. They watched as Madge raised a shotgun, pointed it at the cowboys, and demanded they leave or get shot. As the two drunks staggered toward the door, Jonesy said, "You have to admit, we've got no entertainment like this back home in Aberdene."

When she arrived from the kitchen with their orders, Clay asked, "Would you really have shot those fellas?"

"Maybe," she said. "Maybe not. They're good customers."

They ordered more beer, enjoying being out of the saddle. A brief argument broke out at one of the nearby poker tables but was short-lived and no cause for Madge to threaten bodily harm. None of the customers said so much as a "howdy" to the travelers.

"So I'd admire to know your thinking on what our plan is now that we're here. You think some of these rowdy folks might have been associates of Cal?"

"If so, they would have known him as Will Darby, since that's the name he took on after his leave-taking from the army. Until we get a better idea of who these folks are, I think it best we keep our purpose to ourselves."

"I think you done already spoke with one person who knows everybody in town and what their business is," Jonesy said, looking toward the bar, where Madge was busy refilling whiskey glasses.

T HE LIVERY OWNER told them that since there was no cattle drive in town or expected in the next few days, there were plenty of tents available to rent. "And there's a water pump out back of the stables that you're welcome to use. Rest assured your horses will be fed and well cared for," he said. "How long you boys stayin'?"

"Not sure," Clay said. "Couple of days, maybe longer. We're just passing through."

They hadn't been settled in their tent long before Pate was snoring gently. Breckenridge, however, lay awake, his mind racing with questions. Was this godforsaken place where his brother had escaped to? What had drawn him here to associate with people unlike any they had known growing up? Had he become an outlaw, doing harm to others? What had he done to make a murderous enemy? What had he done to be called a coward?

And how far would Clay actually go to make things right if he found answers to his questions? Since the war ended, he'd had a recurring nightmare of that day on faraway Palmito Ranch when he killed the Union soldier. He'd vowed it would be the last act of violence he would ever commit.

Yet now he felt deep and burning anger that was fueling this journey. And it made him uncomfortable. He'd felt no remorse when he'd cracked the skull of the rustlers' sentry or shot another. And now, God help him, he wanted to kill again.

It was almost daylight when he finally gave way to restless sleep.

CHAPTER EIGHT

ELI RAYBURN, OWNER of the Tascosa livery, was standing outside the tent when Breckenridge and Pate emerged. "I got coffee up in the barn," he said. "It's a service I provide all paying customers. Clean washed cups are available. Both of you look as if you could use some."

He then pointed in the direction of the rising sun. "See that little shack down there near the creek? That's where the Prices—husband and wife—offer laundry service if you're so inclined. And the old man will heat up bathwater, given a little notice. He also does barbering. You'll find their prices fair."

As they walked toward the livery, Rayburn kept up his banter. "Don't see no limping or bruises, so it appears you boys made it through your first night in town unharmed."

"We did watch a woman threaten to blow the heads off a couple of drunks down at the saloon," Jonesy said.

"Ms. Madge," Rayburn said. "She's got herself a bark way bigger than her bite."

Clay eyed the man with interest. His graying beard, slumped shoulders, and bowlegged walk made it easy to guess his age. Somewhere in his seventies, probably. In all likelihood, he'd been in Tascosa long enough to know everybody in town.

By midday the visitors had taken advantage of the laundry and bath services and were in the saloon, finishing up a lunch of beef stew. "Don't know about you," Jonesy said, "but I'm feeling about half pretty after getting all cleaned up."

"You've still got a ways to go, I'd say," Clay replied.

They moved outdoors and sat on a bench, discussing how best to go about asking if anyone had known Clay's brother. They agreed it would be best to proceed with caution until they had a better idea of what he might have been involved in and with whom. "We're going to need to do something in the near future," Breckenridge said, "or folks will start to wonder why a couple of strangers are just hanging about with no obvious purpose."

As they talked, a commotion began taking place on the southern edge of town. When it got closer they could see a rider leading a buckboard. Trailing it were a dozen or so additional horsemen. When the party neared the saloon, a wooden casket in the back of the wagon came into view.

Along the way, several men removed their hats as the procession made its way through town. Madge emerged from the saloon and stood next to Clay and Jonesy.

"Going to be a funeral," she said before they could ask. "That's Ben Baggett riding up front. His employees are behind. It's Ben's boy, Dell, they'll be laying to rest up on Boot Hill."

Clay removed his hat as the casket went by. "How is it he came to pass?"

"Most likely got himself shot," Madge said, "but I got no details."

As the wagon turned onto the caliche road leading to the cemetery, the townspeople who had stood silently hurried back into buildings, closing doors and windows. In a matter of minutes, Tascosa took on the look of a ghost town.

"I get the impression people don't take too kindly to your Mr. Baggett and his lot," Clay said.

"That's a fair assessment," said Madge. "A word of advice to you and your friend: Once the burying is done, they'll all be coming here to drink themselves crazy as rabid skunks. They'll not take kindly to outsiders intruding on their gathering, so I'd suggest you stay away." With no further explanation, she turned and reentered the saloon.

Jonesy was quiet until they reached their tent. "See anybody familiar-looking among that bunch?" he finally said.

"Wasn't paying that much attention."

"The man driving the wagon. Wearing that big floppy hat. A sombrero. He had his leg bandaged and in a splint. Like maybe somebody shot him recently."

Clay was silent for a time, then said, "Seeing as how we're not welcome at Madge's place of business, maybe it's time we had a conversation with Eli up at the livery. It's a good bet he knows something useful that he could share about these Baggett folks."

R AYBURN WAS MUCKING out a stall when they arrived. "You boys appear a bit troubled by something," he said.

"Just been watching the funeral parade," Jonesy said. "Didn't notice you among the crowd. I take it you and this fella Ben Baggett must not be the best of friends."

Eli stopped his raking. "If he's got a horse in need of new shoes or doctoring, I do it. If he needs hay or oats, I load his wagon. That's where our relationship ends." He spoke in a humorless voice. "Suits me fine if he remains at his place down in the canyon and leaves the folks here in Tascosa to tend their own business."

"The canyon?"

"Him and his men got a place south of here, somewhere down in the Palo Duro Canyon. Never actually been there myself. I've heard him refer to it as a ranch, but I think if truth be known it ain't nothing more than a hideout."

"You saying Baggett ain't law-abiding?"

"I'd have to say that's an accurate statement." Rayburn returned to his work, clearly uncomfortable with the direction of the conversation.

Clay continued to press. "You on a name-knowing basis with those who ride for him?"

"I've spoke to a few of them down at the saloon from time to time."

"Is the name Will Darby familiar to you?"

Rayburn shoveled soiled hay into a cart and made no reply.

"He's about my size, with red hair. Shoulders are broader than mine. A few years younger than me and likes talking and carrying on."

"Can't recall ever meeting one of the Baggett boys I'd call fun-loving. Sorry. The name doesn't ring a bell. This Darby, he a friend of yours?"

"He was," Clay replied.

IN THE EVENING, Clay and Jonesy sat cross-legged in front of their tent, a small fire warming coffee and two cans of beans they'd found in a saddlebag. The day's wind had calmed and boisterous sounds of arguing and occasional drunken laughter could be heard from the saloon.

"Ol' Eli doesn't seem like one to be easily spooked," Jonesy said, "but I sensed a genuine fear of this Baggett and his gang."

Clay munched on a dry biscuit and nodded. "Too much gossiping might get him killed or his livery burned down. My guess is everybody in town dreads seeing these men coming. That being said, I've got a strong feeling we're getting close to what we come looking for."

"You thinking your brother might have hooked up with them and met his end on account of it?"

"That's now my fear."

"So we got us a plan?"

Clay stood and stretched, looking in the direction of the noisy saloon. "I'll need to do some sleeping on it," he said.

IN THE SALOON, it was nearing midnight. Madge stood behind the bar, silently observing the mayhem and assessing the damage. Several chairs had already been broken, and the floor was littered with broken glass. The smell of spilled beer and tobacco juice that hadn't made its way to a spittoon filled the room. Several patrons had already passed out, heads down on tables, uttering occasional groans. The poker games underway had dissolved into constant accusations of cheating and rowdy fistfights.

Ben Baggett sat alone at a corner table, drinking whiskey. He said nothing, his cold blue eyes focused on the near-empty bottle in front of him.

Come sunup, the saloon would be closed for the day as Madge cleaned and did repairs.

* * *

CLAY WAITED UNTIL midday before visiting Madge. When he entered the empty saloon, she was on her knees, a scrub brush on hand and a bucket of soapy water beside her. "We're closed," she said, not bothering to look up.

"I realize you're busy, but I was wondering if we might have a private conversation," Breckenridge said as he reached for the mop leaning against the bar. "Be glad to help out while we're talking."

She looked up from her kneeling position, pushing hair from her face. "You going to truthfully tell me why you and your friend are visiting this miserable town? You the law?"

"Trying to learn about someone who might have once lived here. Could be he was affiliated with that bunch that was tearing up your place last night."

Madge shook her head as she put down the brush and got to her feet. "Any questions you've got about that bunch can't do anything but cause you grief. And any questions I might choose to answer won't likely help me neither."

"That's why I suggested us keeping this conversation private."

"Who is it you're hoping to learn about?"

"You ever acquainted with a man called Will Darby?"

The name clearly took her by surprise. "I've heard the name," she said, "but we have no friendship. Can't recall when I last saw him."

"'Cause he's dead," Breckenridge said.

Madge put her hands to her mouth. "I feared as much," she finally said. "There's somebody needs to hear your information."

"Who might that be?"

"Her name's Jennie Broder. She's a friend of mine. Lives with her pa on a little goat farm between here and the canyon. She's a sweet and fragile little thing whose mama died giving birth to her."

"And what was her relation to Darby?"

"They were talking of getting married."

Breckenridge felt a lump in his throat. The idea of his brother settling down, marrying with plans for a domestic future, had never occurred to him. It wasn't the young man he'd known. "I'll be needing to speak with her," he finally said.

She saw the pain on his face and gently placed a hand on his shoulder. "If you don't mind, I'd be glad to accompany you and show you the way. Won't hurt for this place to remain closed for another day. I got a buggy out back we can take. When is it you'll be wanting to go?"

"Now," Clay said. "Right now."

THE ROAD LEADING to the Broder farm was rutted and difficult to travel. When they finally arrived at a clearing and could see the cabin and barn, they heard the bleating of curious goats anticipating their arrival. A dog barked.

Cyrus Broder, wearing overalls and a straw hat, waved a corncob pipe in the air when he recognized Madge's buggy. "Wasn't expecting visitors," he said, "but it's good to see you. Hope it ain't goat-meat jerky you've come for because it's not yet smoked properly. Proud you didn't bust an axle on my road."

Before stepping from the buggy, Madge leaned toward Clay and whispered, "I'm of a mind to speak to Jennie first."

"I'd appreciate it," Clay responded.

Madge introduced the men. "We've come to talk with Jennie," she said.

"She's out in the barn," her father said, "bottle-feeding a couple of newborns. Twins. Their mama can't properly feed them both."

Madge excused herself and found Jennie seated on a mound of hay, a kid goat in her lap. Her eyes lit up when she saw her friend.

In the yard, the men stood in the shade of a mesquite tree. "Mr. Broder," Clay said, "I'm afraid I've come with some bad news for your daughter. As we speak, her friend is telling her that Will Darby has been killed. Reason I know is I'm his brother, and it was me who buried him."

Broder shook his head in disbelief. "This'll put a mighty ache in my daughter's heart," he said. "She thought highly of him, more than she let on to me. But, you know, a daddy can tell. And I liked the young man. He showed good manners when he visited. Told me he grew up on a farm and showed an interest in raising goats himself one day. To be honest, I never cottoned to his being associated with that Baggett outfit, but he told me he was planning to take his leave of that life. How was it he was killed?"

"That's what I'm hoping to find out," Clay said.

As they spoke, the women approached from the barn. Jennie Broder, a baby goat still cradled in her arms, was crying. She was a petite young woman with long blond hair and piercing blue eyes. Even in her buckskin britches, flannel shirt, and scuffed boots, she was pretty. His brother had chosen well, Clay thought.

Broder lovingly hugged his daughter before she turned to Clay and extended her hand. "He spoke of you often and with ever so much affection," she said. "He promised I would meet you once he and I returned to join you on the farm."

Breckenridge hoped she didn't notice the moisture forming in the corners of his eyes. "I'm sorry it had to be this way," he said.

CHAPTER NINE

JONESY WAS SITTING on the steps in front of the saloon when Breckenridge and Madge returned. Clay waited until he'd unhooked the buggy and returned it to its place before telling his friend about the trip. Without a word, Madge disappeared inside to resume her cleaning chores.

"Did the young woman have any idea who might have been responsible for your brother's killing?" Jonesy said.

"When she was talking with Madge, she mentioned somebody who had kept coming around, even after my brother started to court her. Said she didn't like him, but he apparently wasn't inclined to take no for an answer."

"She give his name?"

"She doesn't recall it, but said he worked for Baggett." He paused for a second, then added, "So did my brother."

It was late in the afternoon when they walked toward the tent encampment. "I spoke with Rayburn earlier," Jonesy said, "and he informed me that we'll be needing

to take leave of our tent tomorrow. A herd's coming in
to make a rest stop."

Routinely, cattle drivers would camp their herd a
mile or so outside of town, leaving a small crew of wranglers to watch over the grazing cattle. The others would
enjoy the luxury of Tascosa, sleeping in Rayburn's tents,
visiting the saloon, and stocking up on necessities at the
mercantile.

"I'll be interested to see if there's any contact between
Baggett's folks and those driving the cattle through,"
Clay said. "If we're going to be sleeping in the open
again, I suggest we pick us a spot that will provide us a
chance to keep an eye on this incoming herd." He already had a good idea what they would see.

"So what's our plan between now and then?"

"We might see about helping Madge with the cleaning of her saloon," Clay said.

She was surprised when they entered.

"We were wondering what kind of wages you pay
for doing cleanup work."

Madge laughed. "For pushing a broom or mop," she
said, "I can set out a bottle of whiskey. For anybody
knowing how to mend broken furniture, I'd be inclined
to cook up a steak."

Clay reached for a broom while Jonesy asked Madge
if she had any tools.

"Out back in the shed," she said.

It was past midnight by the time things were back in
order. The floors were swept and mopped. The chairs
and tables that could be repaired were; the others had
been hauled out back for kindling. The remnants of a
mirror were taken down, replaced by an unimpressive
painting of the saloon's exterior a drunk customer had
painted years earlier.

"I'd say things look presentable enough for business,"
Madge said as they sat at the bar. She had cooked a late

dinner of steak and potatoes and was bringing bowls of blackberry cobbler from the kitchen. "I'm appreciative of what you boys have done."

Breckenridge explained that he'd told his friend about their conversation with Jennie out at the Broder farm.

Too tired to sleep, they continued talking by the light of nearby lanterns.

"If it's none of my business, feel free to say so," Clay said, "but I can't help wondering how a woman like yourself got here to run this establishment."

Madge smiled and took a sip of her whiskey. "Some years back my husband and I came here from Kansas City after learning this was a little town just getting started. It sounded like a place with a future, what with more and more cattle drives passing through. We came and used some money my father had gifted me after his success silver mining to open this saloon."

In time, she said, her husband decided it was too much work for too little profit. He began spending more time losing at poker than he did tending bar. "He also became an enthusiastic consumer of the whiskey we'd stocked to sell."

In time, he began disappearing, sometimes for several days and without explanation. "Every time he returned, he would have a good amount of money in his pocket—which he quickly set about losing at the poker table.

"This went on for some time before he finally got drunk enough one night to tell me what it was he was doing. He talked of this man Ben Baggett, who knew ways of making money. Good money, he put it, not like the piddling wages one earns selling drinks in a saloon.

"He talked of Baggett like he was some kind of genius, but actually he was just a common thief, the leader of an outlaw gang of good-for-nothings. A sorry lot my husband happily joined up with."

Madge was getting tipsy as she talked of things she'd shared with no one before. "Finally, I'd had my fill and told him his choice was either me or being a thief. He slapped me hard against the side of my head, went behind the bar, grabbed a bottle of whiskey, and took his leave. It was the last time I ever saw him, and good riddance. I'd have divorced him if this two-bit town had a lawyer. These days, if I was to learn he's dead and gone, I wouldn't mind a bit. Fact is, it would be doing the world a favor. At least he's had the good sense not to show himself in here."

Clay felt a twinge of guilt as he listened to Madge's miseries. Still, he pressed for more information. "What is it he does for Baggett?"

"Like all of them," she said, "takes from those who can't afford it or are unable to do anything about it. They rustle cattle, rob stagecoaches, take goods from traveling wagons, always careful to carry out their foul deeds where no law's nearby."

Her speech was becoming a little slurred as she passed along the information her husband had told her. He had described a rustling operation unlike any Breckenridge or Pate had ever heard of. Rather than making raids on large ranches, Baggett would dispatch groups in various directions to prey on small, unsuspecting ranchers. Each raid would result in a dozen or more stolen cattle and often go unnoticed. By the time a sizable number of cattle had been assembled, arrangements would be made with cattle drivers headed north. They would mix them with the herd they were moving until they got to the sale site, then cut them out and enjoy the profit. So cattle stolen from poor folks got sold off twice.

"Pretty clever thinking," Jonesy said. "Downright sorry behavior but clever."

Madge's eyelids were becoming heavy. "Time I get to

bed," she said. "I'm about talked out anyway. Again, I much appreciate your helping me out . . . and listening."

Clay had one more question as they walked toward the door. "Why do you stay here?"

Madge faintly smiled. "I got nothing else," she said.

Two nights later Breckenridge and Pate left the comfort of their tent and were camped out on a hillside near where a large herd of cattle grazed in the moonlight. Around a fire, a half dozen trail drivers sat, sharing stories. Occasionally, the sounds of laughter and curses echoed in the still night.

It was well after midnight when the quiet was interrupted by a gentle rumble of approaching hooves. Soon the flicker of torches appeared on the horizon. "Looks like they're coming to do business," Jonesy said.

They watched silently as the arriving cattle were driven into the main herd. Then there was the exchange of a saddlebag from one of the trail drivers to the leader of the group that had arrived with the stolen cattle.

The transaction was over in a matter of minutes. As the visiting riders left, their torches still aflame, Clay watched them disappear.

"I think," he told Jonesy, "it's time we figure out a way to see what's going on down in that canyon. I'm of a strong mind that's where we'll find the man I'm looking for."

CHAPTER TEN

PALO DURO CANYON is a thousand-feet-deep, ten-mile-wide geographic scar that runs along Texas' Caprock Escarpment. A half day's ride south of Tascosa, it was an unwelcoming landscape of jagged ledges, massive boulders, dark caves, and a terrain only the most sure-footed of man and beast could safely travel.

Once large herds of buffalo, antelope, and mule deer roamed its basin along the banks of a winding offshoot of the Red River, but when discovered by Indian tribes, they were soon wiped out, leaving only coyotes, rattlesnakes, and the haunting winds that constantly whistle through strange formations and scrubby mesquites and along narrow pathways.

It was an excellent place for a hideout. And it had been Ben Baggett's home for almost a decade.

Over the years, he had organized his operation to military-like efficiency. There were scouts who often traveled in pairs, sometimes alone, searching out potential rustling targets, carefully instructed to focus on

small farms and ranches that were located a considerable distance from sheriffs and marshals. The scouts
would report back with locations, routes of escape, and
hiding places to await buyers from cattle drives.

Throughout northern Texas, west into New Mexico
Territory, and along the southern border of Indian Territory, favored routes of wagon and stagecoaches had
been located and reported to Baggett.

Once targets were determined, men he relied on as
lieutenants would lead small groups of raiders to carry
out the thefts. Sometimes as many as three groups
would be at work simultaneously in different regions.

In the canyon, Dell Baggett was assigned to oversee
the building of living quarters for the men—dugouts,
log-and-mud cabins—and corrals for the horses. He
saw to it that members of the gang ate meals prepared
by an aging chuck wagon cook who had been lured into
the fold. He had planted a vegetable garden along the
riverbank, assembled a flock of chickens, and urged the
raiders to occasionally return with a stolen calf to be
butchered.

It was Dell's responsibility to decide what supplies
needed to be stolen or purchased and how the wages of
each member of the outfit would be paid on a monthly
basis. And it had been his suggestion that the men be
allowed an occasional payday visit to the saloon up in
Tascosa.

So well run was the operation that Ben Baggett had
little to do aside from counting his money and hiding
it away in a canyon cave only he knew about.

Then a freakish accident occurred that briefly changed
things.

Having spotted a chicken-stealing bobcat roaming
the canyon rim one afternoon, Dell got his rifle and
went in pursuit. While negotiating the rugged terrain,
paying more attention to the route being taken by the

animal than his own footing, he slipped and fell into a crevice. The fall itself was short and not harmful, but at the bottom of the opening was a large den of rattlesnakes.

Before he could climb to his feet, the young Baggett had been bitten repeatedly, in the face, on the limbs and torso. His calls for help went unheard for some time, and by the time he was found and rescued, his entire body was badly swollen, the toxic venom having spread from head to toe.

Ben Baggett ordered that his son be stripped and damp clothes applied to his body in an attempt to reduce the swelling and rising fever, but there was little positive effect. Using their knives, several of the men cut small Xs into the spots where bite marks were visible and attempted to suck the contaminated blood from his system.

Nothing worked. By nightfall, Dell was in a coma. By morning, he was dead. For all his careful planning, his father had never thought to include someone with medical knowledge among his gang.

Two days later, after a coffin had been built and a grave marker fashioned, the father and his men made the journey into Tascosa so that Dell might have a proper cemetery burial.

The elder Baggett's grief, such as it was, passed quickly.

CHAPTER ELEVEN

THE BRIGHT MOONLIGHT and torches carried by the rustlers made following them back to their canyon hideout easy. The distant flames danced like fireflies traveling in single file. The purpose of watching Baggett's men was no longer to determine what they were doing or even how they carried out their thefts and exchanges. Breckenridge and Pate simply wanted to learn the location of the outlaws' hiding place.

They were convinced that the cattle thefts, dating back to the one outside Aberdene, were all the work of Baggett's men.

As they rode through the night at a leisurely pace, Clay's mind wandered. The journey, begun in anger and driven by a quest for revenge, had become something more. He thought about young Lonnie waiting back at Nester Callaway's farm and wondered how he was dealing with the loss of his parents and what his future held. He thought of his own family, all now gone, and of Jennie Broder, like him mourning Cal's death. And there was Madge, a strong, hardworking woman who was a virtual prisoner in a worn-out saloon in a dusty little town at the tail end of nowhere.

Pate broke the silence as day was about to break. The rustlers' torches no longer lit the way. "Can't be much farther," he said. Even as he spoke, the distant riders began to disappear from the horizon. "Appears they're riding down into the canyon."

They stopped and dismounted to stretch their legs. "We've come far enough," Clay said. "This is where they can be found."

Jonesy scanned the horizon, seeing nothing but cacti, scrub brush, and blowing sand. "Ain't much to look at, is it?"

E LI RAYBURN WAS seated at the end of the bar when Breckenridge and Pate returned to Tascosa. It was late afternoon and the evening customers were yet to arrive. "Glad to see you boys back," he said. "The herd's on its way out of town, so I've got tents available again if you're interested."

Madge's only acknowledgment was to place two glasses of beer on the counter.

"Stars shining have a tendency to keep me awake," Jonesy said, "so we'll again be accepting your hospitality. Our horses would likely appreciate more comfortable accommodations as well."

"I'll see to it your tent is cleaned and ready and the stalls have fresh hay." Rayburn finished his drink in one gulp. "I have to admit, I wasn't expecting you boys would be hanging around so long."

"We're hoping to have our business done shortly," Clay said.

Only when the men rose to leave did Madge speak. "Mr. Breckenridge," she said, "might I have a word?"

She pointed toward one of the tables generally reserved for poker games. "I've been doing considerable thinking about our conversation the other night," she said. "I've got something that needs saying."

Clay removed his hat and put it on the table, running his fingers along the brim. "If your intent is to persuade me to abandon my purpose," he said, "you'll be wasting your time. I came here with a job that needs doing."

"Go home. Please. Go back and tend your farm. Forget about this awful place," she said. "I fear you're going to wind up dead yourself, trying to avenge the killing of another. You're facing a fight that's nowhere near fair. Unless I'm mistaken, all you've learned is that the person who claimed the life of your brother is likely a member of Ben Baggett's lot. Without more specific knowledge, you're looking at a fight with the whole bunch of them. They're bad people, bad unlike any folks you've ever known. They'd kill a man without bothering to even know his name. And, if you were paying attention the day they came to town to bury Baggett's boy, you saw there is a considerable number of them."

"How many total you think there are in the canyon?"

"I can only guess, but from what I've seen come in here from time to time, I'd say at least fifteen, counting Baggett himself. You can't kill the lot of them just to make sure you get the one who murdered your brother."

For the first time, Madge noticed the darkness in Clay's eyes.

"Why not?" he said.

PART TWO

———— ◇ ————

WILL DARBY'S STORY

CHAPTER TWELVE

I N THE DAYS that immediately followed his desertion
from the Confederate Army, the most difficult thing
for him was to remember that his new name was Will
Darby, no longer Cal Breckenridge. As he rode through
the Mexico desert, stopping only to visit one dingy cantina after another, he constantly repeated the name,
hoping to burn it into his consciousness. Will Darby . . .
Will Darby . . . Will Darby . . .

When he'd had enough tequila, he'd even put it to
song.

> My name's Will Darby
> And I ain't real smart.
> My name's Will Darby
> And I need a head start. . . .

If he wasn't memorizing, he was trying to consider
a future for himself, one that didn't include returning
to Aberdene and the family farm. His father, he knew,

would never welcome a deserter home and most likely he would forever be judged an embarrassment by his older brother.

He would have to make his own way. Maybe there was some cattle ranch up the way that needed an able-bodied hand. Or a newly established town that could use help with building a schoolhouse or a church.

Even in his drunken state, he was already doubting the wisdom of his hasty decision. He knew the army pay he'd managed to save wasn't going to last long. And while hiding out in Mexico for a time was possible, making it his home wasn't an option worthy of consideration.

Once again, he'd made himself a fine mess. He'd done it often enough as Cal Breckenridge, and now was about to do the same as Will Darby.

He rode on until dark, swaying in the saddle. His empty tequila bottle had been tossed into the Rio Grande some miles back.

Making camp on the sandy bank of the river, he managed to remove the saddle from his horse and tether him to a scrub mesquite. Without even bothering to remove his boots, Will stretched out on the saddle blanket and was immediately lost in a drunken sleep, his restless dreams mixed with bloody war battles and boyhood memories of happy times spent with his brother, Clay. They were still young, chasing fireflies near the house, laughing as they ran.

Then the dreams turned into a real nightmare. Someone was kicking at him and cursing. When he opened his eyes, he saw the huge form of a man dressed in buckskins pointing a pistol at his face. Two others stood nearby, toothless grins on their tobacco-stained faces.

"Get to your feet," the man with the pistol said, "and show us where your money is. I'd advise you do it quick."

Highwaymen. Will had heard about them: outlaws who roamed the open country looking for people to rob.

He felt the sharp point of a boot slam against his rib cage even before he could get to his knees. The other two men grabbed his arms and pulled him into a standing position. One slapped him hard across the face. The other held a Bowie knife, its blade glinting in the moonlight.

"The choice is yours to make," the leader said. "You can tell us where your money is, and we'll be on our way, leaving you no worse than you are. Or we can cut your throat and search it out ourselves."

Will was suddenly wide-awake and sober. "I ain't got much," he said. "Some is in my saddlebag, and there's a little in my boot."

The thieves rummaged through Darby's meager belongings, taking his money, his pistol, a half box of ammunition, and his binoculars.

"Wasn't hardly worth it," the leader said as he delivered a series of hard punches to the side of Darby's head.

ISTER . . . MISTER . . . YOU dead?"

Will had a foggy awareness of dirt in his mouth and sun in his eyes. He could hear a young girl's voice somewhere far in the distance. Shielding his face, he looked up at a child who could have been no more than nine or ten. The bottom of her gingham dress was wet from her wading in the river. "My pa wants to know if you're dead or still alive," she said.

"Can't say for certain," Will said, wincing at the pain as he tried to stand. "Who might you be?"

"My name's Darla, and I'm near ten," she said. "My mama's teaching me how to read. That's my pa over there on the other side of the river."

Though his vision was blurry, Will could see that

the child's father was making his way through the shallow water toward them.

"Lordy mercy," the man said. "If there were any railroad tracks nearby, I'd guess you got yourself run over by a train. More likely, though, you got acquainted with the same fellas we did."

Will could see bruises and cuts on the man's face.

"After they finished looting our wagon and turning it on its side, they gave our mules a scare, sending them running. Didn't catch up to one of them until just now. That's how we come to see you."

He sat on a tree stump and poured water from his boots. "Name's Cawthorn Bradley," he said. "You already met my girl, Darla. The wife and the other young'uns are back with the wagon, which I fear is badly broke. I see them thieves did you the courtesy of leaving your horse, so if you're up to riding, you can come back with us. If they didn't steal the coffeepot, my wife can cook some up. She might do some bandaging to your wounds as well."

"I'd be grateful," Will said.

B RADLEY'S WIFE HAD built a fire and buried a covered pot in the coals, cooking biscuits. There was a welcome aroma of coffee. The children were gathering the items scattered by the robbers and piling them next to the overturned wagon.

"A terrible mess, ain't it?" Bradley said as his wife handed him a cup.

The coffee stung Darby's mouth but warmed his throat. He limped toward the wagon to survey the damage. One wheel had been broken loose, and the canopy had collapsed. The tongue was buried in the sandy soil. "Only worse thing they could have done," he said, "was set it afire. I'd say our first order of business is to see if we can set it upright."

"Mister, in your condition I have my doubts about you being able to do much more than stand up straight."

Darby ignored his concern. "You got a hatchet or an ax they might have left behind?" As Bradley went in search of his ax, Darby walked in the direction of a stand of mesquites. "We'll need a straight and strong tree trunk," he said. As a young farm boy, he'd often helped lift the family wagon from ditches and mud holes, using a handmade fulcrum to do the lifting. "We'll also need ropes if you have them."

The plan worked. With the men lifting on the tree trunk that had been pushed beneath the wreckage and Mrs. Bradley and the children pulling on ropes from the other side, the wagon groaned and creaked and finally settled in an upright position.

Exhausted, Will examined the damage, shaking his head. "Fixing it ain't gonna be easy," he finally said, "but I think it can be done. But it'll need proper repair with proper tools before you go much farther. If you can find a settlement somewhere nearby, I'd make that my destination with hope it has a capable blacksmith."

Mrs. Bradley gently hugged the child sleeping in her lap. "Praise the Lord," she said.

They rested in the shade of the wagon, eating warm biscuits and strips of jerky. The younger children slept while Darla sat with a Bible in her lap, mouthing each word she was able to read.

"Where you folks headed?" Will asked.

"A place called Albuquerque, over in northern New Mexico Territory," Bradley said. "To be more specific, the San Augustín de la Isleta Mission." He pulled an envelope from the pocket of his britches. "I got this letter a while back, offering me the opportunity to watch over their flock. My wife will be teaching in their school. I'm told their priest is elderly and in failing health and that I was to arrive as quickly as possible."

"And where is it you're coming from?"

"San Antonio. I had a small church there, located near the Alamo, which you've no doubt heard of. Once all that ugly business was finally ended, we was ready to go somewhere else, some new place where the memories weren't so painful. God answered, offering a new start for us and our young'uns."

Will shook his head. "So I should be addressing you as Father?"

"Cawthorn will do fine. And don't worry none. I'll not be trying to convert you from your evil ways."

R EPAIRING THE BRADLEYS' wagon was no easy task. The men used rocks to pound the damaged wheel back into shape. The shattered tongue was replaced by a sturdy tree limb while Mrs. Bradley did her best to patch the tattered canopy. Their belongings were loaded.

"It's fixed as best we can manage," Will said. "I think you can be on your way tomorrow morning. You'll just want to take it slow."

"And which way will you be headed?"

Will shrugged. "I got no urgent business in any direction," he said. "If you like, I'd be happy to ride along with you for a ways. Not that I'll be much protection, seeing as how my sidearm was taken."

Bradley turned and briefly disappeared into the wagon, emerging with an old shotgun and a leather pouch that contained shells. "As I suppose you've figured, I'm not a man enamored of firearms. Truth is, I've never fired this gun myself. We brought it along, thinking we might occasionally shoot us a rabbit or some squirrels for supper." He handed it to Darby. "Might be better protection than none at all."

Will pressed it against his shoulder and looked down the barrel. "My preference would be a Colt that's well sighted," he said, "but this'll beat throwing rocks at an attacker."

A FTER TWO DAYS' travel, it was Darla who first recognized they were approaching a settlement. She'd heard a rooster crow, then a dog barking. As the wagon slowly creaked up a rise, Bradley pulled the mules to a halt and looked down at the small scattering of buildings and tents in the distance.

"Doesn't look like much," he said.

"Better than anything else we've seen of late," Will replied.

Bradley's assessment of Las Lunas didn't change as he guided the wagon into town. There were a general store, a saloon, and a dusty corral that housed a half dozen horses. Will pointed in the direction of a forge sitting in front of a ragged tent. "Maybe we can find some help there," he said.

The children looked on silently until Darla spoke. "Papa, I don't see that they have a church here."

"I shouldn't be making judgments," her father said, "but if I had to guess, there are few folks here who feel need of one."

The blacksmith was a short, pudgy Mexican with huge hands and bowed legs. His eyes sparkled, and he smiled broadly at the prospect of a customer. "You got some fixing needs doing?" he said, wiping his hands on his soiled apron. "You've come to the right place."

Bradley climbed down from the wagon and shook the man's hand. "We were attacked back on the trail," he said, "and robbed. What money we had was taken. So what I was wondering is, would you consider taking one of my mules in exchange for your service?"

The blacksmith moved to the front of the wagon and examined the animals. He ran his hand along their flanks, opened their mouths to look at their teeth, and checked their hooves. He paced back and forth for several minutes, his eyes never leaving the mules.

"This one," he finally said.

Bradley shook his hand again. "God bless you."

As he unhooked the wagon, his wife gathered the children and a blanket and took them to the shade of a nearby tree to wait.

Will offered his help to the blacksmith but was quickly dismissed. With nothing else to do, he started walking down Las Lunas' lone street. He hadn't had a drink since tossing his empty bottle into the Rio Grande days earlier, and he wished he had money enough for a visit to the shabby-looking saloon up ahead. But he had no mule to trade. He had nothing.

His thoughts turned to the Bradleys. He marveled at their dogged determination to make such a long and dangerous spiritual journey. Despite their hardships, they seemed happy, content. And he envied them. Though his parents had seen to it that he attend church as a youngster, he'd never embraced the idea of a Supreme Being who was looking over those who believed. He'd never prayed. If there was a God, he clearly had no use for Cal Breckenridge. Or Will Darby. And the feeling was mutual.

As he continued down the street, nearing the saloon, he heard the sound of loud curses coming from inside. Then he saw an elderly man stumble from the doorway and fall into the dusty street. Two men, younger and much larger, followed. One had a blackjack and began pounding the helpless old man. The other was kicking him. Both were laughing.

People had gathered on the front steps of the saloon, watching, but none showed any interest in breaking up the melee.

For a split second, thoughts of his own beating at the hands of the highwaymen flashed through Darby's mind, and he found himself running toward the one-sided fight. He grabbed the man with the blackjack by the arm, spun him around, and delivered a fist to his face. As the surprised attacker fell backward, landing on his backside, Darby began kicking him in the groin. The other man reached to grab Will's arm but was slow in doing so. Will's forearm crashed against his face, breaking his nose. He went to his knees, yelling in pain.

Darby then grabbed the blackjack, which had fallen from the other man's hand, and began swinging it wildly. "You boys can thank your lucky stars that I ain't armed," he yelled. "Otherwise, you'd both be shot dead. We can continue this, or you can quietly take your leave and not allow me to see you again."

As he spoke, one of the men struggled to his feet, his hands covering his injured crotch. He began slowly walking away, doubled over and moaning in pain. The other followed, blood covering his face.

Will went to the old man and lifted his frail and beaten body. He was barely conscious and bleeding from his face and arms. "Come with me, old-timer. I know a lady down the street who can see to your wounds."

The old man tried to focus on Darby with little success. "All I done was ask if they'd buy me a drink of whiskey," he whispered.

MRS. BRADLEY CLEANED the man's cuts, rubbed salve on them, and applied bandages fashioned from strips torn from a sleeve of her blouse. Darby looked on silently, his heart no longer racing, and his anger replaced by concern for the beaten stranger.

"I think he'll be fine," Mrs. Bradley said as she put a cup of water to the old man's mouth.

As she did so, Will felt a hand on his shoulder and turned to see a man smiling at him.

"I've come to say how impressed I was with what you did back there and to ask if I might buy you a drink to demonstrate my admiration," he said.

Will could already taste the whiskey and feel its warmth in his throat. "I expect you can," he said.

"Good," the man said as they began walking back toward the saloon. He extended his hand to Will. "Name's Ben Baggett."

CHAPTER THIRTEEN

T HE SALOON WAS lit by a few lanterns and smelled of cigar smoke and spittoons badly in need of emptying. There were only a few customers in the aftermath of the ruckus out front, and it was quiet. A few curious heads briefly turned as Darby entered.

Baggett motioned toward a table near the only window in the place. A half-full whiskey bottle sat in front of a young man, blond with rugged good looks, who signaled for the bartender to bring another glass.

"This is my boy, Dell."

"Name's Will Darby."

"Pull up a chair, Will Darby," Dell said, "and be assured I have no interest in getting on your bad side . . . not after what I witnessed a while ago."

The elder Baggett laughed at his son's joke. "He's not only good-looking, but he's right smart."

They drank quietly for a time, the hosts sipping while

Will twice emptied his shot glass in a single starved swallow.

Ben broke the silence. "What brings you to these parts?"

Will was usually not one to speak freely to people he didn't know, but the whiskey had loosened his tongue. He said he'd been discharged from the army following General Lee's surrender and was headed west in search of work when he was hijacked and near killed. He talked of meeting the Bradleys and learning of their misfortune. "They're fine folks," he said. "He's a man of the cloth, and his wife's gonna be a teacher once they get to Albuquerque. Same outlaws who attacked me in the middle of the night earlier robbed them of every cent they had and nearly destroyed their wagon. It's down at the blacksmith's now, where he's doing needed repairs before they can continue on."

He served himself another drink, downing it quickly. "To be frank, I'm worried about them making it. They had to barter away one of their mules just to get the work done."

Suddenly aware that he was dominating the conversation, he changed the subject. "What is it you folks do?"

"We're in the cattle business," the elder Baggett said. "We're here to recruit additional hands for our operation." He glanced over his shoulder at three men seated at the bar. "Those boys just hired on."

"You looking for more?"

"You interested?"

"Might be."

"The work ain't easy, but there'll be fair pay, a roof over your head, and something on the table come suppertime," Baggett said. "We'll be staying through the night, so you sleep on it and let us know your thinking in the morning."

* * *

B AGGETT MADE NO mention of his past.
He'd come to Texas from back East, determined to make his fortune as a cattle and cotton bro-
ker. He'd brought his teenage son along but left his
wife behind. Their marriage had been a loveless one
from the start, entered into only because of his wife's
family wealth and business connections. He'd taken
much of her money with him when he headed to Texas.

Settling in Brownsville, he found success elusive.
Young Dell Baggett earned nearly as much as his father, loading Mexican cotton onto European-bound
ships. Soon the grubstake he and his father had arrived
with was all but gone, the elder Baggett's mood turning angrier and more violent with each new disappointment.

Things boiled into disaster one rainy spring morning
when, badly hungover, Baggett shot a local cattleman after an argument. By the time the local marshal
was called to the scene, Baggett had collected his son
from the docks and the two were on their way to
Mexico.

Neither Ben Baggett nor his boy would ever do another honest day's work.

For a time they joined a bandito gang that trafficked
peyote, guns, and livestock stolen from struggling
farmers and ranchers on the Texas side of the border.
Their methods were often ill planned and reckless, but
profits were significant until they were captured or
killed by *federales*. For Baggett, it was a learning experience. He soon came to realize that for someone capable of careful planning and the ability to assemble a
crew of reliable men, the life of a thief could be highly
profitable.

The first part of his plan was to put the dirty, dusty Mexican border towns far behind him.

He selected a handful of the smartest banditos to accompany him, promising that his planned enterprise offered far greater rewards. They, like him, were men on the run and better off if they stayed on the move.

As they advanced northward, through small settlements and past slow-moving wagon trains, Baggett continued to recruit. Disenchanted settlers, weary buffalo hunters, and men wanted for a variety of misdeeds were receptive to his promise of outlaw wealth. Along the way, he made it his business to have conversations with men ramrodding cattle drives, putting his plan into motion.

When Dell would ask about their ultimate destination, his father's reply was always the same: "I'll know when we get there."

D ARBY LEFT THE saloon early in the evening, feeling the welcome warmth of the whiskey in his stomach. There was a smile on his face. Maybe his sorry luck was about to change.

When he returned to the Bradleys, the old man had left. "He insisted he was feeling fine, thanked me kindly, and was on his way," Mrs. Bradley said. "He was limping quite badly, I might add."

"I appreciate you caring for him," Darby said. "I'm feeling a bit wore out, so I'm gonna go bed down over behind the corral. Tell the young'uns I'll see them in the morning." For reasons he didn't completely understand, he wanted to slip away before the children would know that he'd been drinking.

"I'll do what I can to rustle up something for breakfast," Mrs. Bradley said.

* * *

WILL WAS FEELING rested and surprisingly clear-headed the following morning when he checked on the progress being made on the wagon. Father Bradley met him in front of the blacksmith's tent, his spirits high. He was holding a Bible.

"Angels come visiting us last night," he said. "That man you met yesterday—Mr. Baggett—he came by and made arrangements with the blacksmith for payment of repairs to our wagon and the return of our mule. Next thing, he approached my wife and placed a twenty-dollar gold piece in the palm of her hand. Never said so much as a word. What a fine Christian man he is. Certain proof that God does work in the most mysterious of ways."

Will went in search of Baggett and found him and his son saddling their horses. "I heard about your act of kindness," he said.

Baggett didn't respond.

"And," Darby continued, "I'd like to accept your offer of that job if it still stands."

Baggett adjusted his hat and nodded. "We'll ride out soon as we partake of Mrs. Bradley's breakfast. She just informed me that she purchased fresh eggs and sweetbreads down at the mercantile."

AFTER THEY ATE, Will moved to sit next to Father Bradley. "Seems you folks ain't the only ones to experience recent good fortune," he said. "I've been offered a job, which I've accepted. So I'll be saying goodbye and wishing you good luck on the remainder of your journey. I put your shotgun in the wagon."

"God be with you," Bradley said. "It's been a pleasure knowing you, and I'll keep you in my prayers."

Darby walked over to the children and gave them each a hug. "Miss Darla, you keep tending to your reading," he said. He tipped his hat to Mrs. Bradley.

There was a momentary silence, as if there was something left unsaid, before he turned away and mounted his horse.

The children were still shouting their goodbyes as he joined Baggett and his men, headed north.

When the riders reached the edge of town, they saw the old man Darby had rescued standing by the road. As they passed, he removed his sweat-stained hat and waved.

The West Texas terrain was bleak, arid flatland for as far as the eye could see. Once the homeland of bands of Comanches who hunted buffalo and waged war against white man trespassers, it was now the location of a few small, isolated ranches and settlements and a route for fortune seekers on their way to the silver mines of New Mexico.

Baggett and his son rode lead with Darby and the three others trailing. Through much of the day, they kept a steady pace with little conversation. Finally, Baggett turned in his saddle and said, "A short way from here is a creek with a stand of trees on its bank. We'll stop there to allow the horses to drink and get us some shade."

Will wondered about their ultimate destination, but didn't ask. Neither did his fellow newcomers.

They had not anticipated the scene that greeted them as they arrived at the creek. Four men sat beneath the shade of a tree, their horses tethered nearby. The burned-out campfire indicated they had been there a while. Along the water's edge was what appeared to have been a makeshift pen.

"Come and sit a spell," one of the men called out. "We got good news."

He went straight to Ben Baggett and handed him a saddlebag. "Thirty head," he said, "five of 'em calves. All fat and in good health. They brought you top dollar."

Saying nothing, Ben opened the bag and began counting the money.

"Wasn't much of a place," another said. "Little old dog-run cabin in the middle of nowhere. No fences. They didn't even know we'd come. We was on our way and long gone before they even woke up. Last night, we drove the cattle to meet up with the driver who was expecting them, collected our pay without problem, and returned here to wait for you to arrive."

He turned to Dell Baggett, who was still sitting astride his mount. "You bring anything to drink?"

Darby listened to the exchange, then watched as Ben counted out bills and handed them out to the four men. He wondered what he'd gotten himself into.

"There'll be no drinking until our work's done," the elder Baggett said. "I assume we've got another plan."

Another of the men stepped forward. "I rode about a day and a half to the east," he said, "and found two more places. They're little, but they've got a right smart of cows grazing. I'd guess twenty or thirty head at each. And I didn't see no neighbors anywhere near. Quieter than a Baptist graveyard."

He'd drawn a crude map, which he pulled from his pocket.

The man who had been in charge of the saddlebag said, "The folks we did business with last night said they're interested in buying more as soon as we can provide them."

Baggett seemed pleased. "Let's get some rest. Then you boys can head out tomorrow. I'll be going on home, leaving Dell and these new boys to give you a hand."

A campfire took the night chill from the air, its flames playing against the faces of the new recruits, who sat listening as Dell Baggett outlined the operation his father had devised.

Passing the map around, he said, "You'll ride out in two groups, four in each. Two of you will be accompanying the men with experience at this. They'll do any explaining necessary along the way. You'll be pleased to find it ain't a complicated undertaking. Once you've collected the cattle, you'll herd them to a place that's already been scouted out and wait for the buyers to arrive."

The newcomers were silent, contemplating the activity they'd hired on for.

"Anybody got questions?" Dell asked.

Will spoke up. "I got no weapon since mine was stolen."

"It's not likely you'll be needing one," Dell said.

THE LEADER OF Darby's group was a one-eyed man called Bootsy, who enjoyed talking, mostly about himself. He'd come to Texas from Kansas to avoid spending time in jail or dangling from the end of a rope for killing a man he hit over the head with a rifle barrel. The man had "full well deserved it," he said.

"In case you're wondering about our plan, it's a simple one that's worked time and time again since I hired on with Mr. Baggett. We'll schedule our arrival at some time around dusk. We'll get close enough to the ranch only to learn the lay of the land and where the cattle graze. That done, we'll locate ourselves a resting spot and wait until around midnight to carry out our business. I've already been told there's no fencing, so that'll not pose us a problem.

"If you've not herded cattle before, be assured it ain't difficult. They're not very smart animals and will head in whichever direction you point them. I've got makings for torches we can use to light our way to the holding pen once we've distanced ourselves from the pasture."

He scanned the anxious faces of the two newcomers and laughed. "You boys got no need for worry," he said. "This'll be the easiest payday you've ever earned. Unless, of course, you've got bank robbing in your history."

Will found himself wondering how many of those who had hired on to Baggett's "cattle business" were lawbreakers. And how he'd feel once he joined their ranks. In an effort to dismiss such thoughts, he reminded himself of his empty pockets and the absence of any other plan for his future.

"An easy payday's waiting," he whispered to himself.

"I got one other rule," Bootsy said. "It's one I ain't never shared with the boss or his boy and needs to be kept secret among us. Most of these folks keep their milk cow near the barn but occasionally they're allowed to graze with the herd. Wherever they are, they're to be left behind. Stealing a family's milk cow ain't in my makeup. Nor should it be in yours."

J UST AS BOOTSY had promised, it was easy. The cattle were docile and willing. Calves dutifully trailed along behind their mothers. The theft was carried out in a matter of minutes. No lanterns were lit in the ranch house. No booming sound of a warning shotgun blast had broken the night's stillness.

The unsuspecting family, whoever they were, had been robbed of their hard-earned livelihood without anyone even waking.

Twenty-four hours later, the job was done. Wranglers from a herd en route to Kansas City had come and driven the stolen cattle away. The money bag hung on Bootsy's saddle horn.

"Everybody did good," Bootsy said. "Time now we head to the canyon."

CHAPTER FOURTEEN

A S THE HORSES carefully made their way down a narrow trail, the horizon disappeared, replaced by towering walls of jagged rock formations. Darby had never seen anything like it. "What is this place?" he called out to Bootsy, who was leading the way.

"It's called Palo Duro Canyon," he said. "Runs for miles and miles, getting deeper and deeper. The history books say the Spanish explorers came on it hundreds of years back. Wasn't too long ago that the Apaches, then the Kiowas, then the Comanches settled in, using it as a place to do their hunting and to trade horses to the Comancheros. Now it's just us."

"Us?"

"Yep, this here's where Mr. Baggett headquarters."

Shortly, they reached the canyon floor and arrived at an opening where a rambling encampment was alive with activity. Against both canyon walls were rows of small log cabins. In the middle was an open-sided pavilion, where meetings were held and meals taken.

There were a holding pen for the horses and a cistern that provided water for a fenced garden. There were tents and dugouts, firepits, a smokehouse, and a storage building that housed everything from saddles to extra parts for a couple of wagons.

A flock of chickens scattered as the riders approached.

"You'll be bunking in one of the tents," Bootsy said. "The cabins are reserved for those who have been on the payroll longest." He explained that when not on the trail, rustling and robbing, everyone had duties to perform at the camp. "Ol' Duster, for instance, he's the cook. Done the same for a cattle company down south before he joined up. He's got a couple of boys who help him with tending the smokehouse and his garden, which he's mighty proud of. We got fellas who are good at building things or cutting firewood and hauling water. The young Baggett has two or three he handpicks to occasionally accompany him into town for supplies."

"What town's that?" Darby asked.

"There's a little place known as Tascosa that's not too far north. Mr. Baggett don't cotton to us visiting except on special occasions, so don't be thinking about wandering off. I expect in time we'll know what chores you're best suited to. No doubt, there'll be something that'll keep you busy."

As they pulled their horses up to a watering trough, the elder Baggett emerged from one of the cabins. "I see you boys made it back in one piece," he yelled. "The other group's already home." He approached Bootsy, who was lifting the money bag from his saddle horn.

They walked to the pavilion and sat down at a table, where the cook had already placed a pot of coffee and tin cups. Dell Baggett joined them as his father shook out the contents of the canvas bag. "How many?"

"Twenty-eight," Bootsy said. "One of 'em appeared

a bit wormy, so I cut the price by a dollar, thinking that to be good business."

Baggett nodded as he began silently counting the money. Once done, he made four small stacks of bills and pushed one in the direction of each man. Before he could ask, Bootsy assured him that the two newcomers had carried out their jobs well.

"Good to hear," Baggett said. "Get yourselves cleaned and rested," he said. "Then look to enjoying a home-cooked meal this evening. You'll not be going out again for a few days. We've got a group that rode out earlier today, and Renfro's on the trail, doing his scouting. When he comes back with news, we'll consider plans for your next trip."

He folded the money, placed it back in the bag, and left, Dell following. "You boys enjoy your coffee," he said.

Once the pot was empty, the men led their horses to the corral and unsaddled them. "Which tent will be mine?" Darby asked.

Bootsy pointed. "That one over yonder." He placed a hand on Darby's shoulder. "How does it feel, having money in your pocket with more to come?"

"Can't say I mind it."

"My advice is save it and not go spending it need-lessly. That's what I've been doing for quite some time. One of these days, I hope to have me a grubstake large enough to start up my own cattle business."

"Same as Baggett's cattle business?"

Bootsy laughed and rubbed his hand across his blind eye. "What else?"

WILL STRETCHED OUT in his tent, enjoying the first moment of solitude he'd had since leaving Las Lunas. Several times he slid his hand into his pocket to touch his money. Earning the wages had not been difficult yet he had a disquieting feeling that would not go away. Not that he hadn't stolen before, but taking from people who depended on what he'd taken for their livelihood troubled him. Thieving for a living, being part of an outlaw gang, was not a future he'd imagined for himself.

He felt his wages again, seeking some manner of justification for his actions. He attempted to turn his thoughts to other things. He closed his eyes and tried to visualize his pa and his brother, Clay, back on the farm, but the visions were marred by his awareness of the disapproval they would feel. The same happened when he thought of Father Bradley and his family. Will Darby felt desperately alone as he struggled with the most recent of his bad decisions.

I N THE MONTHS to come, his concern only grew.
   The routine was always the same. One of the scouts would return to the camp, describing some hardscrabble farm or ranch where cattle could be easily stolen. They would ride out, do their midnight rustling, then meet up with trail drivers who paid for the herd and rode away.

For reasons Darby never understood or questioned, he wasn't assigned a regular chore. With time on his hands, he occasionally volunteered to help cut firewood or haul water. He even took it upon himself to gather the eggs, making a game of seeking out the hidden nests of the free-range hens.

One evening after supper, he was returning to his tent when the cook called his name. "The boss wants to see you up at his cabin," he said.

Baggett was sitting on the front porch, a glass of whiskey in his hand. "Thanks for coming, Will. Let's go inside, where I can find you a glass. I recall you being a whiskey man, right?"

"Yessir."

"Well, then, let's have us a drink and do a little talking."

The cabin was spare and uninviting. There was a single room with a large bed, a table, and chairs. Against one wall were a fireplace and a shelf that held a few dime novels. The rug in the middle of the rock floor was faded and frayed. Will wondered why Baggett spent so much time in such a colorless place.

He poured Darby a drink and motioned for him to take a chair. "I've been waiting for you to get settled in before having this conversation," he said. "You're no doubt aware you've not been assigned any chores here in the canyon. The reason is I have a special job I'd like for you to consider. I've had it in mind ever since I seen how you fought off them fellows back in Las Lunas."

Will was suddenly feeling uneasy but said nothing. Instead, he sipped at his whiskey.

"Don't know as you've noticed," Baggett continued, "but my boy ain't what we'll call assertive. He's not likely to fight, even to defend himself. I'm aware of a few times when he's taken a whupping, then lied to me about why he came home with a black eye or a split lip.

"As you're aware, he occasionally takes the wagon up to Tascosa to buy supplies. And I know that while he's there, he admires a visit to the saloon. There's folk who frequent that establishment that don't look kindly on us. My fear's that there might be trouble one day that Dell ain't properly prepared to handle."

"I thought he was always accompanied by a couple of the men," Will said.

"That's true, but I have no confidence they're capable of taking care of themselves, much less my boy, should things turn drunk ugly. I've seen that you're blessed with that talent. So what I have in mind is for you to accompany Will when he leaves camp, particularly if his destination is Tascosa. It would give me a great comfort."

For a moment, Will acted as if he was contemplating the suggested arrangement, knowing all the while that Ben Baggett would not accept no for an answer. "I'll do my best, sir," he said.

"Fine, fine. I knew I could count on you." He poured more whiskey, and as Will picked up his glass, Baggett left the table and went to a footlocker at the end of his bed. He returned with a gun belt and a shiny Colt in a hand-tooled holster. "I'd feel better knowing you were wearing this," Baggett said.

WHEN WILL RETURNED to his tent, Bootsy was standing outside, puffing on his corncob pipe. "With it being such a nice evening and all, I was wondering if you might like some company," he said.

Bootsy was the closest thing to a friend Will had in the camp. He didn't even know many of the other hands by name. People, he'd decided early on, didn't sign up with Ben Baggett to develop friendships.

Two cups of coffee were sitting on a flat rock near the tent's entrance. "Cook had some left over from dinner, so he obliged me with the dregs."

"I've just come from Mr. Baggett's cabin," Will said, assuming that Bootsy already knew. "He had a proposition on his mind."

"And?"

He outlined the proposal the boss had made. "I didn't see it as a matter I really had a choice in," Will said, "so I agreed to do it."

Bootsy puffed at his pipe. "Seems to me," he said, "you just got yourself a promotion. Tells me the ol' man sees you as somethin' special. Young Dell's not likely to appreciate having a bodyguard trailing along, doing his bidding, but seeing how it's his daddy's notion, he'll have to make his peace with the idea. Ain't nobody here, Dell Baggett included, who goes against the wishes of the boss."

It sounded more like a warning to Will than an observation.

They sat as darkness arrived and the ink black sky filled with stars. "You ever get weary of all this?" Will asked. "Ever want to just ride away somewhere and be by your lonesome, known to nobody?"

"When I was your age, I occasionally considered such notions. But time passes, and a body gets too tired to even think of such matters, much less act on them. You reach a point where you just accept your lot in life, trying to make it through one day at a time. Still, I have to admit, there are times when I think about owning my own place."

The conversation went silent, the only sounds the wind humming through the canyon and coyotes calling out to their mates.

Finally, Will spoke. "I got another question that I've got no rightful cause for asking. If you consider it none of my business, just say so."

"What's that?"

"How was it you lost your eye?"

For a time it didn't appear Bootsy was inclined to answer. "Back in my younger days, before stealing cattle became my trade, I had it in mind that I'd make my fortune as a buffalo hunter, selling skins and gathering the bones of carcasses picked clean by buzzards. The work was hard and stunk to high heaven, but it turned a nice profit.

"We were up on the Kansas plains and had made camp for the night when this band of renegades—Comanches—came riding down on us, hollering and shooting. Before we could get to our feet and raise our guns, my partner was shot dead. One of them come at me with the biggest knife I ever saw. We struggled for a bit before he slashed my face, cuttin' through my eye.

"The pain was like nothing I'd ever known. It felt like he'd cut plumb into my brain, and I was wishing they'd go ahead and kill me as well. Instead, they bound my hands and feet, propped me up, and forced me to watch as they scalped my dead partner. Then they cut his skin away and opened him up. Last thing I remember was them eating his bloody heart."

Will shook his head. "But you survived . . ."

"Next morning some other buffalo hunters found me and rode me to Topeka for doctoring. For a time I wore me an eye patch, but soon wearied of drunks and smart mouths referring to me as One-Eye. Last one who did got himself killed."

He knocked ashes from his pipe. "So now you know my story."

Then he rose and stretched his legs. "Time to put these weary ol' bones to bed," he said. Before walking away, he looked down at the Colt Will had been given by Baggett.

"Fine-lookin' sidearm," he said. "Hope you'll not have cause to use it."

CHAPTER FIFTEEN

DARBY HAD RIDDEN out on two more raids and would have thought little about watching out for Dell Baggett, had it not been for the occasions when their paths crossed in camp. Dell never spoke, only offering a sullen stare as he passed. Obviously, his father had told him of the plan he'd discussed with Will.

It was after the elder Baggett counted the take from the most recent theft and passed out pay to the men that he called Will aside. "Tomorrow, Dell will be riding into Tascosa for supplies," he said. "Plan on accompanying him. Top Wilson will be along as well, helping load the wagon. Your job will be no heavy lifting. Just keep your eyes open for any trouble that might develop."

They left early the following morning, Dell and Wilson in the wagon, Will riding alongside, wearing his sidearm.

Tascosa had already come into view when Dell finally spoke. "There's no real need for me saying how much I dislike your coming along, but I wanted to bring it out into the open. I ain't blaming you for being here. Still, I got no cause to like it."

Darby didn't reply.

The younger Baggett halted the wagon in front of the mercantile. He pulled a list the cook had written out for him and handed it to Top. "You tend this," he said. "I'll start fetching the other things."

He looked at Will, who was tying his horse to a hitching post. "I suppose all that's asked of you is to be ready should the old store owner—who can't see his hand in front of his face—attempt to draw down on us." His voice was laced with sarcasm.

Gathering the goods went quickly. Top loaded sacks of flour, beans, and sugar into the bed of the wagon, then went in search of coal oil, lard, and canned peaches. Several of the hands had given him money to buy chewing tobacco. Dell wandered the aisle filled with hardware items, collecting nails, a couple of rolls of barbed wire, a water pump to replace one that had recently quit working, and new canvas for making additional living quarters in the canyon.

While Baggett settled the bill at the counter up front, Top disappeared to the back of the store. Curious, Darby followed and found him in the company of a pretty young woman who was dusting and stocking shelves. Though his back was turned to Will, it was obvious that the balding, thin-lipped cowboy's presence was making her uncomfortable.

He had moved closer and was attempting a kiss when Will called out, "Time we're leaving, Top. Right now."

Top turned and glared. The woman mouthed the words, "Thank you."

Outside, Dell suggested a visit to the saloon. "This being the parching work it is," he said, "I think we've earned ourselves a sip of whiskey."

Approaching the doorway, he stepped over a sleeping dog and entered the cool darkness. There was only a handful of customers, locals seated at one of the poker tables. Dell tipped his hat to the owner. "Nice to see you, Miz Madge," he said as he moved toward the bar.

One of the poker players spoke loud enough for the new arrivals to hear. "Looks like Lil' Baggett's come to town to do his daddy's shopping," he said. Dell ignored him and ordered a whiskey.

They drank in silence. Darby sipped at a glass of beer while Dell and Top downed several shots. "Ain't my business how much a man drinks," Will finally said, "but we'll be needing to get on our way if we hope to make it back before dark."

Dell grunted his disapproval but shoved his empty glass toward Madge. "You can put this on my old man's account," he said, "and I'll be needing a bottle of his favorite brand to bring to him."

T HE WAGON CREAKED under its heavy load, and the horses snorted as their riggings tightened. Dell, warmed by the liquor, seemed in better spirits while Wilson was sullen, his hat pulled low over his face.

"Your lady friend you was speaking with back in the store," Will said, "you two sweet on each other?"

Top didn't answer, but Dell began to laugh.

"Jennie Broder, pretty little thing that she is, won't have nothing to do with the likes of Top, no matter how hard he might wish."

"That's hogwash," Wilson said. "She'll come to her senses before all's said and done." He'd obviously had eyes on her for some time.

The conversation interested Darby. "Is the old man who runs the mercantile her daddy?"

Dell answered. "Nah, he's her grandpa, and he don't

cotton to Top Wilson any more'n she does. She lives on a farm outside town. Her, her pa, and her grandpa. She comes into town on occasion to help out in the store."

A FTER THE WAGON was unloaded and supper was served, Darby retreated to his tent. He removed his gun belt and boots and sat outside in the cool evening air, contemplating the day. He was pleased to have reported to the elder Baggett that the trip to town had passed without incident.

And he thought of Jennie Broder and the faint "thank you" smile she'd given him. Dell was right. She was easy on the eyes.

As Ben Baggett's most trusted scout, Top Wilson spent less time in camp than any other employee. Though he was assigned one of the cabins in the canyon, he seemed to prefer the open spaces. His job was to roam Texas and eastern New Mexico in search of new targets for the rustlers, and it wasn't unusual for him to be gone for long stretches of time.

Only after he'd been on the trail for weeks, returning with news of new herds he'd located, did he remain in camp, allowing his horse time to rest or, if need be, have a blacksmith replace his worn shoes. If the boredom of camp life set in, Top would accompany rustlers on a trip to one of the sites he'd scouted or volunteer to accompany Dell Baggett on his errand runs into Tascosa.

Wilson knew that the old man wouldn't live forever, eventually turning his "cattle business" over to his son. Being friends with the young Baggett, he believed, was a good investment in his future. Dell, whom he judged a simpleton with no strong will, would need someone tough-minded to see that everyone stayed in line and that things continued to run smoothly. Top Wilson saw himself as that man.

Of all those working for Baggett, he was the most mysterious. When asked about his people, Top would fabricate tales of his father being a U.S. marshal who had patrolled the Texas–Mexico border, sending a dozen men, not including Indians, to meet their Maker. When asked where he'd come from, his answer was always "Down south."

In truth, he was the son of a South Texas circuit preacher who shouted fire and brimstone in exchange for small donations from believers and an occasional free chicken dinner from strangers. They were never in any one place long. Top's mother had died when he was just a child, so it was just he and the Reverend Wilson, wandering from place to place.

The older Top got, the angrier he became.

It was his duty to pass out the hymnals filled with songs he never memorized and to collect the "love offerings" at the end of each sermon. Top didn't believe in the sometimes loving, sometimes vengeful God his father spoke of, nor did he concern himself with his destination in the Hereafter. He just wanted to ride away and never hear the preacher's voice again.

Finally, after stealing a Sunday offering, he made his escape on his fourteenth birthday. He spent most of the money he'd taken, getting drunk on blackberry wine. He stole from farmers' gardens for food.

In time, he signed on as a messenger for a bandito border gang, first learning the excitement and profit of the outlaw life. Then, a few years later, in a Sonora cantina, he met Ben Baggett, who convinced him there was a promising future in cattle rustling.

WILL DARBY FELT a growing dislike for Wilson, though it was based only on the brief encounter with Jennie Broder he'd witnessed in the mercantile.

The feeling was obviously mutual, considering the silent glares Top gave him whenever they crossed paths.

Will was certain that the moment in the back of the store was not the first time Wilson had sought the young woman's attention or that his doing so had made her quite uncomfortable.

O N A QUIET Sunday afternoon, Darby watched as Top left the pavilion and went to the corral to saddle his horse. As he rode away, it was obvious that he'd not stocked the provisions he took on a scouting trip.

Will quickly followed.

It soon became clear that Top was headed to Tascosa. But, instead of riding straight to the saloon, Will watched Wilson steer his horse toward the edge of town. In front of a small cabin, several buggies were parked, and from inside came the sound of voices singing hymns.

For a moment Darby wondered if Top had come to town to join in the gathering. But, when he simply stood outside, leaning against the wheel of one of the buggies, Will recognized that he was only waiting for the meeting to end.

He dismounted and moved closer, kneeling behind a vacant shed.

Soon, the singing ended and people began leaving, exchanging their goodbyes in the front yard. Will immediately recognized Jennie Broder. She was wearing a gingham dress, and her bonnet hid most of her blond hair. She was smiling as she walked toward her buggy. Until she saw Top Wilson.

They spoke for a few minutes, but from his distance, Darby couldn't hear what was being said. Jennie began shaking her head and turned away. Top grabbed her by the arm, spinning her around until their faces were inches apart. The conversation had taken an ugly turn.

He wasn't aware of Will's presence until hands clamped against his shoulder, pulling him away from the terrified woman. "I think that'll be enough," Darby said. "Seems pretty clear the lady's not interested in your company. Best you be on your way."

Wilson gritted his teeth, let out what sounded like a low animal's growl, and took a wild, ineffective swing at Will. Darby responded with a jarring blow to the side of Top's head and quickly followed it with a breath-robbing blow to the stomach. Top slumped to his knees, the growl turning to a groan.

Nearby, Jennie held both hands to her face, crying.

Will stood over Wilson. "I didn't come here intending you harm," he said, "until you showed your ungentlemanly ways. That, I got no tolerance for. Before you get up and go on your way, I hope you'll come to the decision not to bother this lady again."

Top spat blood into the dirt and got to his feet, cursing. "Next time you attempt this manner of cowardly bushwhacking," he said, "you'd best be wearing that pistol the boss gave you. I ain't forgetting this, Darby. Believe me when I say it."

He staggered away, wiping blood from his ear. He was still cursing as he rode in the direction of Madge's saloon.

Will removed his hat and moved toward the shaken woman. "Miss," he said, "I'd like to apologize for the unfortunate commotion. You okay?"

Jennie dabbed a kerchief at her eyes, then smiled the same warm smile he'd seen in the mercantile. "I thank you kindly once again," she said.

They stood silently for a few seconds before she turned to climb into her buggy.

Will took a deep breath, hoping words would come. "My name's Darby. Will Darby. I wonder would it be okay if I ride along with you to see you get home safe?"

She retied her bonnet and took the reins. "I'd much appreciate it," she said.

As if she had read the question on Will's mind, Jennie began trying to explain her history with Top Wilson. "He's been a pest for quite some time," she said, "though never have I given even the slightest indication I was interested in anything he might have to say. The truth is, he scares me, though he's never done me any real harm. But you've seen the temper he possesses. I don't think he's quite right.

"Seems he knows wherever I am. It was in my grandpa's store that I first encountered him. In time, he began coming in there regular. I also used to occasionally help out Madge with cleaning the saloon, but seemed every time I did, there he was, looking at me, so I stopped going. A few times, he's even come to the farm, acting nice as you please, but my pa always ran him off anyway. And now he shows up at Sunday singing, shaming me in front of my friends."

Darby felt partially responsible for the latter as he listened to the weary frustration in her voice. As they neared the farm, the day was coming to an end, the sun turning to a giant orange ball sitting on the horizon.

He was helping her put the buggy away when her father emerged from the house, hurrying toward them with an angry look on his face. When he saw that it was a stranger removing the halter and reins from the horse, he slowed.

"Papa," Jennie called out, "this is Mr. Darby. He kindly volunteered to escort me home."

She turned to Will. "You're welcome to sit a bit and catch your breath before leaving," she said. "I've got lemonade to offer."

"If you reckon it would be okay with your pa."

Cyrus Broder's voice was gruff, but the anger had eased from his face. "I reckon that'll be okay," he said. "I've got to go out to the barn and see the animals are bedded down and the chickens have gone to roost, so I'll leave you two to it."

They sat, sipping lemonade, when a bluetick hound came onto the porch and curled at Jennie's feet.

"I had me a dog once. Name of Sarge. Me and my brother raised him from a pup," Will said. There was a melancholy tone to his voice.

THE FOLLOWING DAY, several of the men asked Wilson about the bruise on the side of his face and the swelling of his ear. It was his explanation that two drunken buffalo hunters had attacked and tried to rob him when he went behind the saloon to relieve himself. He'd retaliated by taking a board to them, leaving both unconscious.

By noon, he had stocked his saddlebags with provisions and was off on another scouting trip.

Bootsy stood beside Darby, watching as Wilson disappeared up the canyon trail. "Seen you riding away yesterday," he said.

"Yep," Will replied, "I decided on attending Sunday singing."

CHAPTER SIXTEEN

I N THE MOONLIGHT, the ramshackle ranch house looked just as Top Wilson had described it. Built of sod and timbers, it listed to one side and rocks had begun to fall away from the chimney. The outbuildings had seen better days. What little fencing there was hadn't had proper upkeep in some time. It was easy to count the number of cattle lying in a group at one end of the pasture. There were only eighteen.

From their hillside vantage point, Darby stared silently at the scene. *These are dirt-poor folks, barely getting by,* he thought, *and we're here to rob them of all hope for any kind of future.*

"Don't hardly seem worth the trip," one of the rustlers said. "Won't be long before Top has us riding plumb down to the Rio Grande or back over into East Texas. Guess we've about cleaned out all the close-by places. At least this'll be easy."

And it was, until two loud shotgun blasts erupted from the front porch of the house. The owner and his son had been roused by the noise of their herd being driven away.

Though already a safe distance away, well out of range of any buckshot aimed in their direction, one of the rustlers reined his horse to a stop and pulled his Winchester from its sheath. Turning toward the house, he fired a series of rapid shots.

There was a distant yell, and one of the men dropped his shotgun and slumped against the porch railing.

"Teach them to go shooting at me," the rustler said as he joined the others moving the cattle.

Will felt a knot swell in his stomach, then thought he was going to be sick. "There was no cause for that," he shouted as the proud gunman rode past.

"Somebody shoots at me," he replied, "he's going to get shooting in return."

It was that moment, like a vision, that Will Darby knew he needed to get out of the cattle-rustling business. Stealing was one thing. Bloodthirst for no good reason was another. It troubled him that no one had even seemed curious whether the rancher had been killed or just wounded. It was just part of doing business.

Darby suddenly felt hopelessly trapped. He'd left everything behind for his independence, and all it had provided was a growing feeling of regret and guilt. When, after writing that one letter home almost two years earlier, he'd received a response from his brother urging him to return and visit his ailing father while there was still time, he'd stubbornly chosen to ignore Clay's plea. It now weighed on him. He missed his pa and the company of his brother and found himself thinking about them often.

It was not only people he'd left behind, he'd come to realize. It was a place, a peaceful little East Texas farm that had been replaced by a canyon filled with outlaws and no-accounts.

He tried to talk with Bootsy about his feelings after they'd returned but got no comfort. "Thing you gotta realize," his friend said, "is that everybody here has shot and killed his fair share of men, be it in the war or in other less justified times. Me included. That's the way this going-to-Hades life is. I got one word of warning you'll do well to think on. The true fact of the matter is this life's far easier to get into than to escape from."

The only rays of brightness Will found himself clinging to were his thoughts of Jennie Broder. He'd seen her several times since escorting her home, visiting the farm on a couple of occasions to sit on the front porch and talk, and saying hello in her grandpa's store.

He had no idea how she felt about him, but he had no doubt that she'd found her way into his heart. His spirits had soared when she invited him to Sunday dinner. When he briefly hesitated, she laughed. "Not to worry," she said. "Papa has promised he'll not shoot you so long as you display proper table manners and use no foul language."

CYRUS BRODER SAID little during the meal, content to listen as his daughter and her gentleman caller enjoyed each other's company. It was when Jennie was in the kitchen, doing dishes, that he and Will spoke.

Broder had obviously given careful thought to what he wished to say. "I've got great admiration for my girl's good judgment," he said. "That's to the credit of her mama, God rest her soul. I don't know if Jennie's said so, but it's clear to me she has feelings for you. You know, you're the first man ever invited to sit at our dinner table."

He chuckled and added, "Fact is, you're the first I ain't considered taking my shotgun to."

He quickly turned serious again. "From what I've

observed, you seem a good man. What you done to protect my daughter a while back set well with me. My concern is the manner in which you earn your living. I'll be honest and say I've got no use for Ben Baggett, though I've never had occasion to meet him. But you hear things—about his lacking good character and his unlawful doings. That you're on his payroll is highly troubling to me, and I can't shed that worry."

Will was at a loss for a response. Finally, he said, "I ain't proud of what I got into when I signed on with him. And I'm planning to soon remedy that mistake." He paused, then added, "Much of that decision is on account of your daughter."

T HE DAY HAD begun to cool as they walked along a pathway leading to a hillside on the edge of Jennie's daddy's farm. Will praised her cooking and the affection her father obviously felt for her.

"He's proud of this place, you know," she said, looking out on the greening landscape. "Loves it with all his heart and soul."

"And rightfully so. It brings to mind my own homeplace. I wanted to tell you we had ourselves a conversation while you were cleaning up in the kitchen."

"I take it he didn't order you to get on your horse and be gone," she said.

"He was expressing concern about me working for Ben Baggett," Darby said. Though she had never broached the subject, he knew it troubled her as well.

Will took her hand. "He's right, you know. I've done things in my life that I've got no cause to feel proud about. I've done a lot of acting before thinking, things I'd prefer we not discuss. But, like I told your daddy, I'm of a mind to mend my ways as best I can, starting with parting ways with Baggett and his sorry bunch."

Jennie rose to her tiptoes and kissed him on the cheek. "And what is it you plan on doing thereafter?"

"I reckon I'll go home and help my brother tend the farm, if he'll have me. I'd lost sight of the beauty there. Come spring, it gets so green it'll hurt your eye. There's clear streams for fishing and woods for hunting. Folks back home do their Sunday singing in a real church."

They began walking again, now hand in hand, as he continued to describe the little town of Aberdene, its quiet ways and good people quick to extend a helping hand to their neighbors. He talked of Clay—"the good brother"—and their happy times together as young boys. "I'm of a mind there's much I can still learn from him."

"It sounds like a place I'd like to see one day," she said as they turned toward the house.

As they approached the house, Jennie waved to her daddy sitting on the front porch, sipping a glass of sweet tea.

"You know," Will said, "there's good sometimes come outta bad. Had I not been hired by Baggett and come to these parts, I'd never have seen you—or got me a taste of your fine cooking."

"In that case," Jennie said, "I'd say good for your Mr. Baggett."

CHAPTER SEVENTEEN

A COCKFIGHT HAD just ended, and the cook was removing gaffs from the loser's spurs. "He'll be the chicken with my dumplings tonight," he said as he picked up the dead rooster. As betting money exchanged hands, Ben Baggett was walking from his cabin toward the pavilion.

He'd called a meeting, and all hands were gathering. Walking at his side was Top Wilson.

"As you know, Top's been on the trail for a good spell, riding both sides of the Red River. And he's returned with news of a number of new herds and an agreement with trail drivers who say they'll gladly purchase every head we can gather.

"This'll be our biggest operation and will require more planning. There'll be more miles of traveling, a need for more provisions, and more men. We'll be sending out three groups of four this time. The payday's gonna make you think Christmas done come early."

A buzz rolled through the gathering. A few even applauded.

The men were unaware that Wilson, now smiling broadly, had been harshly scolded by the boss after the last raid when only eighteen underfed cattle had been stolen. His recent scouting trip had been motivated by the urgent need to return to Ben's good graces.

Baggett pulled a paper from his shirt pocket and read the list of those picked for the three groups. Will Darby's name was on it.

"I hope the wages are what he's promising," he said as he and Bootsy walked from the meeting.

Disappointed that his name hadn't been called, Bootsy kicked at the dirt. "Whatever it'll be, none will find its way into my pockets. I'd give my left eye—if I still had it—to be making that ride."

"It'll be my last one," Will said.

"Why's that?"

"I'm just weary of not feeling right about what it is we do. This payday and what I've got saved will be my moving-on money."

Bootsy shook his head in disbelief. "Don't be expecting no parade when you take your leave," he said. "I ain't aware of many folks who quit on the old man without regret and a sizable amount of grief."

Again, Will knew his friend was issuing a warning. "I'll be so far gone once he knows it, he'll not be able to do anything about it," he said. "I've thought hard on it of late, and it's the right thing for me to be doing."

Bootsy finally smiled. "A woman figure into your thinking?"

Darby chose to ignore the question, but asked that their conversation be kept a secret.

* * *

THE MORNING THEY were to leave, the men rose before dawn for breakfast, then filled their saddlebags with still-warm biscuits, muffins, and cold-water
corn bread. A packhorse had been loaded with canned
goods, coffee, chewing tobacco, and surprise sacks of
stick candy.

Baggett stood, watching as the men assembled. From
the corral, Top Wilson came riding toward the gathering. "There'll be no need for a map this trip," the boss
said. "He'll be leading your way."

They rode for three days, mostly along the northern
bank of the river. There had been little conversation,
even when they bedded down in the evenings. Will
made a conscious effort to avoid Wilson.

After breaking camp on the fourth morning, Top
led the men farther north into Indian Territory. Shortly
before noon they approached a shallow valley where
tepees were lined in carefully plotted rows. From a distance, they could see women tending small cooking
fires while children played. The men sat in groups,
watching youngsters run footraces.

Nearby, cattle roamed freely, grazing.

"Wasn't ever no mention made of dealing with In-
juns," one of the cowboys said as he rode next to Wilson.

Top returned his spyglass to its case. "They're Comanches who've fled the reservation," he said. "Their
herd has grown since I was last here, so I suspect they're
stealing on a regular basis. All we'll be doing is taking
back what don't belong to them in the first place."

"They'll not likely give the cattle up without a fight."

The leader ignored the observation.

Later, there was no campfire for brewing coffee or
warming beans. The only plan Wilson had provided was

that they would wait until deep night, then approach the herd from the back side and drive them toward the river. It was, he explained, his reason for keeping the three groups intact. "Once we're done here," he said, "we'll split up and go our separate ways. But this one's gonna require all hands."

Darby approached the leader when he was alone. "You right sure you've thought this out?" he said. "You know there's a good chance for bloodshed if we don't get away quickly."

"So be it," Top said. "That's what we're carrying firearms for."

"Was Mr. Baggett told of this plan?"

"All the boss wants is cattle rustled and money made. The details don't worry him," Top said. "Why, you feeling scared?"

Will slowly shook his head. "Stealing is one thing," he said. "Risking more than makes good sense is something else altogether."

"Feel free to turn tail and be on your way if it's your choice," Top said. "Wouldn't surprise me none."

For a fleeting moment, Darby considered doing just that. But a strange sense of loyalty to a group of men he hardly knew overruled the idea. If fighting did break out, every man would be needed.

He was through deserting.

LED BY WILSON, they made a wide single-file loop around the Comanche village. Across Top's lap lay his Winchester. There was no moon, and clouds covered the stars, so the going was slow. Only when they were finally in place was the signal given to light the torches and begin moving the cattle.

In a matter of seconds, young braves were pouring from the tepees, rifles pointed in the direction of the rustlers. A shot whistled past Darby's head as he slapped his rope against his thigh and yelled in an effort to get the cattle moving. Nearby, he heard a loud thud followed by a pained scream. A riderless horse ran past.

The herd began to move swiftly away from the camp. The Comanches hurried to their ponies and gave chase as the rustlers began returning fire. One of the pursuing ponies stopped and reared on its hind legs, then fell to the ground after being struck by a bullet. Its rider lay nearby, writhing in pain.

The chase finally ended when the cattle were herded across a shallow spot in the river. Top then ordered his men to form a line, take a knee, and begin firing on the approaching Comanches. "If you kill them every one, it won't bother me," he shouted.

The gunfight lasted only a few minutes before the Indians, short of ammunition, turned away.

When things quieted, the tired herd returned to the shallows to drink as Wilson raised his arms in celebration. Then he surveyed the damage. Two of the men had not made it across the river, likely shot dead or badly injured and now at the mercy of their captors. Another, a man named Rooster Glover, sat nearby, blood oozing from a hole in his shoulder. One horse limped badly from a bullet wound to his stomach and would have to be put down.

"Might near like being on the battlefield," Wilson said. "There's no use attempting to rescue those left behind on the other side of the river. We'll just continue on shorthanded. It's only a half day's ride to where we're to meet up with the buyers."

He looked out on the resting cattle and started counting aloud. "The bossman will be pleased," he said. "Mighty pleased."

One of the others had bandaged Glover's shoulder and was giving him water when Top approached. "I fear your involvement on this trip is done," he said. "I'm sorry for your suffering. Reckon you can make it back to Palo Duro on your own?"

Rooster, feeling faint, nodded.

"Somebody help load up his saddlebag for him," Wilson said. "Then we'll be on our way before our savage friends decide to return." He walked away and resumed counting the cattle.

Darby glared at him and whispered to no one in particular, "He's gone crazier than an outhouse rat."

B EN BAGGETT WAS returning from his cave hideaway, where he'd been checking on the strongbox that contained his fortune, when he saw the horse and rider slowly making their way into the compound. Moving closer, he saw that it was Glover, badly hurt and delirious, and called out to the cook for help.

They carried the wounded rider inside the nearest cabin and bathed his feverish face with cool towels. After peeling away the bloody bandage, the cook immediately began boiling water and disinfecting one of his kitchen knives. "We need to get the bullet out before more infection sets in," he said. "He's also badly in need of water."

Rooster rolled his head and mumbled incoherently as the surgery was performed, whiskey was poured onto the wound, and a fresh bandage was taped in place.

It was hours before he regained consciousness and was able to speak.

"What was it caused this?" Baggett asked several times before getting a faint, rambling answer.

Glover described the raid on the Comanche village and the violence that had erupted. Two men and one good horse had died.

Baggett picked up a canteen and gave him another sip of water. "Was this foolheartedness Top Wilson's doing? Is he responsible for gettin' my men killed and you lying here shot?"

Rooster weakly nodded.

Baggett threw the canteen against the wall and cursed. When he finally calmed down, he leaned close to Rooster again. "Were they able to get the cattle?"

Glover was in and out of consciousness through the night as the cook remained by his side. His fever continued to rise, having soaked his clothes in sweat by the time Baggett returned to check on him.

"Does it look like he'll make it?"

"Afraid not," the cook said. "I fear we'll soon be doing grave digging."

Two hours later Rooster Glover let out a single deep sigh and died.

WITH THE RANKS depleted and the men showing a lack of enthusiasm, Wilson chose to forgo his plan to split into smaller raiding parties. Fearing that desertion might be on the minds of some, he felt it would be best to keep watch on everyone.

Continuing eastward, they stole cattle from two small ranches without incident and made their sales. For Wilson, the rustling of the smaller herds lacked the thrill he'd felt while battling the Indians, and he missed it. His men, meanwhile, only missed the comfort of their own beds back in the canyon.

His behavior became increasingly erratic. One evening as they were making camp, he became irritated when one of the hands was slow gathering wood for a fire, and he slapped him across the face. He launched into lengthy tirades, waving his pistol in the air and criticizing virtually everyone for the most minor shortcomings. When the rest of the men tried to sleep, Wilson nervously paced about, mumbling to himself.

He made no mention of it, but it was obvious that he was increasingly worried about the reception he would receive from Ben Baggett when they returned home. The pouch full of money earned from the cattle sales, he feared, would not be enough to overcome the fact he'd not told his boss of his misguided plan to rustle cattle from the Indians. Nor would it justify the needless deaths of his men. And now around him, there was a near revolt of those who had long been faithful.

Wilson realized that his hope of one day assuming responsibility for Baggett's cattle business was no more than a shattered dream. And the thought angered him.

In his paranoid state, he weighed his options and decided on a new plan. He would take the money earned from the cattle sales and disappear, riding away until he felt he would be safe from the reach and wrath of Ben Baggett.

CHAPTER EIGHTEEN

O N THE MORNING they were breaking camp and preparing to begin their return trip to the canyon, the party discovered that Top Wilson was gone. In the middle of the night, he had walked his horse a few hundred yards from camp, saddled him, and ridden away.

"Good riddance is my personal thinking," one of the hands said.

"Trouble is," Will said, "he's taken the money with him. Us returning to the canyon empty-handed ain't going to set well with the old man. Nor will it provide a payday for our misfortunes." He told everyone to fan out from the campsite and determine which direction Wilson had headed. "Tracking him shouldn't be too difficult."

When tracks were found in a small grove nearby, it was agreed that he was headed east. Darby began saddling his horse. "You boys start on back," he said. "I'll see if I can catch up with Top and the money. Him and me got some settling up to do."

One of the men loaned him a Winchester.

* * *

THE HEAT OF the day came early as Darby followed the tracks. He pulled his hat low against his brow to ward off the sun and the swirling wind. Top had ridden in the direction of the Red River, alternately galloping, then walking his horse. Following his route became easier when he began traveling along the sandy bank of the river.

Will knew he was on a fool's mission. It mattered not to him if Top Wilson rode until he fell off the edge of the world, vanishing forever. However, the money he'd taken was another matter. The hands, in no way responsible for the unfortunate events of recent days, had risked their lives to earn the pay.

It was midafternoon when Will rode up on a couple of elderly farmers who had just pulled their wagon from a mud hole. They sat resting, fanning their sweaty faces with their hats, while coffee brewed on a small fire.

One squinted into the sun as Darby approached. "Howdy, mister," one said. "Wish you had got here sooner so you could have lent us a hand."

Will climbed from his horse. "Mind if I sit?"

"There'll be coffee ready shortly. What brings you to these parts? You ain't some outlaw on the run, are you?"

Darby smiled. "No, honestly I ain't. But, fact is, I'm tracking one." He described Top Wilson.

"He passed this way, early morning, not even offering to help," one of the farmers said. "A right unfriendly sort who didn't seem to have all his wits about him. He did offer to purchase one of our horses, saying his was getting tired out. But when we turned him down, he just rode away, grumbling to himself."

Darby figured Wilson had better than a half day's lead on him. But if his horse was tiring or going lame, the distance should narrow quickly.

As he continued to follow the tracks, his mind wandered, bouncing from one question to another. What was it that made a man like Top Wilson so self-centered, ambitious, and arrogant? What evil force had taken from him any sense of guilt or remorse over stealing from his fellow workers or treating women like Jennie with such disrespect?

And what about old man Baggett? Was there anything that motivated him other than stone-cold greed? Would he have the slightest feeling of genuine sadness for the men who the Indians had killed? Or were they nothing more than broken parts he'd need to replace so his illegal "cattle business" could continue to thrive and grow?

Most important, Will Darby wondered how he had allowed himself to fall in with such unsavory people.

The thought occurred to him that he had the ideal opportunity to break from Baggett and his gang. He could simply keep riding until he found a new life for himself. If he succeeded in catching Wilson, he could take the money for himself and never look back.

He quickly dismissed the idea. Back in the canyon was the money—his money—that he'd been saving. And not far away was Jennie Broder, whom he didn't wish to leave behind. As to the cash Wilson had stolen, it belonged to those who had earned it, however dishonestly. It didn't escape him that part of it was his as well.

He wrestled with the troubling thoughts for miles, his mood lifting only when they turned to Jennie Broder's smile.

U P THE WAY, Wilson's horse had slowed considerably. At times, Top dismounted to walk and lead the weary animal by the reins.

He, too, had a mind full of worrisome questions. Would

he be able to distance himself to a place where he'd not
be found? Where would that safe haven be? Back to Mexico maybe? How long would the stolen money hold out?
And when it was gone, what would he do? More stealing?
An unsatisfactory job wrangling somebody else's cattle
for long days and short wages?

The only answer he had was there was no turning
back. He'd lied to and stolen from Ben Baggett, not a
forgiving man. By doing so, he had destroyed a future
he'd once believed to be promising and profitable.

And he thought of the Broder girl. Her refusal to
welcome his advances had, at first, disappointed him.
Then, after Will Darby entered the picture, stealing
away her attention, he'd felt only anger and a growing
desire for revenge.

The more fragile his mind became, the more he believed the world had treated him unfairly. It had all
started years ago, back when his father was dragging
him along from town to town, poisoning his young
mind with all of that nonsensical God talk.

Wilson had stolen away from his fellow rustlers so
abruptly that he'd not bothered to bring any provisions.
Thus, for days all he'd had to satisfy his hunger were
mustang grapes and wild onions. On the afternoon of
the third day, he abruptly turned south, leaving the river's edge in favor of the woods, where he might be able
to shoot a few squirrels or a rabbit for a meal.

I T WAS NEARING twilight when Will Darby caught the
scent of smoke and something cooking. "Got you,"
he whispered as he dismounted and led his horse
through the shadowy growth, moving toward a strange
sound. Top Wilson was singing happily as he huddled
close to the fire while his supper heated.

He didn't realize Darby was there until he felt the cool barrel of a Winchester pressed against the back of his head.

"What the . . . ?"

"Remain seated, Top," Will said, "or I'll blow a hole in your noggin before we even have a chance for a proper conversation."

Wilson turned his head and glared. "I should have known it would be you who followed along to bring me more troubles. Kind of cowardly, ain't it, to sneak up on a man's back side?"

"All I come for is the money bag you stole." He picked up Wilson's rifle, which was leaning against a nearby saddle.

Wilson's demeanor changed abruptly. He was suddenly grinning at his captor. "You bring any coffee? I'll gladly exchange part of my supper for some coffee." He was babbling, giddy. "You done right good tracking me. . . . Coffee would taste mighty good about now . . . unless you got something stronger. . . . Whiskey maybe? You come alone? Sit here by the fire and warm yourself. . . . We can have ourselves a talk."

Darby felt a sudden touch of sadness for the crazed Wilson as he moved to the other side of the fire to face him. Top's eyes were red and watery, as if he'd stayed too long in Madge's saloon or hadn't slept for days. Sweat beaded on his brow. His arms were scratched from riding through underbrush, and he smelled like a man who hadn't bathed in some time.

"I'm asking where's the money?" Will said, cocking his rifle.

"Am I allowed to get on my feet?" Top's voice again turned hostile.

Will nodded and watched as Wilson stretched his legs and walked to his horse. "It's probably good you came," he said. "My horse is plumb wore out and wasn't likely to make it much farther." He took the money bag from the saddle horn and pitched it toward Darby.

"What will you be doing to me now?"

Will had no ready answer. He stood there as wind whistled through the trees and a nearby coyote howled. An owl hooted in the distance. "I'll need to do some thinking on it," he finally said.

Doing away with a man as evil and useless as Top Wilson would likely be considered a favor to the world. It could be done with one shot that no one would hear or see fired. In a few days the buzzards and animals would have feasted, leaving little clue whom their meal had been. But, for all his shortcomings, Will Darby was no cold-blooded killer. He would find no satisfaction in leaving Wilson dead.

"I've got what I come for," he said, picking up the money bag. "As to what your sorry future holds, I got no interest. My guess is you'll soon be dead, but it'll not be at my hand."

Darby mounted his horse and turned to ride away. "Enjoy your supper." His horse had taken only a couple of steps when a shot rang through the night air.

When Will had turned, Wilson had retrieved his Peacemaker from beneath a nearby blanket and shot Darby squarely between the shoulder blades. Will let out only a faint cry before slumping forward in his saddle. The last image to flash through his mind was of Jennie Broder.

Wilson, his gun still aimed at Darby, rushed to make sure he was dead and to retrieve the money bag. Then he ate his supper, again singing.

He sat for some time, staring at Will's motionless body, smoldering coals all that remained of the campfire.

Finally, he rose and took the rope from Darby's saddle and began binding him to his horse. He took one of the bills from the money bag and used the charcoal end of a stick to write on it. He stuffed the folded paper into Darby's shirt pocket, then stepped back to examine his handiwork.

Satisfied, he slapped the horse's flank and watched as he and his dead rider disappeared into the darkness, headed east.

PART THREE

$\diamond$

REVENGE

CHAPTER NINETEEN

"FOLKS IN TOWN are beginning to think we're men of wealth and leisure," Jonesy said as he and Clay were returning from the laundry. "Hanging about, riding in and out of town, doing mostly the same thing one day after the next." He was getting impatient.

They were nearing the open livery door when they saw a stranger talking with the owner. As they got closer, they could see that the man was blind in one eye.

"They call me Bootsy," he said, extending his hand to Clay. Pointing toward three horses standing near the watering trough, he explained that he'd brought them to town for new shoes. He walked over and gently touched the swollen jaw of one of the animals. "Might be this 'un here also will need a tooth chiseled out or some kind of medicine to treat an infection," he said. "I could have asked Eli here to bring his equipment out to our place, but the boss don't much like visitors."

Clay and Jonesy had already recognized him as a

member of the Baggett funeral procession that had
earlier ridden into town.

"Too soon in the day for you boys to be having a
drink?"

"Sun's up, ain't it?" Pate replied.

The saloon was empty. Madge was in the kitchen,
chopping vegetables for a lamb stew she was preparing,
when the three men entered. Wiping her hands on a
towel, she appeared behind the bar to greet them.

"Getting an early start, I see," she said. "Morning,
Mr. Breckenridge . . . Mr. Pate." Her only acknowledgment of Bootsy was a quick, dismissive nod. "What
will it be?"

"Three glasses of beer," Clay said.

As she walked away, Bootsy offered an explanation
for her chilly dismissal. "Could be the last time I was
in here I broke one of her barstools. Two maybe. Don't
clearly recall."

As Breckenridge looked across the table at him,
Bootsy could not read his thoughts.

"You boys been in town for a while," he said. "I was
thinking to myself on the ride in that if I was to run
into you I'd inquire about your purpose."

"And what business of yours would it be?" Pate
asked.

Bootsy sipped at his beer and wiped foam from his
lips. "Could be we've got a mutual interest, a friend
we're all wondering about."

"He got a name?" Clay asked.

"Will . . . Will Darby." Bootsy gave a general description and explained he'd not seen him for several
weeks. "And soon after he goes missing, you fellas
show up. In one of our discussions, he mentioned having kin off to the east somewhere. I was wondering if
that might be you boys.

"Since not many strangers come to Tascosa and stay

more than a day, two at most, some local folks been wondering why you're here. From what I hear, there's been considerable rumor and gossip. Me, I just put two and two together and made a guess it has something to do with my friend."

"Has that gossip reached out to Palo Duro Canyon?"

Bootsy nodded. "I'd get skinned alive if it was known I'm speaking to you. Only reason I got this chance was the need for someone to bring the horses in for shoeing. Truth is, I'm fond of Will and concerned harm might have come to him."

Clay remained poker-faced and continued to prod, giving the visitor no indication that he already knew Darby's fate. "You got any idea what might have become of him?"

Bootsy explained that Will had last been seen chasing after some money that had been stolen from his boss.

"That would be Ben Baggett?"

"Likely I've done said too much," Bootsy said as he got to his feet.

"Who took the money?"

Bootsy hesitated, then said, "It was a fella who was working for Mr. Baggett." He turned away to head back to the livery.

Once he'd gone, Madge reappeared from the kitchen. Clay asked, "Can he be trusted?"

"About as far as you can throw the horse he rode to town on."

Breckenridge wasn't so sure.

IN THE CANYON, Ben Baggett was pacing the front porch of his cabin. He'd slept little and drunk a great deal since being told that Top Wilson had stolen his money. Daily, he'd watched the trail that led into the encampment, hoping to see Darby returning with a bag looped over his saddle horn.

With each day that passed, Baggett's rage grew. Finally, the time had come to quit waiting and go in search of the money. "I want two things," the old man told the four handpicked men gathered around him. "My money returned . . . and Top Wilson's body brought back dead." He then added, "If it turns out that Will Darby is involved in the thieving, I'll want his head on a stick as well. If any of you get notions about locating the money, then running with it, consider the decision your death wish. I'll come for you, sure as God made little apples."

None doubted his sincerity.

That evening, just before Madge rang the bell to signal closing time, Bootsy slipped onto a stool at the dark end of the bar. He didn't bother ordering a drink. "Tell your friends," he whispered, "that there will be men riding out first thing in the morning."

T HE SKY WAS still pitch-black when Clay and Jonesy arrived at the mouth of the canyon, ready to follow Baggett's search party. Earlier, Madge had visited their tent with fried egg sandwiches and a canteen filled with hot coffee. As Clay cinched his horse, she had leaned forward and kissed him on the cheek. "Be safe," she said.

They ate their breakfast on horseback, watching for the riders to appear and lead them to the man who had killed Will Darby.

It would not take long.

O N THE AFTERNOON of the third day, Baggett's men were riding single file through a narrow gorge when a shot echoed from a perch above. The hat of the lead rider flittered away as blood spilled into his face.

He was dead before his limp body hit the ground, and his frightened horse galloped away.

The other men quickly dismounted and sought cover behind nearby boulders.

Following a mile back, Breckenridge and Pate reined in their horses and sought cover themselves. "Ambush," Jonesy whispered. As he spoke, there was an exchange of fire from rifles and handguns. "He's got himself a bird's-eye view and can keep them pinned down until their ammunition runs out. Whoever he is, he's right smart about what he's doing."

"I've got a good idea who he is," Clay said. Another volley of gunfire erupted.

As the day wore on, the shooting became less frequent. The sniper held the upper hand and was being careful not to waste bullets. Below, his targets were virtual hostages, crouched in hiding.

Finally, Wilson yelled out, "I got nothing but time for waiting, so let's all get comfortable. If we're still here when it gets dark, figure on me sneaking up and cutting your sorry throats one at a time." Then he laughed.

When one of the men, running short of ammunition, attempted to run from one boulder to another, Wilson stood, aimed, and fired a shot that knocked the runner from his feet. He lay in the dust, clutching his chest, calling for help that didn't come.

"Sounds like it's now down to two against one," Jonesy said.

The shooting silenced, lending an eerie quiet to things. "We've got us a standoff," Clay said. "Ain't likely the fellow up top will be leaving his spot, despite his threat to cut folks' throats. The two left down below are most likely thinking of waiting for dark and trying to make a run for it, which ain't gonna do them much good, seeing as how their horses have run away. Afoot, they'll be easy targets, even with the cover of darkness."

Occasionally, the quiet was broken by the chilling sound of Wilson's laughter. "You boys think to bring any coffee?" he called out. "Maybe something stronger?" Then he would laugh again.

Wilson had known he was being followed for a day and a half, long before he'd settled into his hideaway atop the gorge. When the men finally came into sight, he was disappointed they were not being led by Ben Baggett. His hatred for his old boss had grown to a point where he'd concluded that everything that had gone wrong was Baggett's fault. The disastrous raid on the Comanches, the stealing of the payday money, the killing of Will Darby, and now the deaths of those lying in the dirt below were all the cause of the cowardly, greedy, evil-as-Satan Mr. Baggett.

Top gritted his teeth, regretting that he'd not thought to kill Baggett long ago.

Lying on their stomachs beneath a clump of prickly mesquite bushes, Breckenridge and Pate considered what they should do. "We could just lie here and hope they kill each other off," Jonesy said. "I have to say, for a man whose profession is stealing folks' cows, the guy up top's a pretty good shot."

Clay agreed. "Ain't much chance what's left of the search party's going to kill him. Since he doesn't know we're here, maybe we can use the dark to sneak up to where he's shooting from." He gave Jonesy a determined look. "Rest assured, I ain't leaving here without him dead."

A COOL BREEZE replaced the day's heat when the sun went down. Leaving their horses behind, they slowly made their way up the ridge and began approaching the shooter from the back side. As they did so, the night had gone quiet, no more gunfire or gibberish chatter from above. After almost two hours, Breckenridge and Pate were close enough to see a lone shadowy figure leaning against a boulder, his attention fixed on the floor of the gorge.

"Want to shoot him from here or get close enough to have a chat with him 'fore we do?" said Jonesy.

"I want to see his face and know his name," Clay answered.

They were just yards away when Jonesy's foot slipped on a loose rock that rolled toward the edge, alerting Wilson. He turned abruptly, pointing his rifle in their direction. Before either could lift his weapon into position, he fired.

The bullet struck Pate in the shoulder, shattering bone as it entered. He went to his knees as the shooter turned and began to run. Breckenridge's first instinct was to give chase, but he quickly chose to look after his friend instead.

Leaning close, he could see a good deal of blood but also realized the bullet had made a clear entry and exit. He removed Jonesy's bandanna from his neck and placed it over the wound. "You're going to be okay," Clay said. "You're going to be fine, just fine. . . ."

Jonesy felt dizzy and sick to his stomach. "Feels like I got hold of some real bad whiskey," he said.

"I'll need you to get on your feet soon as you feel up to it so we can get you back to your horse," Clay said. In the distance, he could hear the sound of hooves clicking against the rocks as the shooter rode away.

"Did you get to see his face?"

"He's who I expected," Breckenridge said. "Calls himself Top Wilson."

"Why don't you leave me here to get some rest and go on after him?"

"I'd just as soon he have some time to worry about me coming," Clay said.

"You think he knows who you are?"

"Not yet."

T HE SURVIVING MEMBERS of Baggett's search party had escaped the gorge and found their horses before Clay and Jonesy could reach theirs. "We'll get you some proper doctoring once we're back to Tascosa," he said. "Just bear with it and stay with me."

Pate did the best he could, suffering the pain of the jostling ride in silence. After the first day, however, his head began to sway and his eyes rolled. Fearing he would fall from his horse, Clay climbed on behind him and led his own.

Riding two to a saddle slowed their progress even more.

Jonesy was unconscious and Clay's eyes were blurred from lack of sleep when the dim lights of Tascosa finally appeared on the horizon.

The moment Madge saw Clay enter the saloon, Pate's arm across his shoulder, she began ringing her bell furiously. "We'll be closing early tonight," she shouted out to the handful of customers. When those at one of the poker tables protested, she pulled her shotgun from behind the bar and pointed it in their direction. "Go," she said. "Now."

She helped Clay lift Pate onto the bar and began ripping away his shirt. Dried blood was all over his clothing. "Oh, my Lord," she said as she brushed Jonesy's hair from his face and gave him sips of water. "Is he gonna die?"

"I think it's not as bad as it appears," Clay said. "The bullet went through, and he's got movement in his arm."

"I've got very little in the way of medicine here in the bar," she said. "Go over to the livery and tell Eli what's happened and ask that he bring whatever he's got."

When Rayburn and Breckenridge returned, Madge was bathing Pate's wound with a hot towel and had propped up his head on a pillow she'd brought from her bedroom. She looked as if she had been crying.

"How far has he been riding in this condition?" Rayburn asked.

"Too far," Clay said.

"I suggest you get out a bottle of whiskey," the livery owner told Madge. "I'll be needing to sew a couple of stitches to close up the bullet hole so there'll be less opportunity for infection. I'd just as soon he wasn't sober while I'm doing so."

He pulled a needle and a length of fishing line from his vest pocket and looked over at Breckenridge. "It works for horses and cows," Eli said. "Besides, it's all I got at the moment."

An hour later, Jonesy was awake, sitting on the bar and offering to buy a round of drinks for everyone in the house. "Ain't nobody but us here," Clay chided.

Jonesy, feeling tipsy, laughed. "That's my cause for being so generous." His laughter was quickly replaced by a grimace as a jolt of pain shot through his shoulder.

The wound was patched and lathered in salve. A fresh bandage wound from beneath one arm and over the opposite shoulder. Rayburn injected him with a small dose of the tranquilizer he'd earlier used to calm Bootsy's horse before tending to its bad tooth.

"He'll soon be sleeping," Eli said. "I think he's going to be okay. Seems to be a tough ol' bird."

They lifted Pate from the bar and took him upstairs to Madge's bed. He was snoring loudly before they could even remove his bloody boots.

Clay gave Madge a weary smile. "I much appreciate you taking him in," he said. "Any of that whiskey left?"

They moved a lantern to one of the tables and sat as Breckenridge described the events that had taken place in the gorge.

Madge was silent, a troubled look on her face. It was Rayburn who spoke up after Clay had finished telling his story. "This isn't over, you know," he said.

"I'm going to see to it," Clay replied.

Madge got to her feet, leaving her whiskey glass untouched. "I'd best go clean up the bar and check on Mr. Pate," she said.

TOP WILSON COULDN'T remember the last time he'd slept. He'd ridden until daylight, making sure no one was following, and had finally stopped near a small tree-sheltered spring. After he and his horse drank their fill, he removed his boots and socks and bathed his tired feet in the cool, clear water.

Though his empty stomach and sun-blistered face were distractions, he tried to focus. He was pleased with the way he'd held off Baggett's men in the gorge, disappointed only that he'd not killed them all. And who were the other two who arrived later, sneaking up on his back side? What purpose did they have being there? With any luck one of them was now dead.

He tried to think what he'd do next, but his mind wandered. One thing he did know: He badly needed a new horse. His was more exhausted than he was. Since he had plenty of money and no reason to steal—unless absolutely necessary—his best bet was to find a trail-driving crew headed north. They always had extra horses, most of them young and fit. He was prepared to offer a handsome price if they tried to strike a hard bargain.

He stretched out on the grass, watching as his horse

grazed. His eyelids fluttered, and soon he was asleep, dreaming.

In the dream, he was back in the canyon, the barrel of his Peacemaker pressed against the temple of Ben Baggett, who was begging for his life.

CHAPTER TWENTY

AFTER TWO DAYS in the saloon, Jonesy felt good enough to return to his tent. His arm was in a sling, and he still moved slowly, but was in good spirits. "I'm right glad to be out of there," he told Clay. "That's the longest I ever spent in the bed of a woman wasn't my wife."

He was fast tiring of the constant attention. Clay was never far away, always wanting to know if there was anything he could do. He arrived several times daily with coffee and tended the bandages. Madge brought soup and muffins. A bottle of whiskey sat near his bed.

"Time I get up and about," he said when he finally emerged. Clay argued but to no avail: "I ain't figuring on riding broncos or chopping no wood," Jonesy said, "but I feel a need for fresh air, sunshine, and making myself somehow useful."

With Breckenridge at his side, Pate slowly walked up to the corral, then down toward the laundry. It was good to be moving around, feeling the blood pumping through his weakened body.

"We need to do some talking," he said as they made their way back toward the livery. "You and me both know I'm pretty worthless in this state. And I'm aware of you wanting to get on with the business you come to tend. What worries me is you trying to do it by yourself."

Clay gently placed a hand on his friend's injured shoulder. "I didn't bring you out to this godforsaken country to get you all shot up. I'm being truthful when I say I'm feeling real bad about that. The important thing for now is that you mend proper. Once that's done, we'll make us a new plan. We'll go one day at a time."

As they talked, a clatter sounded near the entrance to the stable. They walked around the corner of the building to see a buckboard pulling to a stop. Holding the reins was the one-eyed man named Bootsy. Sitting next to him, a scowl on his reddened face, was Ben Baggett.

"My man here has told me of making your acquaintance," Baggett said, not bothering to introduce himself or inquire about Pate's injured shoulder. "If what he's saying is true, we're both in search of the same man. I'm of a mind we might be of use to one another."

"And how's that?" Clay's question was directed at Baggett, but he was looking at Bootsy, wondering if their earlier visit had been part of a ploy to involve them in the failed attempt to chase down Top Wilson.

"I'm wondering if you've already attempted to make use of us to tend to your bidding," Breckenridge continued. "If so, it got my friend here shot, something I deeply resent."

Baggett removed his hat and ran his fingers through his unruly hair. "I heard about what happened," he said, "and had no idea you boys were involved until my folks come limping home. They didn't even know who it was who allowed them to escape with their lives until Bootsy fessed up and guessed it was you. Part of my reason for being here is to thank you for saving my men." He made no mention of the two who had died.

"Exactly what's your interest in this fellow Wilson?" Clay asked.

"He's got something that belongs to me, and I aim to get it back. I have no idea why it is you boys have need of him, but clearly you do. I'll not poke my nose in your business, but I've got men who'll ride with you and help catch him. After I get what I want, he's yours to do with as you please."

He replaced his hat and looked toward Bootsy. "I do have one other question. You have any cause to believe that Wilson's accompanied by anybody else? Another of my hands has gone missing, causing me concern."

Clay realized that Baggett was unaware his brother was dead. "Nope," he said. "We're looking only for Wilson."

"Then I've said what I come to say. Think on my offer, and Bootsy here will be back in the morning to learn your answer."

As they rode away, Eli Rayburn appeared from behind the livery door, where he'd been listening. "That man's mighty desperate," he said. "I've never known Ben Baggett to ask help from nobody."

"What's your thinking?" Clay asked Jonesy.

"Sounds to me we've just been offered a deal with the devil."

Breckenridge shook his head. "Not 'we,'" he said. "Me."

THE FOLLOWING MORNING Bootsy was waiting outside the tent when they woke. "So we're clear," he said, "I made no mention to Mr. Baggett about alerting you boys to his plan the other day. Nor did I share with him that we talked about Will Darby and how you might even be his kin.

"Only reason I said anything at all was the fact he was mad enough to kill those two who returned empty-handed and told him of being ambushed. And when I say 'kill,' I ain't choosing the word lightly. Wouldn't have surprised me if he'd shot them both right where they stood.

"Here of late, things have been falling apart on him. He lost his boy, you know, then had three men die at the hands of Comanches. Then the two who Wilson bushwhacked, and Darby's gone God knows where. My boss is a mighty distressed man."

"So what will restore a smile to his face?"

"Take four or five men, more if you want, and go looking for Wilson. He'll provide his best, but, truthfully, he knows his men ain't near as smart as he'd wish once they get past stealing cows. So he'll agree on you being in charge. I've volunteered to come along. We can be ready whenever you say."

Breckenridge accepted the cup of coffee Pate handed him. "Tell your boss I need five men with some muscle and good sense. It would be good if they still had hair and their own teeth. And I'll allow only one who ain't got both his eyes. We'll leave out from here at daylight tomorrow."

Clay avoided the saloon that evening, hoping not to have to try to justify his actions to Madge. Pate's sullen response to the idea was enough to deal with. "Teaming up with a crowd of no-'count outlaws is liable to get you killed," he argued. "Wait until I'm better, and we'll go take care of this ourselves." Clay had never heard his friend curse so much.

The fact that Madge didn't stop by the tent spoke loudly about her feelings on the matter.

* * *

A T DAWN BAGGETT'S men were waiting, each wearing a sidearm. Rifles, in their scabbards, hung from their saddles. They looked like a hurriedly-thrown-together sheriff's posse. Bootsy called off the names of the men—Davey, Tip-Toe, Bear, and Geno—which Breckenridge showed no interest in remembering. Pate, attempting to lighten the previous evening's mood, leaned close to his friend and whispered, "I'll say a prayer you don't get your throat cut in your sleep."

As they rode from town, Clay and Bootsy agreed they would travel directly to the site of the ambush and begin the search there. They would be looking for a needle in a haystack.

When they reached the gorge, they found two sad-dled horses running free, foraging on wild berries and the low-hanging beans on mesquite trees. One had an open wound on its flank where it had been attacked by coyotes or wolves. Lying side by side near one of the nearby boulders were the mangled remains of the two men Wilson had killed. Animals and blowflies had made the bodies unrecognizable.

"We'll stop and see what's left of them gets a proper burying and the horses tended to," Clay said. "Collect their weapons as well."

His first order since they had left Tascosa was met with little enthusiasm.

He instructed one of the men to unsaddle the de-serted horses. "We'll leave the gear behind and hope somewhere up ahead we'll find a home for the animals."

Searching the ridge of the gorge, Bootsy located where Wilson had camped, waiting to carry out his am-bush. There were the remains of a small campfire and burned bones of what appeared to be a couple of rabbits. On a pile of rocks were bloodstains left by Jonesy Pate.

Clay walked the area for several minutes, moving from the campsite to the perch Wilson had fired from, then to where he had tethered his horse. "I'm just making a guess," Breckenridge said, "but since he had cause to take leave in a hurry, I'm betting he continued that way." He pointed eastward.

The following day they encountered a small herd being driven toward the Red River. Clay and Bootsy approached the trail boss and asked if he had seen any strangers recently.

"Few evenings back," he said, "this skinny-lookin' fellow—real funny acting—rode into our camp on a horse that appeared on its last leg. He was wanting to buy a fresh mount and said price was of no matter.

"All we could spare was a mare not in much better shape than the one he had. But he took it and was on his way, happy as could be, especially after we also agreed to sell him a tin of coffee."

"You recall what direction he was headed?"

The trail boss pointed to the south.

"What's down that way?" Clay asked.

"Just more of what you're looking at here, which ain't much."

The following afternoon, as the men's heads bobbed in rhythm with the gait of their horses, Clay rode up next to Bootsy. "We're being followed," he said. "Have been most of the day."

Bootsy shielded his good eye and looked in the direction Breckenridge was pointing. On a distant rise, he could see the faint outline of several horses standing side by side.

"Indians," Bootsy said. "I'd bet money on it. My advice is you don't tell the men, lest they scatter like scared quail. This here's trouble Top Wilson started back when he rustled those cattle from the Comanches."

"And it doesn't appear to be over. Best we start con-

sidering what to do should they decide to do more than
follow along and watch."

"My vote's for getting outta here."

"No way of telling how many there are," Breckenridge said, "but it's likely we're badly outnumbered.
And I don't figure there's any friendly intent to their
following us. The cattle drive we paid a visit to is about
a half day's ride back the way we come. They had six,
maybe eight men who, if they're fair shots, could help
even the odds."

Without explanation, Clay ordered the men to re-
verse direction.

Well before they reached where he assumed the
cattle drive would be, Clay sensed disaster. On the far
horizon he could see black dots in the bright blue sky
lazily gliding in a circle.

Buzzards.

The scene they soon rode up on caused two of the
Baggett men to retch. Others silently looked away.

"Good Lord Almighty," said Bootsy, "it was a massacre. Nobody but a crazy person would do something
of this nature."

"Savages," Clay said as his eyes roamed the horror.

Tied to the wheels of the chuck wagon were two cowboys who had been scalped and their eyes removed.
Their shirts had been torn open and gaping cuts to their
stomachs allowed bloody intestines to spill into the dirt.

Other dismembered bodies lay nearby, pecked at by
the buzzards. Somewhere nearby, hungry coyotes were
already howling.

There was no sign of the cattle.

Clay stood in his saddle, again searching the horizon. In the distance he could see the same horseback
forms that had first alerted him to the fact they were
being followed. "They're playing a game with us, like
a kitten with a ball of string," he said. "They're sending

a message I don't rightly understand. If they wanted us dead, they'd have done killed us."

"What are you thinking we should do?"

"Safest thing would be to head back to the canyon. If we can make it."

Which was just what Silver Hawk hoped their plan would be. He had recognized three of the men from the night his village was raided. The War Gods had instructed him to make the white man lead him to the place those who stole his people's cattle and killed his warriors called home.

As the nervous group made their way homeward, they were still followed, but always from afar.

"Time was," said Bootsy, "when I considered the worst thing could happen would be a tongue-lashing or worse from ol' man Baggett. And you can rest assured that'll be coming when he learns of our decision to retreat. But after seeing what was done to those trail drivers back there, the boss doesn't worry me in the least."

The Indians, on the other hand, worried him a great deal. Clay shared his concern.

CHAPTER TWENTY-ONE

T HE LONGER TOP Wilson continued his aimless wandering, the more he dwelled on settling his score with Ben Baggett. It was one of the few trains of thought that he could hold to without his mind hopscotching from one subject to another.

Without knowing how, he had reached the West Texas community of Santa Angela and, near exhaustion, rented a hotel room. He slept fitfully through two days before feeling rested enough to go in search of something to eat. When he looked into the mirror, however, he decided that a shave and a haircut were necessary. He also paid forty cents for the first hot bath he'd had since leaving Tascosa.

Shortly, he discovered the Santa Angela Saloon and Big Red's Gambling House. Since it was located near the newly built Fort Concho, Santa Angela was a bustling, energetic little town where local farmers and cavalry soldiers coexisted. Even the colored Buffalo Soldiers were invited to the bar and poker tables on payday.

With Baggett's money in his pocket, Wilson was

welcomed and began to think he might stay for a while. He dined on steaks and corn on the cob and apple pie and drank all the coffee he wanted. Though he lost far more than he won, he enjoyed the camaraderie of the card games and played most afternoons.

He was thoroughly enjoying himself, relaxed and feeling better than he had in some time. Until the morning he woke in the Concho County Jail.

A soldier had caught him hiding an ace in the pocket of his jacket, reached across the table, and knocked Wilson to the floor. The soldier not only demanded that Top immediately leave the gambling house but that he waste no time getting far from Santa Angela.

As Wilson was lying on the floor, blood dripping from his nose, his personality changed in an instant. He alternately screamed and cursed, kicking wildly at the stunned soldier. He began to growl like a rabid dog, then pulled his pistol and randomly fired shots into the ceiling.

Fearful that he might make one of his fellow card players his next target, the soldier grabbed a chair and brought it down hard against the back of Wilson's head.

He was still unconscious when the sheriff arrived and took him away to jail, not sure whether he was drunk or crazy or both.

The following morning, Wilson bribed an elderly jailer with a five-dollar gold piece, was given back his gun, and set free.

The whole unfortunate event, he'd decided as he'd spent the night in the darkened, foul-smelling cell, was somehow the fault of Ben Baggett.

I N TASCOSA, MADGE had not spoken to Breckenridge since his return. She'd heard Eli Rayburn's secondhand account of the failed trip and misadventure with the Comanches and wished to know no more.

She struggled to decide whether to focus her anger on Clay's stubborn determination to put himself in danger's way or to dismiss the growing feelings she was privately dealing with.

Clay, meanwhile, focused his efforts on helping Jonesy back to health. He'd heard nothing from anyone at the canyon for weeks. It was as if everyone, himself included, had decided to take a long, deep breath before making the next move, whatever it was to be.

One early morning as they were taking their regular walk, Jonesy posed an out-of-the-blue question to his friend. "You ever find yourself wondering about the boy Lonnie?" he said. "How he's doing? If he's getting cared for properly? Or if he remembers our promise to return for him?"

Before Clay could say anything, Pate gave his own answer. "I do. Quite a lot, in fact. I ain't said nothing about it, but I'd admire to see him. Fact is, I've been thinking that if he's of a mind, I'd invite him to come live with me and the wife. I know she'd be pleased having him."

The boy they'd rescued following the Red River flood was not the only thing on Pate's mind.

"Clay," he said, "we've been friends long enough for me to understand how you think on things. For that reason, I'm of a mind I can say my piece and not rile you. So here goes. . . . I have to admit I can't know how I'd feel if my own kin was to be murdered. But I know wanting to do something about it is a natural thing. That's why I come this way with you. But now I have to be honest. I'm wanting to go home. And I'm thinking you should as well. You've done good, learning what caused Cal to be killed and knowing who done it. But now I fear this whole thing is driving you to distraction. It's my opinion that ain't a good thing."

When Clay didn't respond, Jonesy tried to lighten the

mood. "Besides," he said, "ol' Ruben's likely to have eaten you outta house and home by now. Not to mention that your dog's probably tired of having to sleep at the feet of a snoring stranger."

For a moment, he thought the smile on Breckenridge's face was in response to his remark about Sarge. Then, however, he realized that he was looking toward town, where he saw Madge hurrying in their direction.

"I need you to come with me to the saloon," she said after taking a deep breath. "It's Jennie Broder. She's crying and scared out of her wits." Without further explanation, she turned and headed back, Clay and Jonesy following.

Jennie was huddled behind the bar, her face buried against her knees. She was sobbing.

"She saw him," Madge said.

"Saw who?"

"Top Wilson."

Clay knelt next to Jennie and gently lifted her head and wiped away tears. "Tell me what happened," he whispered.

After composing herself and sipping from the glass of water Madge handed her, Jennie said, "I was out front of the mercantile, sweeping off the porch, when this horse came up and stopped right in front of me. I didn't pay it much mind until I heard the rider say, 'Hidy, little lady.' I looked up and there he was, grinning down at me."

"You're sure it was him?"

"He was skinnier than I remember and looked a bit ragged, but I know it was him. He was wearing a black shirt and black britches. He sat there for a few seconds, just grinning. Then he rode off, laughing like a crazy man."

"You see which way he went?"

Jennie shook her head. "Soon as I saw who it was," she said, "I closed my eyes."

Breckenridge gave her a hug and got to his feet. He took Madge's shotgun from behind the bar and handed it to Pate. "You stay here and look after things," he said. "I'm gonna go saddle my horse."

"And do what?" Madge asked.

"I'm gonna go kill him."

D URING HIS RIDE back onto the High Plains, Wilson had mumbled to himself endlessly. For most of one day, he had repeatedly cursed the fact he'd not remained in Santa Angela long enough to shoot the soldier who had caused him to spend the night in jail. But in the brief times when his thinking was clear, he had only two recurring things of importance on his mind. One, it was time he shot Ben Baggett dead and got it over with. Two, he was going to tell Jennie Broder of his feelings for her and take her away. His plan for carrying out those events, however, was a thought for another day.

B RECKENRIDGE HAD NO real expectations of quickly catching up with Wilson. It was just a way of releasing the renewed energy he felt toward his mission. His spirits were rejuvenated by the knowledge that his prey wasn't far away.

And now his purpose was twofold. He would avenge the death of his brother and, in doing so, provide safety to the woman who had loved him.

Dismissing thoughts of immediately confronting Wilson, Clay turned his horse in the direction of the Broder farm. He wanted Jennie's father to be aware of what had happened.

Cyrus Broder was mucking out a stall when Breckenridge arrived. "He shows his face here," he said, "he can expect to get it blowed off. Meanwhile, I'd just as soon my little girl remain in town, where you can keep a close eye on her until this matter's taken care of."

Clay said that he was returning to town right away and would urge Jennie to stay at the saloon. "I'll request that Madge close for business for the time being. Me and my friend Jonesy will be there keeping watch."

The town was quiet when he returned. The front door of the mercantile was locked, and Jennie's grandpa had left for home. Madge had already placed a CLOSED sign in front of the saloon, and Eli Rayburn sat in front of his livery with a shotgun across his lap.

Word had spread quickly that some manner of trouble was afoot, and the street was empty except for a couple of stray dogs.

Pate had removed his sling and was practicing holding Madge's shotgun in a ready position, aiming, and cocking. "I'd much prefer for you to bring me my sidearm," he told Clay. "I doubt I can hit the side of Eli's barn with this thing. What is it you're thinking he's gonna do?"

Clay shrugged. "All I know is he's got a thing for Jennie and won't likely leave town without trying to do something stupid."

"So we're just going to wait for him to ride up, blowing kisses and professing his undying devotion?"

Breckenridge shrugged again. Madge sat across the room, her arm sheltering Jennie. "We can't hide in here forever," she said.

"It won't be long," Clay replied.

TOP WILSON HID his horse in a small ravine less than a half mile beyond the laundry. By climbing onto a high limb of an oak tree, he was able to see everything going on in town, which wasn't much. Nobody entered or exited the mercantile. The street was virtually deserted. A man sat alone in front of the livery, doing nothing. Just sitting, passing time, in the middle of the day.

Top thought how good it had been to see Jennie again. She was still the most beautiful woman he'd ever laid eyes on.

He had no idea how much time had passed before he saw a lone rider stop in front of the saloon and rush inside. Shortly, he came back out and rode down to the tents behind the livery, stayed only a few minutes, then returned to the saloon.

That's where Jennie is, Wilson thought, *waiting for me.*

He climbed down from the tree and sat in its shade. A cool breeze rustled through the leaves. He'd get some rest while he waited for it to get dark. Then he'd go get her.

Fireflies were already dancing when Wilson climbed back to his perch and watched as the man at the livery walked to and from the saloon. Once, he talked with another man in the doorway. Another time, a woman briefly joined them, but she was too far away for him to tell if it was Jennie.

Waiting for nightfall, Top was getting impatient.

I N THE SALOON, Clay and the others were restless. Madge had heated up some soup and put a platter of pork sandwiches on the bar. No one was hungry.

Breckenridge was standing near the front door, looking out onto the empty street, when Madge approached. "What makes you think he'll come and try to take her?"

"Just a gut feeling. It appears he's not right in the head, so he's not thinking on what will result from his actions. Odds of him succeeding at whatever he's got in mind to do ain't good. Even if he knows it, I doubt he cares. If I had a decent notion of where to find him,

I'd be out there looking. But since I don't, it's best we stay here together and force him to come to us. My guess is he's just waiting for dark."

She curled an arm into his and rested her head on his shoulder. "I'm sorry for the way I've been acting since you got back to town. Thinking how you might have been killed . . ."

Clay gently put his fingers to her lips and smiled. "I got a question I've been meaning to ask you," he said.

"What's that?"

"We've known each other for a time now, and I've still not been told your last name."

"Dunning," she said. "I'm officially Elizabeth Margaret Dunning, but I've been called Madge ever since I was a little girl."

Clay held out his free hand. "I'm proud to know you, ma'am."

CHAPTER TWENTY-TWO

IT WAS DECIDED Eli Rayburn would serve as a look-out from a position in front of the livery. If he saw movement or the horses in the corral became suddenly agitated, he was to fire a warning shot to alert Clay and Jonesy.

"Shooting straight up in the air's about all I'm good for," he said. "With a little luck I can at least hit the sky." At sunset he got a lantern from inside, lit it, and set it on his bench alongside his coffeepot. And waited.

A man who had avoided violence all his life, Rayburn had no idea what role he might play in the event that was to unfold. Still, he'd volunteered without hesitation. Madge had been a good friend for years, and though he didn't know Jennie well, he and her father had come to Tascosa at about the same time and had gotten along well from their first meeting. He'd occasionally had a drink with Jennie's grandpa after he'd closed the mercantile for the day.

Too, in the brief time he'd known Clay Breckenridge

and Jonesy Pate, he'd come to admire them. Watching them as they interacted, joking one minute, arguing the next, made him long for a close friend of his own.

It was well past midnight, and he was fighting to keep from nodding off when the sound of a high-pitched voice sent a chill down his spine.

"Let that shotgun slide to the ground and kick it away," Top Wilson said. He was pointing his pistol at Eli's head. "Any coffee left in that pot?"

Wilson had taken a slow zigzag route from his hide-away, sometimes even crawling on hands and knees. When he reached the barn, he slowly slid against the wall that faced away from town. He barely breathed. The familiar night calls of birds and insects were the only sounds Eli heard until Wilson stepped into the yellow light of the lantern and spoke.

Taking Rayburn by the shirt collar, he pulled him inside. "What I'm wanting to know," Top said, "is who it is down there in the saloon."

"Saloon's closed."

Wilson delivered a backhanded slap that sent Eli to his knees. "I know Jennie's hiding there, and Madge is likely keeping her company. But who are the menfolk, and what's their interest in this matter? They part of Baggett's crew, maybe?"

Still on his knees, Rayburn raised his palms and shrugged. Wilson cursed and kicked him in the chest. "Old man, you're going to tell me what I'm asking for," Top said. "Only question is how bad hurt you're gonna be before you get around to it." He leaned forward and delivered a stinging blow to the side of Eli's head, then began to laugh. "I'm in no real hurry, so just go right ahead and bleed all over yourself while I have me some coffee."

After retrieving the pot and lantern from the bench outside, Wilson squatted in front of the moaning Rayburn. "Hey, I know you, don't I? It's you who used to shoe my horses for me back when I was working for that devil down in Palo Duro Canyon."

And with that, he was again off on a rambling harangue about the evils of Ben Baggett. "I'm going to kill him, you know? Kill him and cut his tongue out. Maybe worse than that. Whatever it will be, I'll make sure it hurts. But first, I got business to tend to over at the saloon."

CLAY STEPPED OUT onto the porch and saw that Rayburn's lantern was no longer burning. The bench was empty. Rushing back inside, he shook the dozing Pate awake and called out to Madge and Jennie.

"Something's happening," he said. "Eli's no longer sitting outside. . . ."

"Could be he just had need to stretch his legs or tend to personal matters," Jonesy said. "If there was trouble, wouldn't he have fired a warning shot like we discussed?"

Breckenridge didn't bother to answer. Nor did he voice his concern that Rayburn might be in serious trouble.

"Madge, you and Jennie go back in the kitchen and stay put. Jonesy, there's stairs out back that lead up to the roof. Leave Madge her shotgun, and you take my Winchester. Anything you see from up there that doesn't look right, shoot it."

Clay positioned himself by the front door, squinting into the darkness. "He's out there," he said. "Close."

WILSON'S PATIENCE HAD run out. He stuffed a gag in Rayburn's mouth and tied him to a spare wagon wheel that was leaned against the livery wall.

"I'd shoot you now and get it done with," he said, "but I fear the noise would alert your no-name friends."

Rayburn, unconscious, heard nothing he said.

Wilson struggled to concentrate on his next move, his head throbbing. Why did a simple matter like getting Jennie Broder have to be so complicated? Why couldn't he just walk up to the front door of the saloon, politely call her name, take her by the hand, and be on their way out of this good-for-nothing town? Why were people always making things hard for him?

Now there was probably going to be shooting and some killing before his job was done.

The more he assessed the situation, the angrier he got. Yet for a moment he was suddenly thinking clearly. He checked that he had ample ammunition for his Peacemaker and filled one of his pockets with shells for Rayburn's shotgun. Anticipating need for a quick getaway once he had Jennie, he saddled a horse being kept in a nearby stall and tethered it near the livery doorway. Probably a better mount than the one he'd left down in the gulley anyway, he thought.

After taking inventory of his arsenal, he extinguished Rayburn's lantern and dug in the battered owner's pockets for his matches. From a shelf, he took down a jug of coal oil.

One way or another he was going to get Jennie and her defenders out of the saloon.

The first shot rang out after he'd made it just a few steps from the livery door. It had come from the rooftop of the saloon and had missed by a considerable margin. Slowed by the load he was carrying, Wilson stumbled to a water barrel and hunched down behind it. More shots kicked up dirt.

In return, Wilson emptied both barrels of Eli's shotgun toward the roof before abandoning it to lighten his load. "Listen up," he yelled. "I ain't aiming to hurt nobody. Just send Jennie out the front door, and we'll be on our way without nobody getting shot."

The reply was three quick pistol rounds.

The moonless night and the fact he was wearing all black worked to Wilson's advantage. Hunched over, he ran toward the mercantile as shots buzzed past. Safely there, he shoved his shoulder into the locked front door, breaking it down. Inside, he knelt beneath a window and fired a rapid volley of shots toward the now-dark saloon.

"Can't neither of us get a decent shot," Jonesy said as he moved to sit next to Clay. "From up on the roof, I didn't even have sight of where he's holding up."

"We may be here until daylight," Clay said. "If he's got a thought-out plan other than hunkering down and waiting, I got no idea what it might be." As he spoke, two more shots thudded into the saloon wall.

Wilson, in fact, was already putting a plan in motion. Crawling through the darkness, he found a wooden barrel filled with mops and brooms for sale. Holstering his pistol, he lifted two of the mops, then continued crawling toward the rear of the store, taking with him Eli's lantern and the coal oil.

He'd decided there were only two people shooting at him from inside the saloon. There had been no activity from the rooftop since he'd reached the mercantile. If Wilson was lucky—and God knew it was time for him to have some luck—the attention of the men shooting at him would remain trained on the front of the store.

Before slipping out the back, he doused the heads of the mops with coal oil. Then, carrying them, the lantern, and the can of fuel, he slowly crept down a pitch-black alleyway that led to the toolshed behind the saloon.

Pate was getting impatient. "I can't say I don't mind

not being shot at," he said, "but this waiting makes me nervous. Think we've got us a standoff?"

Breckenridge was also getting impatient—and puzzled. He fired a shot in the direction of the mercantile and waited for one in return. Instead, what he heard was the breaking of glass in the back, near the kitchen.

Pressed against the building, Wilson had sloshed the coal oil against the wall until the can was empty. He then lit the lantern and set the heads of the mops afire. He hurled the lantern through a window and tossed the mops, spearlike, onto the roof of the saloon. Finally, he put a match to the wall of the building before running back toward the mercantile.

There was a loud *whoosh* as the night wind sent flames racing along the wall. Inside, Jennie screamed when smoke began filling the kitchen.

"Oh, my God," Clay said as he raced toward where the women were hiding. He cursed himself for not having realized the degree of Wilson's insanity. He thought he heard someone laughing in the distance, yelling, "Now you've got to come out."

Which was true.

Flames were spreading fast, and the smoke was making it difficult to breathe. Jonesy's eyes were red and watering as he turned to Clay. "What now?"

"I don't see we've got much choice."

Outside, Wilson had taken advantage of the mayhem to reposition himself behind a water barrel in front of the burning saloon. The night sky had turned red orange as the flames ate away at the ancient lumber. Occasionally, a series of popping sounds could be heard as liquor bottles exploded.

"Come on out, Jennie," Wilson shouted. "I'm waiting. Come out, come out, wherever you are. . . ."

"We can't wait any longer," Clay yelled to Pate. "You and me, we'll walk out shoulder to shoulder, shielding the women. Figure on starting to shoot as soon as we clear the door, 'cause he'll most likely do the same. We gotta count on him not taking us both down before one of us kills him."

When they stepped onto the porch and fired their first shots, Wilson began yelling, "Hey . . . hey . . . let's don't have us no gunfight. I ain't here to kill nobody or be killed myself. I'm protected here, so odds are in my favor. All I want is for Jennie to step forward."

"Ain't happening," Clay replied.

"Then you do your best to shoot me, because I ain't leaving without her."

As he spoke, there was a flash of movement in the shadows behind him. In the rush to exit the burning saloon, Madge had turned away from Pate's protection and slipped out a side window.

Top Wilson was unaware that she was standing behind him when she raised her shotgun and pulled the trigger. It was the first time she'd ever fired it. Instantly, his head disappeared in a crimson burst of blood and torn flesh. For a split second he was a grotesque statue, standing headless, before he pitched forward.

Smoke was still coming from the barrel when Madge let it slide from her hands. She was dazed and crying as she stood, watching her saloon burn, then looking down at Wilson's limp body.

"Good riddance," she said.

IN THE LIVERY, Rayburn was struggling to free himself when Clay and Jonesy entered. They untied him and removed the gag. "It's over," Clay said.

"Anybody get hurt?"

"Only the man who done this to you. He's dead."

Eli smiled. "You finally got him."

"Nope, wasn't me."

Pate brought Jennie and Madge to the livery and did his best to make them comfortable. He tried to lighten the mood, but soon realized it was a futile task. There was little talking. At one point, Jennie walked over and gave Madge a hug and whispered, "Thank you."

Clay sat near Madge but said nothing, even when she asked Eli if he had some salve and bandages in the livery that she could apply to his wounds. He told her he would find something as soon as he unsaddled the horse Wilson had planned to ride out on and returned it to the stall.

Down the street, the blaze was beginning to go out and would soon be nothing but smoke and embers, a charred hole left in the heart of Tascosa.

The quiet remained throughout the remainder of the night. Daylight would come soon, time enough for talk and considering what the future held.

CHAPTER TWENTY-THREE

BEN BAGGETT WAS pumping his arms into the air, sloshing whiskey from a glass held in one hand and dropping cigar ashes from the other. Though few details were known, it hadn't taken long for word of Top Wilson's death to reach the canyon. "I can only hope it hurt like the dickens," he said. "Worse than all the misery he's caused me."

The only thing that kept the news from being perfect was the fact Baggett's money was still missing. "But I doubt he was smart enough to hide it too well," Baggett said. "We'll find it."

He summoned Bootsy to his side. "Ride into Tascosa tomorrow and pay a visit to the Boot Hill caretaker," he said. "I want it made sure Wilson's remains ain't buried anywhere near the grave of my boy."

IN TOWN, PEOPLE quietly milled in the street, taking in the devastation. A few looked for Madge, in hopes of offering condolences, but were unable to find her.

Jennie's father and grandfather had arrived in their buggy early in the morning and taken the women out to the farm. Though he felt the danger had passed, Clay promised to ride out later in the day to check on them.

Even before Bootsy arrived, Wilson's body had been wrapped in a canvas tarp and taken to the cemetery, where a grave had been dug on the far back side, among the nameless who had been buried there over the years. There would be no marker to signal its location.

"You ask me, they should have just tossed what was left of him into the fire," Jonesy said as he and Clay watched the body lifted onto a mule to be carried to its final resting place.

Like everyone else, Breckenridge and Pate hadn't talked much in the immediate aftermath of the fire. Tired but unable to sleep, they sat outside the livery in the event Eli needed something. He was going to be okay, but mending from the beating he'd taken would be slow and painful.

Pate finally brought up the subject on both their minds. "We come all the way out here, and deal with all manner of misfortune and foolishness, all to rid the world of the man who killed your brother. Then, lo and behold, a lady who ain't never even fired her own shotgun before gets it done while he's not even looking."

Clay was silent for a few seconds. "You think she's gonna be okay?"

Pate nodded. "About blowing the guy's head off or seeing her saloon get burned down? I wouldn't worry on either count too much. She's a strong lady. I've seen that as we've come to know her. I'm of a mind she'll get past all this sooner than you expect."

He smiled and added, "But it could be she might need a little help with her suffering. You know, my main sorrow's reserved for the loss of a mighty fine saloon. What's a man gonna do about getting himself a drink around here now that it's gone?"

T HE LAST THING Breckenridge had expected to feel once Top Wilson was dead was guilt. Yet, as he rode out toward the Broder farm, he measured the misfortune his presence and purpose had dealt Madge. It had cost her everything, and he felt he was to blame.

When he arrived, she and Jennie were in the garden filling their wicker baskets with vegetables. Both stopped and waved. Cyrus Broder came onto the front porch and did the same.

Clay had not yet bothered to clean up, and he smelled of smoke and coal oil. As he walked toward them, he could see that both women looked exhausted.

"How you ladies doing?" A foolish question.

It was Madge who answered, "Keeping ourselves busy."

"I was wondering if you might have a minute or two for us to talk," Clay said.

Madge handed her basket to Jennie and moved toward Breckenridge. "I guess we should," she said.

They walked toward the stream at the far edge of the pasture, quiet at first, as if each was waiting for the other to begin the conversation. It was Madge who did. "I haven't slept a solitary wink," she said. "I close my eyes and see it all over again. The fire, that man."

"That'll soon pass, I expect. I can't tell you how badly I feel about all the troubles I've brought into your life. I wish I knew how to make it up to you."

"He was a bad man, wasn't he?"

Breckenridge was quickly reassuring. "He caused bad things to happen to a lot of people, not just my brother. He was one of those men with an evil soul who thought only of himself and the hurt he could cause others. He was bad, and he deserved to die. It just should have been me who killed him," Clay said.

Tears came to Madge's eyes. "I thought I was cried out," she said.

"What are your plans?"

"I'm thinking about that, but don't yet have any answers. Jennie's pa has invited me to stay here with them for the time being, and I've accepted his kindness. And though I've got no interest in returning to town anytime soon, I've promised Jennie I'll accompany her to the next Sunday singin'."

Clay gently hugged her. "One day at a time," he whispered. "The saloon . . ."

"To be honest, part of me is glad it's burned and gone," she said. "I always hated that place. It was a bad mistake from the start. Too many bad memories of my no-good husband, drunks, cussing, card cheating, all that fighting going on. Never was a business I could feel any pride about. But like I told you a while back, it was all I had. I got up this morning without even any clean clothes to wear until Jennie loaned me some of hers. I know it's improper for folks to discuss their money worries," she said, "but since you're no doubt wondering, I might already have a solution for that. At least for now. Jennie's grandpa's getting up in years, and while we were talking on the ride out here, he mentioned that he'd like to retire and let me and Jennie run the mercantile. I'd like that, though I suspect it will only last until he gets bored and wants to come back to work."

"You got good friends, Madge," Clay said. "And even with all that's happened, I'd like to be considered one of them. Jonesy feels the same."

She kissed him softly on the cheek, and they turned

back toward the cabin. Both were smiling. "I guess Mr. Broder will invite you to stay for supper," she said. "We got vegetables, fresh from the garden."

I N THE LIVERY, Jonesy and Eli sat dozing. Weary from the sleepless night, they would wake, talk a bit, then sleep and snore some more. During one of their alert moments, Pate began to laugh. "Ain't we a pair?" he said. "Me with my broke shoulder bandaged up and you all bruised and swollen, looking like death warmed over."

Rayburn tried to return the laughter, but it was too painful. "We're alive, ain't we?"

Just as they were about to doze off again, Paul Price, owner of the laundry, appeared in the front doorway. He was wearing overalls a couple of sizes too large, and his shoulder-length hair covered his face. He was leading a horse.

"I was down near the gulley squirrel hunting this morning when I found him. I yelled out, hoping to alert his owner, but got no response. So I untied him and took him up to the house for some water. Wasn't sure what I should do with him, so I brought him here."

Eli examined the horse, still saddled, and determined there was nothing physically wrong with it. "I'm glad you did, Paul. I think I might know who he belongs to. Leave him and I'll see he gets fed and rid of that saddle."

He was certain it was Top Wilson's horse, left in the gulley so he could make a swift getaway.

Price, glad to be relieved of the responsibility for the horse, turned to leave. He stopped for a moment to view the charred remains of the saloon. "Real shame about the fire, ain't it? Man done that should be shot."

Eli smiled. "He was."

As soon as Price left, they freed the horse of his saddle and placed him in a stall with fresh hay and a bucket of oats. Rayburn removed the saddlebags and laid them on his workbench. Inside, he found a large pouch and a small tin of coffee. Emptying the pouch, he and Pate watched speechless as bills and coins spilled out.

"That's a right smart of money," Jonesy said. "I'd say Wilson was near rich."

"Wasn't his money," Eli said. "He stole it."

"That's what Ben Baggett's been in such a stew about, huh?" Pate said.

"And if you'll agree to make no mention of us finding this, he can continue his stewing." Even as he spoke, Eli was trying to think of a good hiding place.

CHAPTER TWENTY-FOUR

THOSE WHO HAD patronized Madge's saloon regularly—local farmers, ranch cowboys, buffalo hunters—began arriving with their tools and wagons to clear away the debris. It was something of a last salute to a place that had been special to them. Even a few of the Tascosa women, despite their disdain for the place where their husbands had gotten drunk and lost grocery money at cards, brought sweet tea and lemonade for the workers.

Meanwhile, Eli Rayburn limped about in search of the ideal hiding place for the money. For the time being, it was buried in the bottom of his grain bin, but he wanted a safer place, somewhere far removed from the livery. It needed to be impossible for Ben Baggett or his men to find.

He and Jonesy had told Clay about their discovery.

They spent one whole evening tossing around ideas for a perfect hiding place. Finally, in the dead of night, they walked to the cemetery and found the grave of

Colonel Basil Jay Hawthorne, a rancher said to have been the richest man on the High Plains before a strike of lightning claimed his life. As the legend went, he was out in a pasture helping a cow to birth her calf during a storm when it happened. The calf, which survived, was named Colonel by Hawthorne's grieving widow.

There, beneath the largest tombstone on Boot Hill, they buried the money pouch in a strongbox.

"Anybody ever asks," Jonesy said, "we can just say it appeared the colonel was just trying to take his money with him."

"It'll not need to remain here long anyway," Rayburn said. "Just until a little time has passed so ol' man Baggett will have forgotten about it, or died, whichever comes first."

ALMOST TWO WEEKS had passed since what locals began referring to simply as "the Fire," and neither Clay nor Jonesy had said much more about leaving for home. When the subject did come up, it was quickly quieted by a litany of excuses. It might still be a bit early for Pate to travel long distances. . . . They needed to keep an eye on Eli's healing process and lend a hand at the livery. . . . And they would both feel better knowing Madge and Jennie were in good frames of mind before they left.

The decision to stay even seemed to put Jonesy in better spirits. "Truth is," he said, "it could be that my wife hasn't even discovered I'm gone yet. And if we get to running low on pocket money, we can always sneak out and rob the colonel of whatever we need."

For a while longer, the tent would continue to be their home.

With the saloon no longer a destination, a new quiet settled over Tascosa. Only those in need of supplies

braved the sweltering summer heat to visit Madge and
Jennie at the mercantile. Blacksmithing needs were
put on hold until Rayburn's health returned, so there
was little activity at the livery. Rarely was anyone from
the canyon seen in town.

Even the pace of Baggett's operation had slowed
while he sought to recruit new manpower to replace the
rustlers he'd lost. Bootsy was promoted to head scout
and spent much of his time searching the New Mexico
Territory for new ranches to raid.

Though he didn't mention it as often, a day rarely
passed that Baggett didn't think about the money that
had been stolen from him and curse the memory of
Top Wilson. He had been delighted when he finally
learned the details of the killing.

When Bootsy had told him that it was Madge who
was responsible, Baggett walked down to the canyon
corral, where Calvin Dunning was mending a fence.
"Don't I recall you being married to that saloon woman
in town?"

Bootsy had also made him aware of Madge's recent
fame. "We ain't been together in a long time," Dunning said.

"But according to the law, you're still husband and
wife."

"I guess." Aware that others were listening, Dunning was uncomfortable with the conversation.

Baggett was enjoying the embarrassment he was
causing. "When you come to work here, I had no idea
you was hitched to such a famous person. Me, I had a
woman like that, I'd stick close so she could protect me.
Blow the head off anyone giving me grief. Of course, a
fellow would need to be careful not to get her mad, lest
she aim her shotgun in his direction. Think there's any
chance I might be able to hire her?"

There was a smattering of laughter among the other

workers at the corral as Dunning turned and walked away.

"Next time you're in town," Baggett called out, "you be sure and tell the little lady how proud I am of what she done."

"I don't go to town," Dunning mumbled.

P AUL PRICE WAS likely the least sociable resident of Tascosa. Aside from those who visited his laundry or sought a monthly shave or hot bath, few townspeople ever saw him or his wife, Anna. It was generally assumed that his shyness had something to do with his having been kicked in the head by a mule when he was a youngster. It was safe to assume he was the only person in town who had not heard details of the saloon burning.

Price was good at washing, folding clothes, and making chin whiskers disappear, but social graces eluded him.

When he'd appeared at the livery with Wilson's horse, it was only the second or third time Eli had ever had a conversation with him. And then he was back. And again he was talking about a hunting trip he'd made in the wooded area beyond his place of business.

"I was wondering," he said, "if we've got reason to be concerned about Indians attacking."

"Far as I know," Rayburn said, "it's been a long while since we had those worries. I think the last time they were seen in these parts was when the army ran them out of the canyon and onto the reservation over in the Territory. What causes you to ask?"

"I thought I saw some the other day. Two of them riding bareback and carrying long guns."

"Was they wearing warbonnets and have their faces painted?" Eli regretted the condescending remark as soon as it left his mouth.

"I'm telling you, I saw them."

"Didn't intend making fun. I'm sure you did. But I got no explanation for them being in these parts."

Breckenridge, however, did when Eli mentioned the conversation that evening.

"Remember me saying how I thought there was something strange about those cattle drivers being killed the way they were? It seemed more message sending, like they were of a mind to even the score for what Top Wilson caused over at that Comanche village. They replaced their stolen cattle, but maybe ain't yet satisfied they've properly avenged their dead."

Rayburn spat tobacco into the dirt and cursed. "How long until we get all of Wilson's messes cleaned up?"

"I recall a few of them following us home. Didn't see them after we made it to Tascosa, but it could be they continued trailing Baggett's boys on to the canyon. Might have recognized them as members of that rustling party Wilson led."

Eli had a solemn look on his face. "You think we've got cause for concern here in Tascosa?"

"I don't think so," Clay said, "but if I was living down in Palo Duro Canyon, I might be inclined to start sleeping with one eye open."

MADGE KNEW NONE of the hymns but faked singing as best she could. Jennie, seeing her brave effort, smiled from across the room. For both, it felt good to be among people again. It also pleased them that none in attendance had so much as mentioned the events at the saloon.

As was tradition, Sunday singing ended with a prayer and refreshments. On this afternoon there was gingerbread cake and apple cider.

On the buggy ride back to the farm, Madge wasn't

sure how she felt about the experience. The people, other women mostly, had been nice, but she was uncertain about a person placing so much blind faith in a divine being who watched out for people from somewhere high above the clouds. Where had He been the night her saloon burned?

She decided not to mention her doubts. Instead, she asked Jennie about Will Darby.

"He was a man trying very hard to mend his ways." Jennie's voice took on a wistful quality. "In his past, he had made a lot of wrong turns and bad decisions. He admitted that. But he had good qualities as well. Even Pa could see that once he got to know him. I told him once that he was like watching a rosebud opening into a beautiful flower."

"And you loved him," Madge said.

"I loved what he was becoming . . . a good and honest man. He told me of his mistakes and shortcomings, even why he gave up his Christian name to be called Will Darby."

"What did he tell you about his brother?"

"Clay was the man he wanted to someday be. Will felt he'd been a great disappointment to his brother and wanted to make it up to him. He spoke often about one day returning to the family farm—me with him—and working side by side with Clay. He loved him."

"I'm sorry that wasn't allowed to happen," Madge said.

The lantern was already lit in the cabin when they arrived. "In a way," Jennie said, "I could understand his feelings about his homeplace. It's much the same for me. I always feel everything's right and as it should be once I get home."

Madge reached across the buggy and gave Jennie a hug. She felt a slight tug of jealousy. The closest thing she'd ever known to a real home was a small bedroom located upstairs from a smelly saloon. And now even that was gone.

While they watched Cyrus unhitch the horse and store the buggy away, Madge felt a shiver run down her spine. She had the sudden feeling they were being watched.

"What is it?" Jennie said.

Madge forced a smile. "Nothing," she said. "The devil just walked over my grandma's grave."

CHAPTER TWENTY-FIVE

SILVER HAWK CONTINUED to brood over the rustlers' midnight attack on his village and the deaths of his three young warriors. In time, he left on a solitary trip into the Indian Territory wilderness to seek counsel with the spirits.

The small band of hostile followers who had joined him in escaping the confines of the reservation and the restraints of the white man's government anxiously waited for him to return and provide guidance.

One of the tribe's most revered war chiefs, he had been shamed, and the only way he could restore his reputation was to take bloody revenge on his enemy. He summoned rebel leaders of several other Comanche camps for a council meeting to discuss combining forces and attacking an enemy hidden away in a High Plains place called Palo Duro Canyon.

When he returned to the village in full battle gear, chants promising death to the white devils went up from the braves. Then there was a ceremonial bonfire and prayers to the War Gods that their aims would be true.

In the generations before, Comanche warriors had fought battles against the white man in a spontaneous and near-suicidal way. There was no planning and very little concern for the number of casualties that might be suffered. When young braves died, others simply stepped up to take their places. Such was the Indian tradition of range war in the early days of the new West.

Guidance and tactics were delivered by the spirits.

Then the soldiers brought a new style of warfare. Their military approach featured careful planning and strategy, measuring of all odds and advantages before the first shot was fired. Tribal leaders, weary of losing battles, soon began to adopt the white man's battle plans.

Though he had never been to Palo Duro Canyon, Silver Hawk could see it clearly in his mind. Scouts, traveling in pairs, had been there and returned to the village with details of everything from the jagged walls to the number of men living there. What they described was an ideal place for a surprise attack. For the unsuspecting white man, it was a death trap.

The first shot fired was symbolic—a flaming arrow that arced high in the twilight sky before landing on the roof of one of the cabins. Afterward came a barrage of rifle fire.

Silver Hawk's raiding party, almost fifty warriors strong, had split into two groups that lined the canyon on both sides of the Baggett encampment. The order was simple. They had come to take nothing but the white men's lives, avenging the loss of their fallen brothers and the theft of their cattle. What they could not kill, they would burn.

So sudden was the attack that several men fell dead even before they had time to search for cover. Others began firing harmless shots toward the canyon rim.

Those who looked toward the trail that led out found that it was already blocked by rifle-bearing Indians.

Ben Baggett frantically raced about his cabin. "Who are these people?" he yelled from a window. He held a gun, but had no idea where to aim it. "Who . . . are . . . these . . . people?"

A rifle shot tore away the canvas window curtain near him, and he ducked to the floor. "Somebody do something," he said in a childlike voice.

Bootsy was trapped under a wagon with a couple of other men. With no visible enemy, none had yet fired a single shot.

"Why don't they show themselves?" one of the men asked.

"Why should they?" Bootsy replied. "They got every advantage. We're no more than target practice."

The Comanches had planned the assault for the evening of a full moon, so even after nightfall, visibility remained good. Adding an eerie glow were the flames licking at the roofs of several cabins.

"How many dead you think we've got?" said one of the men crouched beneath the pavilion table.

"Maybe half," someone said. "And more to come. This ain't no fair fight . . . and I fear it's likely to end pretty soon."

"What if we surrender?"

"That ain't what these folks have come here for."

Even as he spoke, the attacking warriors began to descend from the walls of the canyon. If their prey insisted on hiding, it was time for hand-to-hand fighting to begin.

The Comanches knew they had the upper hand and were emboldened. The drone of war chants began to echo through the canyon as the warriors neared its floor. Down the trail, additional attackers were coming on horseback.

As they ran through the compound, they would occasionally stop to fire shots into the bodies of those already dead. Scalping and mutilation could wait until later.

Despite a volley of fire, they charged the barn, where several of the cowboys were making a stand. The defenders were quickly overwhelmed. Some were shot point-blank; some had their throats cut. And when the last white man was dead, the building was set afire.

When Bootsy saw three warriors headed toward him, he got to his feet and took aim. "Might as well get this over with," he said. He got off only a single shot before a bullet tore into his stomach. Another hit him in the neck. Choking and spitting blood, he fell to the ground and was soon dead.

A few tried to run, but escape was impossible. If anyone mounted a horse in an attempt to ride away, the animal was shot from beneath him.

Finally, when the last spattering of gunfire ended, the warriors began a methodical search of each cabin, tent, and outbuilding, looking for survivors. When none were found, the structures were also set on fire.

Ben Baggett's cabin was already ablaze when braves checked it for occupants. Finding no one inside, they walked away and let it burn.

The fires gave an orange glow to the night sky as the attackers gathered the dead and piled them in the middle of the now silent compound. They, too, were set afire. All except the one-eyed man.

Silver Hawk instructed two of his braves to take the body into the place called Tascosa. It would send a message. The tribal leader wanted it known what had just happened in the canyon: that revenge had been taken. He also wanted to show he had no interest in causing the deaths of the innocent townspeople he had no grudge against.

* * *

B OOTSY'S BODY WAS found in the vacant lot where the saloon had stood. He had been scalped, and his one good eye was gone.

"So it was Indians that Price saw," Pate said. "Pretty mad ones, I'd say."

Breckenridge's worst fear had been realized. The Comanches, angry over the rustling of their cattle, had telegraphed that this manner of revenge would happen when they slaughtered the trail drivers.

"I guess we'll need to take a ride out and see what's happened," he said, "though I'm guessing I already know."

Several farmers joined Clay, Jonesy, and Rayburn on the trip to Palo Duro Canyon. The stench of burned flesh greeted them long before they reached what had once been the headquarters for the Baggett gang. At first sight, the carnage seemed like something from a high-fever nightmare.

All that remained were the skeletal remains of burned-out buildings, the still-smoldering pile of human remains, and the carcasses of dead animals. The only sound was the slow-turning blade of a windmill. Vultures were already gathering.

"Good thing is there won't be no more cattle rustling," Eli said. "Bad thing is we've got to decide what it is we'll need to do with the deceased. Ain't no way to identify anybody, but we can either bury them here or take them back to Boot Hill. Whatever we decide, we're gonna need to get busy with the grave digging."

Clay stepped closer to the charred mound of bones and flesh, holding the sleeve of his shirt to his face. He was looking for the remains of Ben Baggett, but there was no way to recognize anyone.

A vote was held, and it was decided volunteers would help transport the victims of the massacre to Boot Hill.

"How many graves you thinking?" Pate asked.

Rayburn looked back at the mound of bodies and again shook his head in disbelief. "One," he said. "A big one."

CHAPTER TWENTY-SIX

B EN BAGGETT SAT at the back of the pitch-dark cave, a rifle between his knees, pondering the sudden and dramatic change that had just occurred. This place had been his comforting getaway since he and his men had settled in Palo Duro Canyon, a secret only he knew. It was here he hid his money, safely locked away in a strongbox. Here, in this place he'd discovered by chance years earlier, he could come to be alone in the calming quietness that was only his.

Now, suddenly, it was just a hiding place he hoped the attacking Indians would not discover.

While the terror was being played out in the compound, as his men were being slaughtered, he had struggled to understand what was happening until a volley of flaming arrows landed on the roof of his cabin, setting it ablaze. It was then he had slipped out the back way and run onto the narrow path only he used. Not far, hidden by scrub brush and a large boulder, was the entrance to the place he'd always privately thought of as his money cave.

He'd remained there as the shooting went on, hearing the victorious war chants, then smelling the burning flesh. Even after silence had returned, he didn't move. He was still sitting motionless, barely breathing, when he heard new voices discussing what to do about those who had been killed. Something was said about Bootsy and Boot Hill and the word "massacre" was spoken several times.

Even when he later heard the slow grind of wagon wheels coming down the entrance path, he remained in his hiding place.

In time, his thoughts turned to what awaited him once he ventured beyond the mouth of the cave. Would he be safe? How did one rebuild his world when it had been so completely destroyed? He was still asking these questions when he finally emerged and viewed the unbelievable carnage.

The only sound was the cawing of circling buzzards still hoping for another meal until, from behind the burned rubble of a wagon, he heard a voice. "Howdy, boss."

It was Calvin Dunning, the hand he'd made fun of just days earlier. Upon hearing the first shot of the attack, Dunning had run from the compound and hidden beneath a brush pile on the bank of the creek.

THERE WERE FEW at the cemetery when the canyon victims were laid to rest. Those who did come were there mainly to view the size of the mass grave that had taken a full day to dig. There was no prayer, no hymns sung, no Bible verses quoted.

At Clay's request, Bootsy was afforded his own grave.

"I was of a mind these parts had seen the last of this

kind of Indian raid," Rayburn said as Pate helped him apply liniment to his healing cuts and bruises. "With the soldiers taking a no-foolishness attitude and the Oklahoma reservations operating, I thought things would quiet down."

"Never will completely, as long as there's Comanches and Apaches around to cause trouble," Jonesy said. "Since the buffalo are getting harder to find, killing white folks is about all they got left to do for pleasure."

Eli thought for a moment. "Before you know it, that fella Ned Buntline'll be showing up to write one of his dime novels about this one. I done got his title picked out—'Massacre at Palo Duro Canyon.'"

As he spoke, Clay entered the livery to announce that the burials had been completed.

"I have to ask," Pate said, "why were you so set on that one-eyed fella being allowed a grave all to himself?"

"Because I liked him," Breckenridge said. "There's people who do bad things but still have a good heart. I believe Bootsy was one of 'em."

THIS TIME, IT was Clay who brought up the subject. "Time we head home," he said. Though both had lost track of time, their journey had lasted almost three months.

Pate offered no argument. He'd already begun packing his gear. "I got to be honest. I'm not going to miss this town or this tent," he said, "but I admit I've come to appreciate some of the folks living here."

So had Clay. "I got some goodbyes I want to tend to," he said. "But first I'm going to visit the Prices and have me a shave and a hot bath." He smiled. "Since it's likely you've been smelling of late, you might consider doing the same. Maybe ask Paul to splash a little of that lilac water in your tub."

It was midafternoon when he made his slow walk toward the mercantile. He stopped briefly at the vacant lot where the saloon had stood, watching a dust devil stir the last remnants of ashes. He'd rehearsed what he wanted to say but was far from confident.

Madge was dusting shelves, and Jennie was behind the counter when he entered. Both smiled as he tipped his hat. The smiles disappeared, however, when he explained that he'd come to purchase supplies for his and Jonesy's return home.

The atmosphere suddenly turned uncomfortable. "I'd be happy to help you with your shopping," Madge said, a strained formality in her tone. "What is it you'll be needing?"

Clay was already flustered. "Some coffee . . . flour . . . uh, jerky if you got it . . . probably some hard candy for Jonesy's sweet tooth . . . maybe a little bit of . . ." He stopped. "Truthfully, what I've come for is to talk with you about something other than supplies."

"I'm gonna go out front and sit," Jennie said, smiling as she hurried toward the door.

Fumbling with the brim of his hat, Breckenridge moved toward Madge. "I was wondering if you've given any more thought to your future plans. . . ."

"Like you said, one day at a time. But I know I can't go on living at the Broder house forever. They've been nice as can be, but, between you and me, I've got no use for those smelly goats they raise."

"Have I ever spoken to you about my little farm?"

When Madge didn't remind him that he'd bragged about it on several occasions, he began his rehearsed description. When he'd finished painting a picture of the farm, he began extolling the virtues of Aberdene, another subject he'd already discussed with her.

"It all sounds nice," she said.

"It's just me and Sarge," he said. "What I'm wondering is, would you have any interest in joining us? We got plenty of—"

Madge put her hand to his lips. "Mr. Breckenridge, am I to understand that you're proposing we get married?"

"Yes, ma'am, I am. I know a preacher in Aberdene, and there's a church. . . ."

"I know. You've already told me." She placed her arms around his neck. "I've got nothing to pack and no money to help with the purchase of provisions."

"No need to worry," Clay said as he let out a relieved breath and smiled.

Madge called out to Jennie. "You can come on back in," she said. "I got good news and bad news I want you to hear."

Jennie was giddy with anticipation as she reentered.

"The bad news," Madge said, "is that you'll soon be running the store by yourself. The good news is that Clay's asked me to marry him. Wasn't exactly the kind of proposal they write songs and poems about, but it sounded good to me."

As Clay, red-faced and happy, left to share the news with Jonesy, Jennie broke into a jig. Then, for a second, a worried look crossed her face.

Madge anticipated her question. "I'll have no need to get a divorce," she said. "The Comanches solved that problem by doing away with everybody out at the canyon and making me a widow."

Clay was beaming when he walked into the livery. "Eli," he said, "we'll be needing an extra horse and saddle for our trip. I'd prefer one that's sturdy but a gentle ride."

"Wouldn't be for a lady whose saloon recently burned down, would it?"

Clay blushed. "It might be."

The following morning, a small group gathered in front of the livery. Jennie was joined by her father and grandfather. Several ladies from the Sunday singing group were there, bringing freshly made bread and muffins. They had pooled their egg money to buy Madge a new bonnet. Even the Prices showed up and waved bashfully. Rayburn put on a brave front, forcing a smile as he held the reins of a newly shod and already saddled dappled gray mare named Lucy. He had also rolled and tied one of his small tents onto the back of the pack-horse. His wedding gift, he said.

There were hugs, handshakes, and well-wishes. And then they were on their way, leaving one adventure behind and heading toward another.

CHAPTER TWENTY-SEVEN

LONNIE LOOKED AS if he'd grown a foot. He was deeply tanned and bathed in sweat, mending one of Nester Callaway's fences when they arrived. When he saw the horses approaching, he immediately dropped his hammer and began running toward the cabin. The Callaways were already on the front porch, shading their eyes against the noon sun in an effort to see who was coming.

It was Cora Callaway who first recognized Jonesy and began clapping her hands. "They're back," she told her husband. Then she yelled out to the boy running from the field, "Lonnie, honey, they're back." She was hugging Clay before he could completely get down from his horse.

Nester, more frail-looking than he'd been the last time they'd seen him, was smiling. "Seems it's been a coon's age since you was last here. Welcome back."

The most excited was Lonnie. He didn't know whom to reach out to first. Finally, Jonesy solved his problem by slapping him on the shoulder, then wrapping an arm around him. "Good to see you, boy," he said. "Looks like they've been feeding you extra helpings while we've been gone."

Pate stepped back so Clay could say hello. "We missed you," he said, putting his hands to Lonnie's face. Then he turned to Nester and Cora. "We missed all of you."

Madge viewed the reunion from horseback until Clay helped her down and introduced her. "This lady," he said, "is going home with me. We're gonna get married once we get there."

Cora wiped tears from her eyes with the corner of her apron. "Oh, my, isn't that the most wonderful news?" she said, then reached out to hug Madge. "Don't mind me. I cry at just about everything."

"I've heard so much about you folks, I feel I already know you," Madge said as she shook Nester's hand. Then she turned to Lonnie. "Especially you," she said.

Lonnie smiled bashfully and took the reins from her. "Go on inside and cool off," he said. "I'll see to the horses."

As they walked toward the cabin, Madge whispered to Clay and Jonesy, "He's a fine-looking young man. I see now why you were so anxious to get here."

Cora had just taken an apple pie from the oven, and Madge helped her prepare plates for everyone. Nester urged Clay and Jonesy to take a seat at the kitchen table.

"Before the boy gets in here, I want to do some bragging on him," Callaway said. "I've never seen a harder worker in my life. This place looks better than it ever has. Holes in the roof of the barn have been patched, fences repaired. Ain't no weeds in the garden, and he does the milking and a right smart of plowing without even being asked. Sometimes even helps with the cooking. He doesn't know when to quit." The halting manner of his speech and the struggle for breath made it obvious that Nester's health had seriously declined. "Don't know what we'd have done without him. My wife calls him a godsend."

"The hard work will soon be over," Cora said as she placed pie and cups of coffee on the table. "We've reached a decision to sell the place and move into town, where Nester can be closer to the doctor . . . and I can be less worried and nearer church services."

Her husband explained that a neighbor had offered him a fair price for his livestock, "which you folks kindly rescued for us," and the banker in town was searching for a buyer for the property. "He came out and looked it over a while back and seemed impressed with the upkeep. He says more and more folks are moving out this way, looking for land to buy."

"I guess you're gonna miss it," Pate said.

Nester began coughing, then took a sip of coffee. "Not as much as you might expect," he said. "When folks get up in years, they get kinda worn-out, and their attitudes change. The notion of sleeping late and napping on the porch in the afternoons doesn't sound all bad."

As he spoke, Lonnie entered, still smiling. He was anxious to hear about the trip his friends had made. "Were you able to get done what you wanted?"

"Yes," Clay said, "though it took a little longer than we'd expected." He offered no details, which disappointed Lonnie. But instead of asking more questions, he ate his pie.

They sat, enjoying one another's company long after the plates were empty and the coffeepot had been drained. After Madge helped Cora clear the table, she approached Lonnie. "If you're not too tired from your fence mending, I'd like to take a tour of the place," she said. "I understand you've done considerable hard work."

Lonnie was quickly on his feet, putting on his hat.

Once they were out the door, Jonesy cleared his throat and began outlining his plan.

"Since we were last here, I've given thought to what might lie ahead for Lonnie," he said, "and the best idea I've come up with is for him to come live with me and my wife. We'd take good care of him—just like you folks have—and see that he gets proper schooling. My wife was once a schoolteacher and places high value on education. Though you'd never believe it from being around me, so do I. We ain't rich by no means, but we can take care of any needs he'll have.

"My wife—her name's Patricia—loves young'uns, and I know she would be proud to have Lonnie as part of our family. We've never been able to have children of our own, which is one of her great sorrows."

Clay entered the conversation. "We're neighbors, me and Jonesy. Our places are just a few miles apart, so it would really be like Lonnie having two homes if he's of a mind," he said. "I think highly of the boy as well and would like having him around. He'd even be welcome to come live with me and Madge. We've discussed it, and she has no objections."

"Praise the Lord," Cora said. "How I've been praying for this. We've come to love Lonnie like our own, but there's going to soon come a time when we can't properly care for him. What's best for him is what we want, even if it means having an ache in our hearts from missing him."

"I bet we could arrange an occasional visit," Pate said.

Cora came around the table and hugged him, then Clay. "I doubt convincing him will be difficult," she said.

Madge could tell the conversation had gone well when she returned to the cabin. "Lonnie's seeing to chores in the barn," she said to Jonesy. "I told him you would be there shortly to discuss something with him."

Pate, usually outgoing and confident, suddenly appeared nervous. "What if he doesn't like the idea?"

Madge laughed. "He will."

"You want to come with me?"

"Nope," said Clay. "This should be a private matter, just between you and the boy."

Lonnie was stacking cedar posts when Jonesy entered the barn.

"The Callaways tell me you been behaving yourself and earning your keep," Pate said.

"They've been mighty nice, though I worry about Mr. Callaway's health. He's not doing too good."

"I guess they've talked with you about their plans for moving into town."

"I guess it's the smart thing to do," Lonnie said. "They've told me I'm welcome to come with them, but there's been no mention of what I might do about Maizy."

Jonesy had seen Lonnie's mare grazing in the pasture as they'd arrived. Her coat was smooth and shiny, bringing to mind the time they'd found her after the flood, covered in mud and river debris. She was a beautiful horse, and Jonesy could understand the youngster's attachment to her.

"I got a proposition that might work for both you and Maizy," he said. "Take a seat and hear me out."

They sat together on a pile of hay as Pate explained his hope that Lonnie would consider becoming part of his family. He'd been rehearsing the speech since they'd left Tascosa. He talked about his wife, described the ranch, and noted how close Lonnie would be to Clay's farm. Aberdene wasn't far away, close enough for him to ride Maizy in and resume his schooling and meet others his own age. In the summers there was a town baseball team he might even like to join. If Lonnie wanted to learn the cattle business, he'd gladly be his teacher. If he was more inclined to be a farmer, Mr. Breckenridge could provide pointers.

Jonesy tried not to make things sound too idyllic. "I ain't promising it'll be perfect. My wife and me can't no more replace your ma and pa than the Callaways have. But we can give you a home that's permanent and has a lot of love in it if you're of a mind to accept it."

Lonnie was silent for a moment as he rose and walked to the doorway of the barn. He looked toward the cabin for some time. "I wish there was more I could do to pay back the Callaways for all they've done for me. They've given me a place to live and fed me. Treated me good. She's even sewed me clothes."

"I think you've paid them back more than you know. Folks get old, and it's nice having somebody young around. You being here has brought more joy to their lives than you can ever know."

"He's gonna die soon, you know," Lonnie said. "It ain't just Mr. Callaway's coughing and trouble breathing. You can see it in his eyes and hear it in his voice."

"And you'll be one of the good memories he takes with him."

Lonnie turned and smiled. It was his answer.

"Let's go up to the house and tell them what you've decided," Jonesy said.

Cora Callaway was watching through the window and saw them walking from the barn, arm in arm. They looked happy.

"Oh, my stars," she said, "we're going to have to have us a special dinner tonight to celebrate." As expected, she again had tears in her eyes.

IN TASCOSA, ELI Rayburn had been in a foul mood for days. He'd had no idea how much he would miss the company of Clay Breckenridge and Jonesy Pate. And

Madge. A couple of times a day, he would walk down to the mercantile to say hello to Jennie and find she was also in the doldrums.

"At the rate things are happening," he told her, "this place will soon be a ghost town, which, I suppose, won't set too many folks to crying."

He was on the way back to the livery when he saw two horses out front. Neither had a saddle. Their bridles were poorly fashioned from rope.

He was stunned when he walked in to see Ben Baggett and another man standing there. Both were dirty and looked exhausted. "Thought maybe you were closed for business since nobody was around," Baggett said.

"Something I can do for you?"

"We're in the need of two saddles, all the riggings, and blankets. I have to ride one more mile bareback, I'm liable to shoot the horse and just leave him lie."

Rayburn was at a loss for words. He looked at Baggett as if he was seeing a ghost. Same with the man standing next to him. He was familiar to Eli, but Eli couldn't put a name to the face.

Baggett's raspy voice jolted him back to attention. "Saddles? You got any?"

"I've got a couple stored in a shed out back. Let me go get them." Rayburn didn't tell him that one had come off the horse Paul Price had recently brought in—the one Top Wilson had left down in the gulley.

"They'll do," Baggett said, barely looking at them. "We're going to walk down to the laundry and see about getting ourselves cleaned up and more presentable. Then we'll visit the mercantile to see about new clothes and provisions."

"If you don't see Paul soon as you arrive at the laundry, just give a loud holler," Rayburn said. "He's sometimes down in the woods, still on the lookout for Indians."

Baggett showed little interest in the remark. "While

we're gone," he said, "maybe you could feed our horses
and give 'em a good brushing. I'll pay when we get back.
Got any whiskey?"

"Might have a sip or two," Eli said.

"I'll buy that as well," Baggett said.

Rayburn nodded. As they walked away, he called
out, "Where you gonna be heading?"

Baggett turned and gave him a hard look. "As far
away from Palo Duro Canyon as we can get," he said.

PART FOUR

—— ◇ ——

HELL'S HALF ACRE

CHAPTER TWENTY-EIGHT

Five months later

CLAY AND MADGE were married in God's Place Chapel in Aberdene. Jonesy and Patricia were there, accompanied by Lonnie, who was wearing the first store-bought clothes he'd ever owned. Once the brief ceremony was completed, they had walked to the town park, where a celebration was underway.

There were tables filled with fried chicken and sweet potato pies, fresh bread and jars of lemonade. Children were pitching horseshoes and having sack races. Grown-ups sat on benches and blankets spread in the shade of huge pecan trees, talking and watching the kids. Laughter could be heard everywhere. Lonnie had never seen anything like it.

That day, the look on his face pleased the Pates and the newlyweds, assuring them that he was adjusting well to his new home.

Now, months later, they still talked fondly of that "wedding day."

Ruben had done a good job tending Clay's farm in his absence, and the spring rains had continued into the summer, lending an emerald luster to everything. Sarge had been glad to see Clay and quickly welcomed Madge into the family.

She and Patricia became immediate friends and visited each other regularly, as did their husbands. Rarely was Tascosa mentioned, except to wonder how Eli or the Broders were. The money, buried on Boot Hill, was never discussed.

One Sunday, after riding Maizy over for a visit, Lonnie happened upon the graves of Clay's parents and brother and asked about them. His mother and father had been much like Lonnie's, Clay said, loving, hardworking people. When remembering Cal, he spoke only of good times and good deeds.

"Losing family's hard. It leaves an empty place that's difficult to fill unless you're lucky enough to find others," Clay said. "You and me, we've been fortunate to have new folks come into our lives and bring us new happiness."

They walked to the fence line of the pasture and picked wildflowers, then placed them on each of the graves. Lonnie didn't mention it, but he wished the resting place of his parents was closer.

Seeking to lighten the mood, Clay asked about school. "You're now in grade seven as I recall," he said.

"Eight," Lonnie said. "They put me ahead a grade after I showed my teacher I was good at reading and writing. I can thank my ma for seeing to that."

He talked about how much he liked Miss Cochran, his teacher, and his classmates. He bragged that he was the fastest runner in school and admitted there was one girl, named Ginger, he especially admired.

What he didn't mention was the stranger he'd seen riding past the schoolhouse several times recently, his hat always pulled low on his forehead.

For ben baggett, thoughts of the past were constantly on his mind. Somewhere, somebody still had the money Top Wilson had stolen from him, and he was more determined than ever to find it. Through a process of elimination, he'd considered the possibilities.

He had no reason to think that the livery owner in Tascosa might have it. His place was the same run-down barn and corral it had always been. If he had somehow gotten the money, he would have shut the doors of his business and been on his way, headed out West probably. Instead, he continued to eke out a living renting tents to passing cattle drivers and blacksmithing.

Wilson had no friends. There was no way one of the others living in the canyon had gotten their hands on the money pouch. Even on the off chance someone had, his secret was forever safe, thanks to the Comanches. The girl he'd been sweet on had repeatedly rejected him and was now working for her grandpa in the mercantile, and her pa was still raising goats. They'd not likely received any financial windfall. After speaking with the strange-acting fella who ran the laundry and bath, he was scratched from the list of suspects.

Somehow, somebody, Ben had decided, had made off from Tascosa with his money. From what he'd learned from Paul Price—when he wasn't talking crazy of another potential Indian raid—the fella named Breckenridge and his partner, along with Madge, had left for a place called Aberdene over in East Texas.

Find them, Baggett thought, and they would lead him to his money.

First, however, he needed to locate somewhere new

and get his life back in order. The money he'd put away
in the cave wouldn't last forever. Once clear thinking
had returned following the murderous attack in the
canyon, he decided to head for Fort Worth. It was a
cattle town, and he still considered himself a cattleman, however outside the law he operated.

Fort Worth, he knew, was the major stopping place
for those driving longhorns along the Chisholm Trail
toward Kansas City. Once the site of an old army out-
post, it had grown into a bawdy, no-holds-barred town
where an area known as Hell's Half Acre was home to
notorious outlaws hiding from the law for various reasons. A bigger Tascosa. It would be the perfect place
for Baggett to begin rebuilding his gang and a good
place to headquarter.

For the moment, however, all he had was Calvin
Dunning, a partner he considered half-witted and of
little use, a survivor of the canyon raid thanks to his
cowardice. Baggett would keep him around only until
he found someone better.

Still, while he got acquainted with the men in Hell's
Half Acre, he did have one assignment he felt Dunning
would be capable of carrying out.

"Once we get ourselves settled," he said, "I'll be
wanting you to ride over to this place called Aberdene
and locate some folks. Might be interesting for you,
seeing as how one of them's your wife. Meanwhile, I
think we need to go find us a place to drink some
whiskey."

After hearing what his boss wanted him to do, Dunning badly needed a drink.

B AGGETT FOUND THE city life invigorating. He liked
the lights and noise, the constant movement of
people. There were numerous saloons to choose from

and places where you could order a steak well into the night. No one ever seemed to sleep. It brought to mind his days in Brownsville, on the Texas coast, and he regretted spending so many years in a place as remote as Palo Duro Canyon.

At the first saloon they visited, they saw two fights break out. In another, a drunken cowboy won a poker hand and, in celebration, pulled his pistol and fired several shots into the ceiling. Few patrons even bothered to look up from their drinking. Things were free-wheeling and apparently lawless. The latter was just what Baggett was looking for.

Dunning, meanwhile, wrestled with mixed feelings. He was glad to be riding out of the city, alone for a while, but was anxious about the job he'd been given. He had no wish to see Madge and considered ways to avoid her. Hopefully, the bushy beard he'd grown would provide some disguise.

He'd felt relief when Baggett had instructed that he only determine that Clay and Jonesy were there, not approach anyone. Just find them, then report their activities and location back to him. Once that was done, Baggett would figure out the next step.

Dunning, aware that his boss didn't hold him in high regard, hoped it would not involve him.

It was easier than he'd anticipated.

The first day in town he was having breakfast in the hotel when he heard Jonesy Pate's name mentioned by a man at a nearby table. Dunning went over, introduced himself as Haley Johnson, and said he'd overheard the name of an old friend.

"I'm just passing through," he said, "but if Jonesy's living anywhere nearby, I'd like to drop in on him."

He was immediately given directions to Pate's ranch. "You're in luck. Him and his friend returned from a trip somewhere out West a few months back," one of the men said. "And Jonesy came back with a youngster who's now living with him and his wife."

"Lordy mercy. Jonesy's got himself a son?"

"Oh, no. As I hear it, this boy's an orphan who Jonesy took a liking to and invited to move in with him and Patricia. Nice-looking young man. Don't recall his name, but I'm sure you'll meet him."

"I look forward to it," Dunning said. "Now, once again, which road is it I want to take to get to his place?"

The man pointed his napkin in the direction of the kitchen. "Go north and just follow the one that runs out past the schoolhouse. It ain't far. You'll first come to the Breckenridge farm. Then Pate's place is just a mile or two on down the way."

As if feeling left out of the conversation, the other breakfast eater spoke up. "Clay Breckenridge, he's who went on the trip with Jonesy. And, believe it or not, he came back home with a lady he married just a while back. Real pretty woman."

In five minutes, Dunning had learned everything he wanted to know and more, thanks to the gossipy old men. Not only had he found out that Breckenridge and Pate were, indeed, there, but also that his wife had married again.

For reasons he couldn't fully explain, the latter didn't interest him nearly as much as Pate taking in an orphan.

Later that day, he was hiding in a creek bed near the caliche road entrance to the Pate ranch when Lonnie rode past. *Likely returning home from school,* Dunning thought.

On the way back into town, he decided against trying to get a glimpse of Clay or the new Mrs. Breckenridge. Instead, he rode past the schoolhouse several times the following day, trying to get a better look at the boy. He had begun formulating a plan that he thought might put him in the good graces of his boss.

The orphan, he thought, could well be the key to finding Baggett's stolen cash.

CHAPTER TWENTY-NINE

WHEN CALVIN DUNNING returned to Fort Worth, he found Baggett sitting at a corner table in his favorite saloon. There was a half-full bottle of whiskey on the table and two cutthroat-looking cowboys across from him. Dunning didn't even wait to be offered a drink before he began telling his boss he'd located the people he'd been sent to find.

"Everybody's there, just like you thought, living right outside of Aberdene. I can draw you directions right to their front door," he said. "And I've got some additional information you might find of interest." He glanced across the table toward the two strangers, who had not spoken a word.

"You can talk freely," Baggett said. "These boys have just joined up with us."

Feeling confident, Dunning took the liberty of pouring himself a drink. He told Baggett of Pate bringing an orphan home with him. "The boy looks fifteen, maybe sixteen, and he's attending school there in Aberdene," he said. "Way I was told, he's thought highly of by both Pate and Breckenridge."

"Where did he come from?"

"That I wasn't able to learn."

"So what's he got to do with my money?"

It was the question Calvin was hoping to hear. "Hard-headed as Pate and Breckenridge are likely to be," he said, "I'm betting they ain't going to be inclined to readily discuss the location of what you're looking for. But if they were to fear harm might come to . . ."

Baggett was way ahead of him. "We kidnap the boy," he said, "and hold on to him until I get my money."

From across the table, the silent strangers smiled.

THE TWO MEN were brothers named Doozy and Alvin, short and stocky, both barely in their twenties when they started robbing stagecoaches and wagon trains. They had never been much good at it and had spent several stretches in various Texas jails. Just recently released by the Callahan County sheriff, they had come to Fort Worth in hopes of starting a new and more financially rewarding career.

They had stayed drunk for several days and gotten into a few fights before they met Ben Baggett.

He could tell an outlaw when he saw one. He'd introduced himself, bought them a couple of drinks, and asked if they were looking for work.

In chorus they said, "Yessir."

Baggett sealed the deal by buying them a bottle of cheap whiskey and said he would be back in touch in a couple of days. "I've got to do some thinking," he said. "Then we'll talk about a job I'll need you to do."

The following day he sent Dunning in search of Doozy and Alvin.

"Calvin here's got directions to where you'll be heading," he said as they sat at the same table. This time there was no liquor since he wanted them stone-cold sober when he gave them instructions. "He'll also describe a young'un who comes and goes from school every day. Your job will be to grab the boy without being seen and bring him back here. I've written out a message you're to leave behind."

Dunning spread a piece of paper on which he'd drawn a map that showed the directions to Aberdene. On one side he'd drawn a route to the East Texas community. On the other were the locations of the school and the ranch where Lonnie lived. He thought his role in the plot was over until Baggett had a final thought.

"Now that I think on it, it might be best if Calvin accompanies you so you don't get lost," Baggett said.

Dunning's heart sank. Baggett slapped him on the shoulder and smiled. "Why don't you go down to the café and tell them to cook us up some steaks?" he said. "Don't want you boys riding out on empty stomachs. Me and these boys will discuss their pay, then be there shortly."

After he'd left, Baggett placed his elbows on the table and leaned toward his new employees. "Not to worry. You'll get paid well," he said, "but I got some rules you'll need to abide by. First, there'll be no drinking until the job's completed. Second thing, don't do the boy no harm.

"Third, I don't want you bringin' Dunning back with you."

MISS COCHRAN HAD spent most of the day teaching arithmetic, the subject that least interested Lonnie. He was glad when she dismissed the students for the day and was looking forward to stopping by the

Breckenridge farm on the way home to spend a few minutes playing with Sarge.

Jonesy, seeing how much he enjoyed Clay's dog, had already promised he'd soon have a pup of his own, so long as it didn't interfere with his chores and studies.

At the hitching rail he pulled an apple from his lunch bucket and fed it to Maizy, then led her to the watering trough before leaving the schoolyard. Since she waited for him all day, Lonnie chose not to burden her with the discomfort of a saddle and rode bareback to and from town. As he left, he turned and waved goodbye to Ginger.

They were just a few hundred yards from the school when two riders suddenly emerged from a stand of trees and were quickly on each side of Maizy. One of the men grabbed the reins while the other pointed a pistol. A third man appeared and grabbed the lunch bucket from Lonnie, stuffed a piece of paper inside it, and tossed it to the ground.

"Climb down and get on back," the gunman said, pointing to his partner's horse. "We'll not be taking yours."

"Where are we going?" Lonnie said. There was the treble of fear in his voice.

"Just shut up and climb on," one of the men said. "That fellow pointing the gun will be riding right behind you, in case you get thoughts of doing something foolish."

In less than two minutes, it was done. Doozy was laughing as they galloped away. "That," he said, "was easy."

PATRICIA PATE WAS uneasy when Lonnie was late arriving home. She had baked gingerbread and had it cooling for him. Her concern grew to full-blown horror when Jonesy burst into the kitchen, his face ashen. "Maizy just showed up at the barn," he said, "and Lonnie's not with her."

She slumped to a chair and buried her face in her hands as her husband hurried away to saddle his own horse.

He was sweating and out of breath by the time he reached Clay's place and told him of the situation. In a matter of minutes both were riding toward town.

It was Jonesy who first saw the lunch bucket in the middle of the dusty road. He quickly reined his horse to a stop and dismounted.

"I think it's Lonnie's," he said.

"See if there's anything inside."

Jonesy unfolded the piece of paper and read the note written on it aloud.

I got your boy. And you got my money.
Let's make us a trade.

Though he rarely did, Clay yelled out a curse. "Ben Baggett ain't dead," he said.

CHAPTER THIRTY

A FEW OF the town children were still in the school-yard, playing games. None, when asked, had seen anything but Lonnie riding toward home, as he usually did. Inside, Miss Cochran was gathering up books and dusting her blackboard. She was horrified by the news but knew nothing.

Clay had never seen his friend so frantic. "I'm having difficulty thinking what we should do next," Jonesy said.

"Let's go see the marshal."

"We'll get a search party together," Dodge Rankin said as he bolted from his chair. "Got any thoughts on who might have taken him? You sure his horse didn't just pitch him, and he's lying hurt somewhere?"

Pate raised his voice and waved the note. "He's been kidnapped, Marshal, plain and simple. And we have to find whoever it is who took him."

"Lord, Lord," Rankin said. "I can't recollect us having a kidnapping since way back when the Comanches was stealing women and children. I'll get some of the boys together, and we'll get to looking." He then added a warning. "Ain't likely to be easy since nobody seems to have seen which way they went. Plus, there's not that much daylight left."

While the marshal summoned a search party, Pate and Breckenridge headed for the ranch. Madge was already there, attempting to calm Patricia. The four sat at the kitchen table as Jonesy told of finding the note.

"You sure Ben Baggett's involved?" said Madge. "Everybody thought he was killed in that Indian raid along with everybody else."

"It's Baggett," Clay said. "I got no doubt. He somehow survived."

"What's this about money?" Patricia asked.

"It's a long story," said Jonesy. Then he told it.

"So you stole money from somebody who stole it from him?" his wife said. "I never heard of such a thing. And hiding it in a graveyard . . ."

"We weren't planning on keeping it for ourselves," Jonesy said. "What I don't understand is how he knows it was us and Eli who wound up with it."

"I suspect he's just guessing," Clay said, "which isn't that important at the moment. What we gotta do is find Lonnie before any harm comes to him."

AFTER COVERING SEVERAL miles and feeling confident that they hadn't been followed, Doozy suggested they give their horses a rest. Alvin bound Lonnie's wrists and ankles and had him sit against a tree trunk.

The brothers were elated by their success. "Think Mr. Baggett's gonna ask for ransom?" Alvin said. "Maybe thousands of dollars?"

"Hope so," Doozy said. "I'm wondering how much of it we'll be getting."

Dunning sat nearby, silently staring at the young boy who was shivering despite the heat. He was wishing he'd never mentioned that Jonesy Pate had brought him home.

After a short rest, Doozy said it was time to mount up. "We can keep riding until dark, then camp for the night. Be in Fort Worth by this time tomorrow."

The moon was just coming over the horizon when the kidnappers arrived on the bank of a swift-running creek. A nearby grove of trees looked like a good place to camp. Doozy, feeling emboldened by their success, had appointed himself leader. "There's to be no campfire," he said, "and we'll take shifts standing watch. We don't want nothing going wrong now that we've come this far." He looked at his brother. "Get the boy a drink. Then see to it he's tied up good and tight."

Then he smiled. "Our work's already half done." Alvin knew to what he was referring.

The night passed slowly as Lonnie slept fitfully, often whimpering when in the middle of a bad dream. Doozy and Alvin snored in harmony when they weren't standing watch. Sleep completely evaded Dunning, who was glad to finally see the first rays of daylight.

While the brothers stretched and cursed their stiffness, Calvin walked to the bank of the creek to splash water on his face. He was on his knees, bent forward, when he felt the barrel of Alvin's pistol pressed against his back.

"The boss said to tell you that your services won't be needed any longer," Alvin said just before pulling the trigger.

Dunning's body quivered, then slowly toppled forward into the water.

Nearby, Lonnie screamed and frantically tried without success to free himself. "Why did you kill him?"

"Not to worry, little man," Doozy said. "Our instruc-

tions was to kill only him and see to it you got good care.
Think on it this way: Now you got a horse of your own
to ride the rest of the way."

S OON AFTER IT was discovered that Lonnie was missing, a dozen men joined Marshal Rankin and his
two deputies to begin a search. Since there was little
daylight remaining, they looked in secluded areas near
town. "Check every barn and shed you come across.
Come morning, we'll split up in groups and head out in
every direction," Rankin said. He called out the names
of the searchers who would make up each party.

By dark they had found no trace of the boy or his
abductors.

When daylight came the next day, they broadened
the search. "This seems to be well planned out, so I'm
guessing they'll head toward where they can find water
for their horses. Grayson Creek's to the east of here,"
Rankin said. The marshal asked Pate and Breckenridge to be part of his group, which would head in that
direction.

It was late in the afternoon when they reached Grayson Creek. They rode along the bank for almost a mile
before finding Calvin Dunning's body. He was on his side,
and the crimson wound in his back was plain to see. He
looked dead as they dragged him away from the water.

Only a faint groan convinced them otherwise.

Clay was leaning forward, his face almost touching
Dunning's chest, when he saw the other man's eyes
flicker and open slightly. In a slurred whisper, Dunning said, "Tell Madge . . . sorry . . . all I done." Then
there was a loud gasp and his eyes closed. His last
words sounded like "Fort Worth . . ." and "Bagg . . ."

Breckenridge slowly got to his feet. "Baggett's got
Lonnie somewhere in Fort Worth," he said.

"I know the marshal there," Rankin said, "but truth is, he's one of the biggest outlaws the town's got. Don't know how much help he can be to us, unless you've got money to pay him."

"Doesn't matter," Jonesy said. "We can take care of what needs doing."

CHAPTER THIRTY-ONE

M Y, AIN'T YOU a fine-looking young fellow," Ben
Baggett said as Lonnie was brought into the
room. As instructed, Doozy and Alvin had waited until
long past dark before coming to town. "I'm sorry, but
it'll be necessary to keep you tied up and gagged so you
can't speak out. Don't want to be disturbing nobody."

He turned toward the brothers. "You boys did good,"
he said. "I'm assuming nobody saw you or followed you
back."

"No, sir."

"The boy been fed?"

"I rode in and got us some meat loaf and corn bread
while waiting for it to get dark," Alvin said. "We've
treated him kindly, just like you said to."

Baggett was pleased. "You can now get rested up.
Then we'll discuss the next part of the plan."

"Next part?"

They hadn't been told that the note left in Lonnie's

lunch bucket had made no mention of how his captor could be contacted and the stolen money returned.

Baggett was smiling when the brothers left. It was obvious he was enjoying the game he'd set in motion.

THE WIVES WERE on the front porch, taking turns pacing, when Clay and Jonesy returned. The women's faces showed disappointment when they saw that Lonnie wasn't with them.

"We ain't found him," Jonesy said, "but we've now got a fair idea where to start looking. Like we expected, this is all about the money, so it's not likely he'll be harmed if we give Baggett what he wants."

"Then let's do it," Patricia said. "Get him his money and get me my boy back home."

"It's gonna take some patience," Clay said. "We've gotta consider what Baggett's plan is before we go off half-cocked." He looked over at his wife and signaled for her to follow him into the yard.

"The reason we know Lonnie's likely being held in Fort Worth is from what we was told by one of the men who took him. He was near dead when we found him and passed shortly after providing us the information. He did us a big favor."

Madge listened with only mild interest, her thoughts focused on the safe return of Lonnie.

"Reason I'm telling you this is I need you to know who the fellow was."

A puzzled look crossed Madge's face.

"It was Calvin Dunning. Somehow, he survived the attack in the canyon, just like Baggett."

"You mean . . . You're saying I was still married when we . . . Oh, my God."

"That don't matter. But before he died, he asked

that I give you a message. He said to tell you he was sorry for all he'd done. I thought you should know that."

Without a response, Madge turned and walked back to the house. As she did, Marshal Rankin was stepping onto the porch. "Morning, Mrs. Breckenridge," he said, tipping his hat. She hurried past him and into the kitchen without responding.

The marshal was there to discuss what to do next.

"My vote is we head out for Fort Worth and get on with finding him," Jonesy said. "Right now."

"It's a big place, you know. My guess would be that they're hiding out somewhere in the Hell's Half Acre part of town, but it'll still be like looking for a needle in a haystack," Rankin said.

"If we ask enough people," Jonesy said, "we'll get some answers. It'll be better than sitting around here. Me and Clay, we've done this before."

"You know this Baggett fellow you've mentioned ain't going to willingly give up the boy unless he gets his money," the marshal said.

"There ain't time to travel out to Tascosa and dig it up," Jonesy said. "Best we can do on short notice is give him the location and let him go get it himself."

"Or," said Breckenridge, "we can find him and shoot him dead. Then we can bring Lonnie back safe with no worries about what Baggett's going to think of pulling at some future date. Only way this will end right is for him to be dead."

"You know I can't agree to that kind of thinking," the marshal said.

"Not asking you to. We're heading out first thing in the morning."

Clay followed Rankin to where his horse was tethered. "Just so you know," the marshal said, "Doc

Franklin's tending to the dead man we brought back. He'll see to it he's buried properly."

"Less said on that matter, the better."

THE YOUNG MORNING sky was still burnt orange as Clay and Jonesy were preparing to leave. Madge had remained at the ranch and was helping Patricia prepare breakfast. Ruben was again on the way to watch over the Breckenridge farm and keep Sarge company.

As the women busied themselves in the kitchen, they heard Marshal Rankin arrive. He didn't even bother getting off his horse before handing a piece of paper to Jonesy. "Miss Cochran arrived early at the schoolhouse and found this on her door. She brought it to me straightaway."

Pate looked at it, then handed it to Clay. Two days from now, it read, they were to bring Baggett's money to the Longhorn Saloon in Fort Worth at exactly three o'clock in the afternoon. If they did so, and there was no fighting or shooting, they would be told where they could find the boy. This time the note was signed: *Your Friend, Benjamin J. Baggett*.

"At least now we won't have to look for that needle in a haystack," Jonesy said.

As he made the observation, his wife appeared at the kitchen door. "Everybody come on in while it's still hot," Patricia said. Seeing Rankin, she said, "You're more than welcome to join us, Marshal."

As they finished their scrambled eggs and biscuits, it was Patricia who noticed that Rankin wasn't wearing his badge. "I think this is the first time I've ever seen you without it," she said.

"Not gonna be needing it for a couple of days," he said. "I informed my deputies I'll be taking a short vacation from marshaling." He drained his coffee cup and looked across the table at Clay and Jonesy. "I've invited myself to go along with you," he said.

I N THE REAR of a dimly lit bar on the far edge of the Half Acre, Doozy and his brother were well on their way to getting drunk. "I didn't hire on to be no Pony Express rider," Doozy said. "I might near killed a good horse getting back over there in the middle of the night to leave that letter at the schoolhouse."

"And we ain't yet been paid a cent," Alvin said, sloshing some of his drink onto the table. "Seems to me if you do a man a good job on a kidnapping and a killing, it ain't asking too much to be fairly paid."

Doozy nodded in agreement. "Not to mention delivering mail."

"You don't think he's gonna try and cheat us, do you?"

"Be sorry if he does."

"Hey, I got an idea. Maybe we should think about kidnapping the boy ourselves and make the old man pay us for his safe return."

They staggered out the doorway, arm in arm, into a still-crowded backstreet, pondering the fuzzy outline of a new idea. Alvin took a deep breath of the warm air. "Before we call it a day," he said, "I wouldn't mind to find me somebody to have a real good fistfight with."

Later, he did.

CHAPTER THIRTY-TWO

SATURDAYS IN FORT Worth were day-and-night carnivals. For cattle drivers and stockyard workers, it was payday. Buyers and sellers came to town to hammer out high-dollar deals at the same time petty thieves and two-bit cardsharps practiced their shady crafts. In the saloons and gambling houses, it was standing room only around the clock. And in the streets, fights and gunplay were commonplace. It was difficult to know whether it was greed or alcohol that lit the fuse to such bawdy behavior. Probably both.

It was because of the throngs that arrived and mingled in Hell's Half Acre on the weekend that Ben Baggett had picked it for the meeting with the men who had his money. On Saturday, he had learned, most people become faceless, self-absorbed, or just too drunk to pay attention. A meeting to arrange an exchange of money for a kidnapped young boy was no more likely to be noticed than some poker player cursing another for hiding an ace up his sleeve.

Of all the saloons in town, the Longhorn would be the rowdiest.

"Being as I'm the only one your man doesn't know," said Rankin as they reached the city, "I think it best we split up. I know the Longhorn from visits in my younger days, so I'll arrive early and locate me a good place from which to view your sit-down. Whether it goes off as planned or not, I still might be able to follow our man back to the location where Lonnie's being held."

Clay was the least optimistic about success. "I'm afraid if he doesn't see cash in a canvas bag, he ain't going to be inclined to hear anything else we've got to say."

"That's why I'm thinking following him might wind up being our best bet," the marshal said. "Could even be good if he gets mad and storms off."

SINCE THE ARRIVAL of the boy, Baggett's mood had changed constantly. One minute he was excited, the next wary and impatient, then angry over having to babysit. Rather than sleep, he repeatedly played out the Saturday meeting. First, he'd considered sending the brothers while he remained with the boy. But since he didn't completely trust Doozy and Alvin, despite the fact they'd done everything he'd instructed them to do, he felt it best he attend the meeting himself. One of them could babysit while the other would provide him protection and stand by to signal that the money had been received and it was okay to release the youngster.

Alvin could stay with the kid and Doozy could accompany him to the Longhorn. He was sure there would be two waiting for them—the boy's new pa, whose name he couldn't recall, and his friend Clay Breckenridge.

The only detail he'd not completely worked out was how to distance himself from them after he got the money. If he had more men, he could simply order them done away with, but there wasn't time to put a plan like that in motion. Maybe Doozy could occupy them for a time by suggesting his brother would harm the boy if they chose to become aggressive.

Hopefully, the men coming to town had no interest in violence and would just do whatever was necessary to see the boy returned safely. He'd tried to get a reading on them from Lonnie without much success.

"I want you to know I'm sorry to mix you up in this," he said. "This business is none of your doing. But your new pa's got something of mine I want returned. That's how simple it is. So if whoever shows up Saturday wants only to take you home safe, everything's gonna be fine."

He'd finally removed the bandanna that covered Lonnie's eyes and mouth after the youngster had nodded a promise to remain quiet. With a pistol in one hand, he used the other to hand the boy a glass of water. "I'd be interested to hear what you think they're going to do when we have our meeting."

Lonnie was still afraid, but during the time he'd been tied to the chair, he'd become increasingly angry and worried about what might happen to the people he hoped were coming to rescue him.

When he was able to adjust to the light, he saw Baggett for the first time. He was smiling, showing teeth that were yellow and crooked.

"What I'm wondering," Baggett said, "is whether your thieving friends have the good sense to see to this matter peacefully. You got any thoughts?"

Lonnie glared. "They're not thieves," he said. "They're good, honest people who weren't looking for any trouble until you and those other men came along. I suspect now they're pretty mad about all this."

"You saying I'm gonna have to kill them to get what's mine?"

"If there's any killing done," Lonnie defiantly answered, "it'll most likely be you who gets killed."

Baggett got to his feet and slapped Lonnie hard across the face, sending him and the chair tumbling to the floor. "Boy, I can't tell you how glad I'll be to be shed of you," he said.

MARSHAL RANKIN ARRIVED at the Longhorn well ahead of Clay and Jonesy and found himself a place along a balcony rail. The saloon was filled and noisy. He let his eyes roam the floor below, not knowing whom he was looking for since he'd never seen Baggett or the men who had abducted Lonnie.

He watched as Breckenridge and Pate finally entered and stood briefly in the doorway. It was exactly three o'clock. It was Rankin who first saw a man near the back of the room stand and wave a hand.

When they saw him, Clay and Jonesy began elbowing their way in his direction.

As they reached the table, Baggett motioned for them to sit. As he did, a man neither recognized moved to stand behind Baggett. He had a hand on his holster.

"Just wanted to make things even," Baggett said.

"Is my boy okay?" Jonesy said.

"I don't see you boys carrying anything with you," Baggett replied.

"We've got a good reason for that," Clay said. "We ain't got your money with us, but we know where it is. You ain't given us much time to put our hands on it. But if you return the boy, we'll gladly see you get it."

Baggett cursed. "Where is it?"

"It's back at Tascosa, where we came by it in the first place. We found it by chance after your man Wilson was killed. Here's the offer we've come to make.

You give us the boy and I'll ride with you out to Tascosa, and show you where it's hidden. You can bind me and take my weapon. That sound fair?"

The proposition took Baggett by surprise. He was silent for a moment as his bodyguard shifted from one foot to another. "I done made myself a promise never to go back out to that part of the world," he finally said.

"Well, that's where your money is."

"Tell me where you hid it."

"Be happy to, if you bring us the boy, unharmed."

"And if I don't?"

"Then I'm gonna kill you dead in a way you ain't never imagined," Clay said.

Doozy nervously put his hand on the handle of his pistol. This wasn't going the way it was supposed to, he thought to himself.

As the men talked, Rankin had made his way down the stairs and through the crowd to stand behind Doozy. He moved his face to the back of the bodyguard's neck and whispered, "Slowly take your hand away from your holster. Loud as it is in here, I doubt many would even hear if I was to shoot you right now. Those who do probably won't much care."

When he became aware of what was going on behind him, Baggett reached for his own pistol. Before he could raise and point it, Jonesy said, "You want to be real careful. There's two just like it pointed at you under the table."

Baggett cursed again and laid his face on his arm and pounded his fist against the table. "Nothing's working out the way it's supposed to," he said.

"Give us your gun," Clay said, "and tell us where Lonnie is."

Baggett raised his head and glared, not moving.

"This doesn't have to be hard," Clay said.

"I can walk you to where he is," Baggett finally said, slowly getting to his feet. "Will I still get my money?"

Jonesy laughed. "We ain't even decided yet if we're going to allow you to keep living."

I N THE STREET, they made their way through the crowd. Baggett and Doozy walked in front with Clay and Jonesy close behind, poking gun barrels in their backs. At one point they had to step over a cowboy lying drunk on the sidewalk, laughing at something only he knew was funny.

"This is it," Baggett said. It was a shabby-looking two-story hotel that didn't seem to have a front entrance. They walked into an alley and up a rickety stairway.

"Keeping my boy in a place like this ought to be reason alone for putting a bullet in your ugly face," Jonesy said.

They reached the door to room eight.

Marshal Rankin, who had said nothing since they'd left the saloon, cocked his Peacemaker and signaled everyone to get behind him. Gun pointed, he shouldered his way through the doorway, the others close behind.

All they found was an empty room. The only evidence that anyone had previously been there was a chair that had been turned over, an unmade bed, Baggett's half bottle of whiskey on a table, and a few of his clothes hanging in a wardrobe whose door was off its hinges.

T HEY WERE HERE, I swear," Baggett said, sweat beading across his brow. "I left your boy in the care of Doozy's half-wit brother. No more than an hour ago."

Doozy was also sweating as the marshal turned to him. "Where did he take him?"

"I got no idea," Doozy said before Jonesy hit him in the temple with the barrel of his pistol. "He's crazy. No telling where they went."

CHAPTER THIRTY-THREE

"I DONE TOLD you the law here is crooked as snakes," Rankin said, "but if we take these two to jail and I explain how they're involved in kidnapping, a killing, and anything else I can think of, they'll be obliged to lock them up for the time being. I'll explain that I'll come back and take custody shortly and lock them up in Aberdene."

"That or we can just shoot them," Pate said.

The marshal ignored his comment. "I'll stay here with these two while you boys find the marshal's office and tell him I urgently need his help. He knows me, so just tell him where I am." Under normal circumstances, Rankin would have gone himself, but he was leery of leaving Jonesy and Clay alone with two men they would have dearly loved to see dead.

"By doing it this way," Rankin said, "we can focus all our attention on finding where Lonnie's been taken. And why."

"The second part ain't hard to answer," Clay said. "Whoever it is who has the boy is likely thinking he'll hold him for ransom. Being a participant in Baggett's plan, he had to know there was money involved somehow. Now I figure it'll be him contacting us."

Rankin shook his head. "If all this wasn't such a serious situation, I'd have to laugh. You boys stealing money that was already stolen. Somebody kidnapping a boy already been kidnapped . . ."

"You're right, Marshal," Clay said, a deadpan look on his face. "This is a serious situation."

Dodge Rankin blushed in response. "Then let's see if we can figure out what to do."

L ONNIE'S HANDS WERE tied behind his back, making it difficult to keep his balance as his horse moved along at a steady gait. Alvin was leading it by the reins as they headed south out of Fort Worth, their destination a deserted farm near the Brazos River where he and his brother had hunted and hidden from the law in the past.

The plan was for Alvin and Lonnie to wait at an old shack on the property until Doozy arrived.

"You're getting to do a right smart of traveling, ain't you?" Alvin said as they reached the shack. "Nobody's yet told me why you're so important, but seeing as you must be, you can expect me to treat you like we were best friends."

He had removed Lonnie's gag but left his hands tied. "When we get inside and make ourselves at home, I'm sorry to say I'll be needing to secure your ankles again. But I ain't going to hurt you."

Lonnie gave a mock laugh. "Like you didn't hurt that man at the creek you shot in the back of the head?"

"That was different. We were told he needed killing. And Doozy said it was my turn," Alvin said. "Ain't nobody said nothing about doing you harm."

Near the shack were the remnants of an old vegetable garden where watermelon vines were growing wild. Alvin selected a ripe melon and cut it in half with his pocketknife. He then sat on the floor next to Lonnie, slicing off bites to hand-feed him.

"Yep," Alvin said as juice ran down his chin, "you and me, we're going to be friends. And after my brother gets here and says it's okay, I'm gonna untie you so you can head on back home." He wiped the watermelon juice from his chin and shirt and smiled.

M ARSHAL RANKIN SAT in the shade of a tree next to the jail. Clay and Jonesy were pacing. "Hardest part of my job," the marshal said, "is waiting. I've always said if a fellow hopes to be a success as a lawman, he best have the patience of Job."

Once Baggett and Doozy were jailed, they had considered their next move, only to realize they didn't have one. "No telling where they are," Rankin said. "We could run in every direction like chickens with our heads wrung off, but it wouldn't do us no good."

They needed to know where to look if they were to find Lonnie. And Rankin at least had an idea. During his lengthy career as a marshal, he had become fairly good at thinking like the criminals he was pursuing.

"I ain't met too many folks with a high IQ who make their living rustling cattle or robbing stagecoaches," he said. "I'm of a notion that Baggett is of no use to us. But I think Doozy and his brother have something up their sleeves. Somehow, they're planning on using Lonnie to get some of Baggett's money. I don't know about his brother, but Doozy doesn't exactly seem like a genius. Still, he and what's-his-name must have had some kind of plan once Baggett left the hotel to come see you boys.

And I bet if we can separate him from the old man, he just might give us some useful information."

Clay and Jonesy liked what they were hearing. They had stopped pacing and were kneeling next to the marshal.

"I can probably talk the jailer into letting him out for a while," he said, "but what occurs next will have to be up to you boys while I look the other way. I swore an oath long ago that I'd not break the law."

Twenty minutes later he was walking down the steps of the jail, Doozy at his side, handcuffed and not looking at all happy.

W E BEEN HAVING us an argument over who gets the pleasure of killing you," Clay said as he shoved his hands into Doozy's chest. They had taken him into a shed on a nearby vacant lot. A rat scurried over Doozy's boot. "Whoever gets to do it, this here would be a good place to leave you. Let the rats eat your eyes out, then crawl inside your mouth. . . ."

"What is it you want with me?" Doozy said. There was panic in his voice. "The old man back there in the jail is who you need to be killing."

"We'll get around to that soon enough," Jonesy said. "But for now we wanted to give you a chance to keep breathing."

"Where's the boy?" Clay said as he drove a fist hard into Doozy's stomach. "Tell us where we can find him and your brother, and we'll be done here."

"You'll let me go?"

"Might give it some consideration."

"This ain't our fault, me and Alvin. It's Mr. Baggett who made us do it. And he ain't even paid us."

Clay delivered another gut punch. "Was it his idea

for your brother to run off with the boy while we were
in the Longhorn?"

"Well, no, that was our plan so we could get our
money for the work we done."

Jonesy was getting impatient and drew his pistol.
"We're wasting our time. He ain't going to cooperate,"
he said. "Let's end this and get on with our business."

Doozy's eyes widened as Pate cocked the hammer.
"We ain't hurt him," he said. "We were just planning to
keep him until we could get some money from Baggett.
My brother's got no idea I've been put in jail."

"So he's somewhere waiting for you, not aware you're
not coming?"

"That's about the size of it."

"Where? That's the last time I'm asking." Clay's fist
crushed into Doozy's face. There was a crunching sound
that indicated his nose had been broken; then he began
choking on the blood that flowed into his mouth. Breckenridge stepped back and let him sink to his knees.
Jonesy stepped up and delivered a kick to his stomach.

"Okay, okay, enough," Doozy said, putting his
handcuffed hands to his face. "I'll tell you what you
want to know."

His voice was weak as he gave directions to the
shack. "That's where they're waiting. It'll take you no
more'n a two-hour ride to get there. You going to let
me go now?"

They lifted him to his feet and led him out of the
shed. "Rats are gonna be mighty disappointed," Jonesy
said.

Across the street, Marshal Rankin waited, sitting
on the edge of a watering trough, puffing on his corncob pipe.

"We had us a good conversation," Clay said. "You
can take him back to jail now."

* * *

Iτ was almost sundown when they reached the deserted farm. They dismounted and approached the shack on foot. "They're likely inside," Clay whispered, "and probably the brother's keeping watch. Best we wait until it gets dark before we make our move."

"I ain't sure I can wait," Jonesy said.

"Remember what I told you about patience," Rankin said. "It won't be much longer."

Waiting for darkness, they huddled in a thicket, no more than a hundred yards from where they knew Lonnie was being held. Clay was rubbing his swollen fist.

"Too bad that fellow took such a bad fall back there," Rankin said, attempting to ease the tension.

Soon, the glow of a lantern lit the inside of the shack. They could see a shadow of movement.

"Here's our plan," the marshal said. "Jonesy, you make your way around to the back side of the place and wait until you hear me call out. Me and Clay, we'll approach from the front. Don't get rambunctious and make yourself an easy target."

Moving in a crouch, Pate was on his way before Rankin finished his sentence.

They gave him a few minutes to get in place, then slowly approached the shack. "Hello the house," the marshal called out.

"That you, Doozy?"

"Nope, this is Marshal Dodge Rankin from Aberdene. I've come for the boy and to place you under arrest. Step outside with your hands raised and you can avoid getting hurt."

There was a moment's silence, then a shot from the window. "Get on back," Alvin yelled, "or I'll have to shoot the kid, which I don't want to do."

Clay was on his feet, his pistol drawn. "I'm going," he said as he rushed toward the house.

"Don't be shooting blind," the marshal said as he followed. "Don't want the boy getting hurt." Another wild shot came from the shack.

"We got the advantage that he can't see us," Rankin said, "so let's do this quick."

Clay burst through the door and saw Lonnie, tied to a chair. Standing behind him, a gun pointed at the youth's head, was his captor.

"You boys come a step closer, and I'm gonna do what I promised not to," Alvin said. He was nervous, the gun shaking in his hand. "Where's Doozy? He was supposed to be here."

"If you don't want to get killed where you stand," Clay said, "you'll holster your gun and put this to an end."

"Doozy told me he'd be here." It sounded as if he was crying.

"He ain't right in the head," Rankin whispered. "Be careful what you do."

Terrified, Lonnie called out to Breckenridge, and Alvin delivered a hard slap to the back of his head. Rankin grabbed Clay's arm to prevent him from rushing forward.

There was a loud noise as Jonesy burst through the back door, raced across the room, and flung himself at the surprised Alvin, knocking him to the floor. Lonnie's chair toppled as Breckenridge and Rankin rushed to apprehend his abductor. Alvin, dazed and lying on his back, pointed his pistol at the oncoming men. "No," Lonnie yelled.

Then the room filled with smoke as a shot was fired. The gun fell from Alvin's hand and his eyes widened, then slowly closed. Back on his feet, Jonesy fired a second shot to make sure he was dead. Then he rushed to Lonnie and began freeing him from his bindings.

Both were in tears as they embraced. "You okay, son?" Pate asked. All Lonnie could do was nod.

"Come on, let's go home."

Rankin and Breckenridge were smiling. As they walked into the night, a breeze rustled in the trees and the rush of water in the nearby Brazos could be heard. Somewhere, an owl hooted.

Clay turned and looked back toward the shack. Through the doorway he could see Alvin's body lying on the floor. "What are we going to do about him?"

"Not my concern," Rankin said. "This ain't my jurisdiction."

P ATRICIA WAS ALREADY halfway down the pathway as they approached the ranch house. Running just behind her was Madge. The men had ridden straight through, stopping only to occasionally give the horses a rest and a drink of water. They were exhausted but all smiles.

The women almost pulled Lonnie from his horse. They didn't know whether to hug or kiss him first. "How I've been praying for this," Patricia said. She and Madge were both crying.

"I'm all right," Lonnie assured the women. "Just a little hungry."

Everyone was laughing as they stepped onto the porch. "We're going to fix you boys a breakfast like you've never seen before," Patricia said. She had turned her affection from Lonnie to her weary husband. "I don't know what all you had to do to bring Lonnie home," she said, "but I'm so proud. Of all of you."

Only then did she notice that Marshal Rankin wasn't with them.

"He had some business to tend to at the Fort Worth

jail," Jonesy explained. "He'll be along shortly. He was a mighty big help to us."

"I'll have him a pie baked by the time he returns," she said. "Maybe two."

Clay led the horses to the barn with Madge close at his side. He removed the saddles and filled buckets of oats as she talked nonstop. He'd never seen his wife so giddy. "I about worried myself sick while you were gone," she said. "It's a relief to have my husband back safe."

He knew to what she was referring. "I hope you've not worried yourself on that matter," he said. "I'm now the only husband you've got. Or gonna have from now on."

She put her arms around him and kissed him. "This," she said, "is a glorious day if I ever saw one."

In the kitchen, the men marveled at a table filled with eggs, bacon, redeye gravy, biscuits, and two huge stacks of flapjacks. Patricia couldn't take her eyes off of Lonnie as he filled his plate for a second time. "Once you've had your fill," she said, "I want you to get cleaned up, then sleep for two solid days."

"What about school?" he said.

"It'll still be there after you're properly rested."

"Before I take a bath," he said as he got up from the table, "I'd like to go check on Maizy."

It was almost dark when Marshal Rankin arrived at the ranch. He, too, received a hero's welcome from the women. Patricia insisted he come in and have some supper.

"The boy's already gone to bed, or he'd be thanking you again," Jonesy said.

"Sometimes things just have a way of working out," Clay said as he handed the marshal a bottle of beer.

"Not everything," Rankin said. "When I went to the jail to check on our friends, they wasn't there. Somehow they managed to escape, I was told."

CHAPTER THIRTY-FOUR

B EN BAGGETT LAUGHED when he saw Doozy's condition as he was returned to the jail cell. "Looks like you fell off a building," he said as a deputy helped the semiconscious prisoner onto a bunk.

"Maybe so," Doozy said, "but I didn't tell them nothing."

"Where's your ignorant brother and the boy?"

"Honest to God, Mr. Baggett, I ain't got the faintest," he said before passing out.

By late in the evening, the adjacent cell was crowded with drunks, cursing, vomiting, and soiling themselves. A couple attempted to fight but quickly realized they had no room and passed out instead. The stench was overwhelming.

During a lull in the noise, Baggett called out to the young jailer working the late-night shift. Reluctantly, he approached the cell.

"Back in the safe at my hotel," Baggett said, "there's a duffel bag belonging to me that's filled with money.

What would be your price to unlock this door and set us free? You could claim a jailbreak somehow occurred. And honest truth is, we haven't done anything to deserve being here in the first place. And as you can see plain as day, my friend here is in bad need of a doctor."

The deputy turned to walk away from the overwhelming odor.

"You can name your price," Baggett said, "and you're welcome to accompany us to the hotel to see I'm being truthful and that we won't just run away."

An hour later, they were riding out of Hell's Half Acre. Doozy was hurting and could barely stay on his horse, but Baggett urged him on. The bottle of whiskey he'd brought along helped to dull the pain.

Baggett despised the man riding alongside him and didn't trust him, but at the moment, he had no better option. He wasn't going to attempt the journey he had in mind alone.

J ONESY ARRIVED AT Clay's farm to find his neighbor sitting on the porch, petting Sarge. Feeling rested but restless, he'd ridden over to report that Lonnie was doing fine and planning to return to school in the next day or so.

"I've been doing some thinking," Clay said. "Baggett ain't gonna find any peace until he gets that money back. He's plumb obsessed. And now that he knows it's somewhere out in Tascosa, he's probably going to head there. . . ."

"And Eli might find himself in harm's way," Pate said.

Clay scratched behind Sarge's ears. "The women ain't gonna be happy to hear it," he said, "but I'm thinking we got one more trip we need to make."

* * *

E LI RAYBURN SQUINTED into the sunlight, attempting to count the number of Tascosa residents in
attendance at Cyrus Broder's funeral. There weren't
many. Jennie's father had died in his sleep two nights
earlier, and she hadn't even realized it until she returned home from work at the mercantile to find him
still in bed and the goats not tended.

Well-wishers passed along condolences, then whispered among themselves how sad it was that Cyrus had
passed before his eighty-six-year-old father. They also
quietly wondered how Jennie could keep the farm going
while also running the mercantile for her grandpa. Asa
Broder would likely have to come out of retirement and
return to minding the store. But for how long?

Several men in the community, including Rayburn,
had already volunteered to help on the farm, but there
was some question how long it could continue without a
full-time caretaker. "I don't know anything about raising
goats," Eli said, "but I'm available to do whatever I can."

E LI AND PAUL Price were walking toward the livery,
eager to get out of the sun. "How many funerals
you guess you've attended here?" Price asked.

Rayburn thought for a moment. "Way too many,"
he finally said. "One of these days I'll look up and
there won't be nobody but me left." As they moved
closer to the barn, Eli saw two horses he didn't recognize. "Looks like I got company," he said as Price
turned to head back to the laundry.

He did recognize the voice he heard as he stepped
into the darkened building. "Howdy, Mr. Rayburn,"
Ben Baggett said.

When his eyes adjusted, Eli saw that there was another man with Baggett whom he'd never seen before. His nose was misshapen, and there were bruises on the side of his face.

"You needing something?"

"Just come for a visit," Baggett said. "We might be wanting to rent a couple of your tents and have you tend our horses."

"That'll be seventy-five cents a day," Rayburn said. "A dollar if you want oats in addition to hay for your animals."

"While we're here, we also hope to get some questions answered," Baggett said. There was a menacing tone to his voice.

Rayburn was feeling uneasy. "If I got answers," he said, "I'll give them."

"I know you'll recall that Top Wilson, God rest his miserable soul, stole a sizable sum of money belonging to me. Money I ain't yet been able to recover," Baggett said. "Now, recently I was told that it's hidden somewhere here in Tascosa. Got any knowledge of that?"

"Can't say I do."

"Well, let me put it this way. If you were me, where would you begin looking?"

Eli shrugged. "I got no idea, Mr. Baggett."

"I see. Well, I'd much appreciate your thinking on it. Meanwhile, if you'll show us to our tent and feed our horses, I'd be obliged." As he stood to leave, he asked, "Think that fellow who runs the laundry is down at his place?"

"I ain't sure."

"And that pretty Broder gal, Jennie. She's still working up at the mercantile, I assume."

"Not today," Eli said. "She just buried her daddy a while ago."

"I'm right sorry to hear that," Baggett said. "Right sorry indeed."

Price was hanging bedsheets out to dry when Baggett and Doozy approached. "If you're needing bathwater heated, it'll be a few minutes. I gotta get these things hung out," he said.

"Baths can wait another day or two," Baggett said. "We were just talking with Eli up at the livery, and he said you might know the answer to a question I've got." He went through the same scenario about the money that he'd done with Rayburn.

"First I've heard of it," Price said. "Top Wilson, huh? From what I been told, he was a real bad sort."

"No doubt about that."

Baggett and Doozy were turning to leave when Price said, "It was me who found his horse, you know."

"Where was that?"

Price pointed toward the south. "He'd left it tied up down in a gulley. All saddled and ready."

"And what happened to the horse?"

"I took it up to the livery and gave it to Eli."

When they were settled in the tent, Baggett told Doozy to find a pick and shovel. "Steal them from the mercantile if it isn't open. I want you to go down to that gulley and do some digging."

Doozy nodded as he slowly chewed a piece of jerky. Each bite was painful. He still hadn't said a word since they'd arrived in Tascosa.

"While you're tending to that, I'm going to have another conversation with my friend Eli," Baggett said.

C LAY HAD BEEN right. Madge and Patricia weren't at all happy about their leaving. Nor was Lonnie.

"My guess is we'll be needing to bring presents and maybe wave a white flag when we make our return this time," Jonesy said.

Despite the urgency both were feeling, they rested

their horses along the way. Sitting in front of a small campfire, waiting for coffee to boil, they talked about what they would encounter once they reached Tascosa.

"I regret telling him his money was hidden there," Clay said, "but what's done is done."

As he poked at the fire, he gnashed his teeth. "This foolishness has got to end. It's way past time for Ben Baggett to be out of my life. Yours as well. He's been a troublesome thorn since even before I met him, luring my brother into his outlaw ways. To my thinking he's at least partially to blame for Cal being killed. The harm the man's done people ought not to be tolerated. My worry now is for Eli's safety. He's a fine man, but he ain't one who can put up a fight against the likes of Baggett."

"He ain't violent, but he'll use good sense," Jonesy said. "You know, I never considered myself a violent person either, but if I had my way, Baggett would already be dead, and I'd be home, digging postholes, mending fences, and eating my wife's cooking."

"Soon," Clay replied.

D OOZY HAD BEEN searching in the gulley all day without success. He was bathed in sweat, and his muscles ached. "Nothing here but rocks and snakes," he said when Baggett arrived.

Ben slapped his hat against his thigh and cursed. "They ain't gonna make this easy," he said. "Come on, your work here's done. I got something for you to help me with up at the livery."

Rayburn was burning a pile of soiled hay when they approached.

"Seems you didn't tell me all you knew when we last spoke," Baggett said.

"Not sure what you're referring to."

"What did you do with Wilson's horse and saddle when Price brought it to you?"

"I recall selling the saddle sometime back," Rayburn said. He didn't mention the irony of it being Baggett who bought it after he'd come to town riding bareback. "The horse is out in the corral."

"Was there saddlebags?"

Eli struggled to maintain his composure. He slowly raked embers from the fire, then said, "Yep, I seem to remember there was. All I found in them was a half-full tin of coffee makings."

"You're lying," Baggett yelled. "My money was in them bags, wasn't it?"

"Not that I seen."

Baggett nodded to Doozy, who grabbed the rake from Rayburn and swung it at his head. "I don't want him dead, but see he gets a good beating. Maybe then he'll be inclined to tell me what I want to hear."

WHEN, AFTER A four-day ride, they reached Tascosa, Breckenridge and Pate rode directly to the livery. Inside, they found Paul Price sitting in the dirt with Rayburn's head in his lap. There was a bucket of water at his side and he was attempting to wash away the blood that covered Eli's face.

"I came to deliver his laundry," Price said, "and found him like this. He looks beat half to death."

Clay knelt and tried to determine how badly his friend was hurt. One of Eli's eyes was swollen shut, and there was a bleeding gash behind one ear. It appeared an arm might have been broken. The fact that blood oozed from his mouth was a warning sign that there might be internal injuries. Broken ribs, probably.

The interior of the livery was strewn with tools, and

the contents of Rayburn's desk were scattered. Doors of the stalls stood open, and the oat barrel had been turned upside down.

Livid, Clay slammed his fist against the wall. "We should have gotten here sooner. They're looking for the money."

"Doesn't appear Eli told them where it's at," Jonesy said.

At the sound of his name, Rayburn moaned.

"Eli, it's me, Clay. Jonesy's here with me. We're going to see you get cared for."

Price was already on his way home to summon his wife and her basket of medical supplies.

Rayburn attempted a faint smile at Breckenridge, then mouthed a single word before slipping into unconsciousness. "Baggett," he said.

"Where you think he's gone?" Jonesy said.

"I'll first check the cemetery," Clay said, "though I doubt he'll be there. You stay here and see after Eli, and I'll go take a look at the tents and the mercantile."

"Make sure Jennie's okay," Pate said.

Clay found her slowly emerging from the storeroom when he entered. When she saw him, she ran to the front of the store and threw her arms around him.

"You okay?"

"I guess," she said. "I just came by here for a minute after Pa's funeral. . . ."

The news surprised Clay. "Your pa's passed?"

Jennie nodded. "Died in his sleep two nights ago." Tears came as she spoke. "Anyway, I wasn't intending to open the store but needed to get some things. All of a sudden, there was Ben Baggett, standing in the doorway with this strange look on his face. Said something about being on a treasure hunt.

"When I told him I didn't know what he was talking about, he started cussing and said he wanted to know where his money was. I said I had no idea, and he began acting all crazy, pulling things off the shelves and throwing them on the floor. That's when I ran and locked myself in the storeroom."

Clay placed a reassuring hand on her shoulder. "I'll wait while you close up. Then I want you to come with me down to the livery. Jonesy's there, helpin' tend to Eli, who's been hurt." He then asked if her grandfather was out at the farm.

"After the funeral, one of his friends was planning to take him home," she said. "His eyesight's beginning to fail him."

W HEN CLAY ARRIVED at the Broder farm, he found Asa locked in the woodshed. He was unhurt but confused.

"I'd just come in from my boy's burying," he said, "and was going to lie down and take me a nap when these men busted in, yelling something about money they thought was here. I can't see too good, so I can't be for sure who they were. I just know there was two of them.

"They started tearing the place apart, cussing and kicking over, not finding what they wanted. When I started raising Cain, telling 'em to be on their way, they locked me up. Guess I'm lucky they didn't shoot me."

"Glad they didn't," Clay said. "I'm going to hitch up the buggy and take you into town, where you'll be safe until we get these men tended to. Jennie's there waiting for you."

"She tending the store? I thought she was planning to close up for the day," Asa said.

He was still trembling when Clay helped him into the buggy.

CHAPTER THIRTY-FIVE

$\mathbf{B}$RECKENRIDGE STOOD IN the doorway, angrily shaking his head as he surveyed the situation. Folks being forced into hiding in their own town and being beaten in their own place of business was insanity. Jennie was helping Anna Price tend to Eli, who had regained consciousness and was sitting up. Paul Price was on the other side of the room, talking quietly with Asa, trying to assure him that a Comanche raiding party wasn't bearing down on the livery.

Clay was contemplating what to do. "If this doesn't end," he told Jonesy, "there's gonna be folks getting killed. Eli nearly was already."

"We going after them?" Pate said.

"Be better than waiting for them to come sneaking up on us. Right now we've got an advantage since they don't likely know you and me have followed them here."

"Then let's make them aware."

Clay walked over to Rayburn and sat beside him. "How you feeling?"

Eli's voice was weak and gravelly. "Like I got run over by a herd of cattle," he said. "But I'll live. It's mighty good to see you boys back in town. I missed you."

"Paul tells me that Baggett and his associate rented tents," Clay said. "You recall which ones you assigned to them?"

Eli thought for a minute before answering. "Down at the end of the third row," he said. "Took them there myself. Baggett paid for two, side by side." He let out a painful chuckle. "If it's necessary to put a few bullet holes in my property," he said, "there'll be no charge."

Clay then went to Price. "I know you can use a rifle," he said, "seeing as how you're a squirrel hunter." He handed him Rayburn's Winchester. "Me and Jonesy, we're going to go see if we can confront these men. In our absence, you're in charge of protecting folks here."

"I wasn't in the war, you know," Paul said, "so I've never shot at a man before."

"You might have to start," Jonesy said. "Just think of 'em as somebody wanting to do harm to your wife."

Price cocked the rifle and moved toward the doorway. "That'll get them killed," he said.

Y OU GOT US a plan?" Jonesy said to Clay as he pulled his rifle from its scabbard.

"I'm thinking they've run out of folks to confront for the time being and are in need of time to think about what to do next. Since they've got no other place to go, they've probably returned to the tents. It's best we approach on foot since horses would alert them long before we got close."

There was a treeless, grassy slope behind the livery that led to Rayburn's tent city. Clay and Jonesy had walked the route numerous times during their earlier stay in Tascosa. "We'll be exposed, but I doubt they're expecting company."

In Baggett's tent, he and Doozy were doing exactly what Clay had predicted. Their horses were staked outside.

Clay and Jonesy, crouching in the high grass, were within thirty yards of the tent when Baggett heard a voice he immediately recognized.

"Baggett, this is Clay Breckenridge. I got Jonesy Pate with me, and we're here to see you dead."

Almost immediately a series of quick shots erupted from the tent, forcing Clay and Jonesy onto their stomachs. Breckenridge again called out, "Doozy, we know you're in there as well. I want you to be aware we've done left your crazy brother dead in that shack down by the Brazos. You should also know we got our boy back."

In the tent, Doozy looked panic-stricken. "I didn't come out here to get myself killed," he said to Baggett. "They've done killed Alvin. Did you hear him? My brother's dead."

"Shut up," Baggett said as he fired another shot toward the sound of Breckenridge's voice.

"No way I'm doing this," Doozy said, getting to his feet. "No way. I ain't getting myself killed for someone who won't even pay a fellow what's owed him."

He dropped his pistol to the plank floor and hurried through the tent opening, his hands high above his head.

"I'm surrendering," he yelled. "Don't shoot."

From inside, Baggett let out a loud stream of curses. "You worthless coward," he yelled, then fired a shot that struck Doozy in the back. His arms fell to his side; then he slowly went to his knees as Baggett shot him again. He was dead before his face was buried into the sand.

Even before Doozy's fall was completed, Baggett was out of the tent, shooting blindly as he ran toward his horse. Clay and Jonesy, briefly surprised by what had just transpired, got to their feet and returned fire but missed.

Baggett was quickly riding away.

Pate turned to head back to the livery. "Let's get our horses," he said, pulling at Clay's arm.

"I don't think there's a need to rush," Clay said. "I got a good idea where he's headed."

B AGGETT WAS PUSHING his horse unmercifully, riding through Tascosa at a gallop and heading south.

In the livery anxious eyes focused on the doorway as Clay and Jonesy appeared.

"We heard gunfire," Price said. "You boys shot or anything?"

"Nope. We're fine," Clay said. "One's dead, but we still got work to do." He told Price to remain on guard.

Jonesy was already saddling the horses. "Where we headed?" he said.

"Palo Duro Canyon."

R ETURNING TO THE canyon, something he'd sworn never to do, gave Baggett a painful knot in his stomach. He felt as if he might vomit as memories of the raid by the Comanches flowed back. As he rode down the path leading to where his compound had once been, the putrid odor of burned buildings and the remnants of death greeted him. The skeletal remains of several horses were scattered about and a large blackened circle where the bodies of his men had been burned was still visible.

Baggett was repulsed, thoughts of his stolen money

no longer foremost on his mind. This time it was survival not greed that had brought him here to the last safe place he knew.

His horse's coat was lathered in sweat as he reined him to a stop in front of where his cabin had once stood. All that was left were ashes. He dismounted and hurried to the hidden trail he'd used so many times before.

A S THEY SLOWLY entered the canyon, the sights and smells also offended Breckenridge and Pate. They stopped as they neared the opening where the compound once was.

"Don't appear to me there's many hiding places remaining," Jonesy said as he surveyed the burned-out buildings. Clay scanned the canyon walls, looking for a vantage point from which Baggett might open fire. Aside from a few circling hawks, he saw no movement.

Hoping their prey might reveal his location with gunfire, Breckenridge called out, "This is the end of the line, Baggett. You'll not get away. Consider yourself a dead man."

The warning was met with silence.

"Where do you think he is?" Pate said.

"I got no idea, but I think we'd be wise to take Marshal Rankin's advice and show patience. Baggett ain't got but one way out of this place, and unless he grows wings and flies, we got him covered. We'll wait him out for a while."

He yelled once more, his voice echoing against the canyon walls. "We got all the time in the world, Baggett."

In truth, they waited less than two hours. "Let's start walkin' the edges," Clay said. "You take the east side, and I'll head west. Go slow, and be sure he doesn't sneak up on your backside. Stay down in the rock formations in case he does decide to start shooting and give away where he's hiding."

As he made his way along the boulders, Clay looked out at Baggett's horse, on its side and struggling for breath. It was dying, and Breckenridge felt a renewed surge of anger. Jonesy, meanwhile, hadn't gone but a hundred yards before a bobcat sprinted from its lair, very nearly causing him to fire off a round. Mostly, however, there was only a disquieting feeling about the place. No breeze blew and only the occasional sound of nature broke the silence.

Breckenridge moved slowly along the ledges and crevices, stopping occasionally to listen for any telling sounds. There was nothing to hear or see until he reached the area directly behind where Baggett's cabin had once stood. There, he saw vegetation, tangled vines and bushes mingled with the cacti.

It hid what appeared to be a narrow footpath. Though never much of a tracker, Clay thought he could see faint boot prints in the crushed rock. They led toward the canyon rim. He followed the path higher until he could see a larger stand of brush and a boulder where the trail seemed to end.

Taking small, careful steps, he reached the brush pile and saw what it was hiding.

He was preparing to move one of the limbs aside when he heard the shotgun blast. It blew the remainder of the brush away from the cave entrance and sent red-hot pain through Clay's thigh. His rifle flew away, tumbling down the side of the canyon, and he was suddenly on his back, feeling as if he might pass out.

He rolled from the pathway as a second blast lit the dark interior. Smoke billowed from the mouth of the opening. There was a faint sound of someone laughing.

Hearing the shots, Pate climbed down from the rocks

and was running across the compound, calling Breckenridge's name. When he reached him, Clay was bleeding badly. He had torn the sleeve from his shirt and
was attempting to bandage the wound when Jonesy
arrived.

"He's holed up in that cave," Clay said, pointing to
the nearby ledge. "We've got to keep him there until
we can figure a way to approach him."

"Any thoughts on how much ammunition he's got?"

"I don't want to make a guess, but probably enough
to kill us both if we don't use our heads."

Pate was staring at Clay's wound. "You ain't gonna
die on me, are you?"

"Not planning on it. You bring any matches?"

Jonesy reached into his shirt pocket. "Good thing I
ain't had time for smoking my pipe today," he said as
he held up a half dozen wooden matches.

"Let's smoke him out."

Jonesy moved away from the path and approached
the mouth of the cave from the side. Brushing some
dried leaves into a pile, he soon had a small blaze. After he moved large limbs of the dried brush over it,
they were quickly ablaze and being thrown into the
cave. Pate repeated the action several times as thun-
derous shots from inside responded.

Shortly, a roaring fire lit the first few yards of the
cave. Pate could hear curses coming from inside.

He found a small bush that was still alive and full of
leaves, pulled it from the rocky soil, and, leaning in from
one side of the opening, began using it to fan the smoke
farther back into the darkness. Then they waited.

"Might as well come on out, old man. If you don't,
next thing we got planned is a rockslide that'll close up
this hole," Jonesy said.

There were more shots from inside, then a long silence.

Finally, they heard the sound of coughing getting nearer and nearer, louder and louder. Suddenly, Baggett was standing at the opening, holding his shotgun and wiping his eyes in an effort to see where to aim.

Whether it was a shot fired from Jonesy's rifle or the one from Breckenridge's pistol that killed Ben Baggett, neither knew. Nor did they care. Clay was on his feet, moving stiff legged toward the fallen body. Pate was already straddled over it, his rifle pointed at the dead man's head.

He and Clay looked at each other, expressions of relief on their faces.

"Now all I gotta do is figure how to get you down from here so we can head back to town before you bleed to death," Pate said. "That or Madge'll be giving me the dickens from now on."

CHAPTER THIRTY-SIX

T HE RIDE BACK to Tascosa was long and painful for Clay. In and out of consciousness, he was unable to stay on his horse. After a short distance, they stopped while Jonesy found a couple of straight mesquite limbs and, using ropes and Clay's saddle blanket, fashioned a sled that his horse could pull.

"I fear this ain't gonna be a very comfortable ride," he said as he helped Breckenridge down onto the blanket.

The constant jostling caused the bleeding to start again, and by the time they reached the livery, Clay was too weak to say anything but "It's over." His voice was barely a whisper.

Price's wife, Anna, normally even more quiet and reserved than he, had assumed the role of nurse in their absence, seeing that Rayburn was made comfortable. His face had been bandaged and his ribs tightly wrapped with strips of a bedsheet. He was feeling much better by the time Jonesy and Clay returned.

"Lay him on a clean blanket and get his britches off," Anna said, "and boil some more water. I'll also need my bottle of sulfur powder and the sharpest knife you can find." She told her husband to hurry down to their cabin and get more freshly washed sheets. He was amazed at the manner in which she had taken command of the situation.

Clay was unconscious as she tenderly cleaned the blood from his wound and tightened a tourniquet above his knee. Jennie knelt next to him, holding his hand and whispering a prayer. Jonesy paced back and forth, then finally decided his best effort would be spent tending to the horses.

The pellets were numerous and deeply embedded. "I'll need some help restraining him," Anna said. "I've already looked everywhere, and Eli's got no drinking whiskey we can give him to dull the pain."

Paul had returned with an armload of sheets and a knife he used for cleaning squirrels and rabbits. He poured boiling water over the blade and handed it to his wife.

"It's good he's passed out," she said. "Let's hope he remains so."

Jonesy held one arm and Price the other. Jennie and her grandfather held Clay's feet. "If he gets to kicking," Anna said, "you might need to just sit on them."

For a half hour she carefully dug the knife into Clay's thigh, lifting out pellet after pellet and placing them on a nearby towel. Jonesy kept count. Anna had removed more than thirty when she wiped her brow and said she was done. "Might be a few more, too deep to get to, but they don't appear to have damaged any arteries," she said, "so he'll just have to carry them around with him." She used some of Eli's fishing line and a needle to stitch up several of the more jagged openings, then liberally sprinkled sulfur powder onto the wound.

After she was sure the bleeding had stopped, she bandaged Clay's leg. "All we can do now is watch to see no infection sets in." She sounded exhausted.

Jonesy positioned a saddle under the leg, then hugged Anna. "I appreciate what you done," he said. "Where did you learn how?"

"My daddy served as a nurse for the Confederate Army," she said. "He took time to teach me a few things."

"God bless him," Jennie said.

THE DANGER HAD passed, but everyone remained in the livery for several days, keeping vigil over Breckenridge. Though he was still in and out of consciousness, his color was returning, and he would occasionally ask for sips of water.

Still in pain, Rayburn had improved to the point where he could walk around, and he was getting more grouchy by the day. A good sign, Anna said.

Jonesy drove Jennie out to the farm in the buggy to tend her goats and milk cow and prepare pots of stew and vegetable soup to take back to the livery.

Several townspeople, aware of what had taken place and that safety had been restored, began visiting, bringing food and offering help. A local farmer arrived with a bottle of whiskey for Clay and Eli. "Last I got," he told them, "but looks like you boys are needing a painkiller worse than me."

One afternoon, as Jennie was cooking, Jonesy asked what her future plans were. "I don't think I got to tell you how sorry I was to hear of your daddy passing," he said. "With him gone, I'm concerned how you'll manage." He didn't mention the increasingly feeble mental state of her aged grandpa.

"At the funeral," she said, "there were some folks, Eli included, who kindly offered their help."

"What worries me," Jonesy said, "is how much help they can be and for how long. Folks got their own business to tend and people to watch over."

"I know," she said as she stirred the stew.

"And what about the mercantile? You been running it by yourself since Madge left."

The mention of Madge changed the course of the conversation.

"In all the confusion, I've not even asked about her," Jennie said.

"She's doing fine, enjoying life in Aberdene and liking being married to Clay. Of course, I ain't sure how pleased she'll be to see the shape he's in when we get back home."

Jennie laughed for the first time in days. "I know how she feels about him. Even if she gives him what for, she'll be pleased just to have him back. Before you leave, I want to pick out something nice at the store for a late wedding present."

I T WAS DAYS before there was any talk about what had happened in the canyon. Even then Jonesy approached the subject grudgingly. "What's done is done," he said. "A bad man is finally gone, and we're all the better for it."

Rayburn, however, continued to press for details. So did Paul Price, who, along with Anna, was spending more time at the livery than at the laundry.

Jonesy insisted they wait until Breckenridge was feeling up to it before they discussed the matter further.

Price mentioned that he'd spoken to the Boot Hill caretaker and the bodies of Doozy and Baggett had been taken care of. "I suggested they be burned," he said, "but they got buried instead."

Clay's healing was a slow process, even with the occasional sip of whiskey when the pain returned. Anna continued her role as nurse, changing bandages and applying sulfur powder twice daily. "I know you're feeling weak," she said, "but soon as you can, you need to stand on that leg, no matter how much it hurts. It'll keep the stiffness away and maybe prevent your having a limp once you've recovered."

Though he had little appetite, Jennie insisted that he let her spoon-feed him her soup.

Jonesy's attitude quickly turned from sympathy to relief that his friend was going to live. "You'll be running footraces before you know it," he said. "And it could be that'll come in handy once Madge learns you allowed yourself to get shot."

"When are we heading home?" Clay said.

"A while yet, according to what Nurse Price says. She and Paul are even talking of movin' you down to their place so you can have the comfort of a real bed."

Eli, overhearing, spoke up. "I think that would be a fine idea," he said. "It's getting mighty crowded here. And I got work to do."

Jonesy laughed at Rayburn's foul mood. "Condition you're in right now, you couldn't even lift a hammer. And I see you ain't been turning down any of the free cooking and attention you're getting."

Rayburn limped away without a reply. As he did so, Jonesy said, "Once you get a smile back on your face, we got us some talking to do."

That evening, after a dinner of fried rabbit and collard greens provided by one of the women of the community, the three men gathered near the doorway of the livery to catch the breeze. Jennie had taken her grandpa home, and the Prices had washing that needed tending.

"I been talking with Jennie," Jonesy said. He explained his concern for her situation. "She's stuck with that goat farm with only the promise of occasional volunteer help. Then there's the mercantile, which her grandpa ain't capable of running. And folks need it for their shopping."

Clay and Eli could see where he was headed.

"If you're asking for a vote," Rayburn said, "it ain't necessary. It's time we go visit the colonel and see he makes a contribution so Miss Broder can have proper funding to hire herself some full-time help with the farm and the store. And maybe someone to lend a hand caring for her grandpa."

Breckenridge agreed. "Not but one of us currently fit to go dig it up," he said to Jonesy, "so that'll be your responsibility."

"Where we going to tell her it come from?"

"We ain't," Clay said.

Ten days had passed since he'd been wounded, and Breckenridge was beginning to feel frustrated. Though he could walk short distances, the leg was still swollen, and the pain remained constant.

The good news, Anna told him, was that there was no sign of infection. The bad news was that it was still going to be some time before he could ride a horse.

It was midday when Jonesy appeared at the Price house and entered the room where Clay was just finishing a bowl of vegetable soup. "Got somebody here wanting to see you," he said.

Clay rolled his eyes. "I don't need more soup," he said.

As he spoke, Marshal Rankin appeared in the doorway, a wide grin on his face. "I've come to make an arrest and haul you back to Aberdene," he said. "Wasn't aware you was laid up."

Clay's mouth hung open before he was able to form a sentence. "I can't believe . . ."

Before he could finish, the marshal stepped aside,

and Madge walked into the room. Clay tried to blink away tears, but his wife didn't. She rushed to his bedside and threw her arms around him. They embraced silently for several seconds before Madge pulled back and placed her hands on Clay's face. "I had to threaten to throw a hissy fit and shoot the marshal before he finally agreed to accompany me out here," she said.

Clay turned to Rankin and mouthed the word, "Thanks."

"I've learned you're gonna live," the marshal said, "so I'll leave you two to yourselves and see if Jonesy can find me a cup of coffee."

"I got plenty of soup you're welcome to," Clay said.

Madge was asking questions faster than he could answer them. He gave her a brief recount of chasing Baggett and the gunfight that had left him injured. He told her of Jennie's father dying and assured her Eli would be back in good health soon. Anna Price, he said, had very likely saved his life with her nursing skills. "I ain't never had so much soup in my life.

"The most important thing for you to know," he said, "is that it's now over."

He then asked about things at home. Madge quickly went through the list. Everything at the farm was fine, thanks to Ruben. Sarge was wondering when he'd return. Same with Lonnie, who was back in school and doing better with long division. "He's got a dog now. Named it after his pa," she said. "Patricia's been just as worried as I have," she said, "and badly wanted to come with us. But the marshal and I convinced her that she needed to stay home and watch after Lonnie. We couldn't leave him by himself for going on three weeks."

"You need to tell Jonesy that," Clay said. "I think he's been about ready to head home without me."

She leaned forward and kissed his forehead. "Get some rest," she said. "I'm going to go talk with him.

Then, if you think it's safe now, I might ride out and say hello to Jennie."

Clay smiled. "It's safe," he said. "That's what we came out here for."

As she rode past the lot where her saloon had stood, Madge was surprised that she had no nostalgic feelings at all. Nothing about the town, aside from a few people, interested her. She now had a better life in a better place.

Jennie screamed and burst into tears when she saw Madge walking onto the porch. Even Grandpa Asa got to his feet and shuffled toward the door to greet her.

"We were talking about you just yesterday," Jennie said. "I can't tell you how much I've missed having your company."

"And I've thought about you a lot, too," Madge said. "I was so sorry when Clay told me about your daddy."

They drank lemonade and laughed, reminisced about times good and bad, and talked of how Clay might never eat another bowl of soup once he gets out of Tascosa.

Jennie admitted her future had never been so uncertain.

"One step at a time," Madge said. "That's Clay's motto—and good advice."

Two days later, Marshal Rankin announced he was ready for everybody to head back to Aberdene. "If I stay away much longer," he said, "the town's liable to turn into another lawbreaking Fort Worth."

Clay was delighted to hear the news, but apprehensive about how he'd be able to make it. The leg was still weak and bothering him considerably.

"Your friend Eli and a couple of his buddies have found a solution to that problem," Rankin said. "If you can make it up to the barn, I'll show you."

Clay hobbled his way up the slope, stopping a couple of times to briefly rest. He felt exhausted when they finally arrived. There, in the center of the room, sat Eli's wagon, freshly painted, its wheels greased. In the bed were blankets laid over a thick bed of straw. There were several feather pillows donated by local residents. "Ain't exactly the way heroes are supposed to make their return home, and you'll be facing backward all the way," the marshal said, "but you can be assured of a fairly comfortable ride."

There was one more thing left to do.

Clay summoned Madge to his bedside just as it was getting dark. "Jonesy's got a chore to attend to, and I thought you might go along and keep him company," he said.

Though puzzled, Madge agreed. Her horse was already saddled when she returned to the livery.

When they reached the entrance to Boot Hill, Jonesy handed her a torch and lit it. "I'll need you to hold this while I do my digging," he said.

"Oh, my stars. Dig what?"

Jonesy laughed into the warm night. "There'll be no dead folks dug up, I promise," he said. "The colonel's just been keeping something for us."

Despite the size of its headstone, it took Pate a few minutes to locate the grave site of the famous Basil Jay Hawthorne. Once he did, it took only a few minutes to unearth the strongbox that contained the canvas bag. He handed it to Madge. "Look inside."

The sight of so many bills and gold coins took her breath away. "So this is what it was all about," she finally said.

"For the most part, yes. Some other matters as well."

They returned to the Price house, where Clay and Eli were waiting. They quit counting after the total reached several thousand dollars. Pate and Breckenridge insisted that Rayburn take a small portion "to make up for earnings lost while being stove-up and so grouchy."

"Also, for the purchase of your wagon, since I ain't planning on bringing it back," Clay said.

Eli argued against it before reluctantly accepting. The rest went into the same saddlebags in which it had been found.

Later that night, when he was certain Jennie was asleep, Jonesy crept onto the porch of her farmhouse and left the saddlebags.

CHAPTER THIRTY-SEVEN

THE WAGON WAS hitched and loaded before Anna Price finished cooking breakfast. There was an uncomfortable finality to the meal, and there was very little conversation. Everyone, even those headed home, was feeling melancholy. Anna gave Madge last-minute instructions for tending to Clay's wounds, insisting all the while that she was confident he would be fine. Eli ate sparingly and said nothing.

Jennie arrived, carrying two boxes she'd stopped by the mercantile to get. In them were Stetson hats for Clay and Madge, belated wedding presents she said. "I hope they're the right size."

She waited until Jonesy and Eli were helping Clay settle into the wagon before she spoke again. "A miracle took place out at the farm last night," she said. She didn't elaborate further, nor did the men ask for details.

Jonesy climbed onto the driver's seat. "Never thought

about having to haul your skinny behind home," he called back to Clay.

"Just be sure you make it a smooth ride," his passenger replied.

After hugs and a basket of hot biscuits from Anna, they were off, the marshal and Madge riding alongside. "I hope never to see this place again," Clay called up to his driver.

Jonesy popped the reins to speed the horses along.

L ONNIE HAD JUST returned from school when his new dog began barking at the sound of the wagon coming down the road. Patricia stepped onto the porch to see what the commotion was about.

She watched silently for several seconds, then said, "Honey, it's them. Thank the Lord." She untied her apron and tossed it aside, then began racing Lonnie and his dog to meet the arriving caravan.

Jonesy jumped from the wagon to embrace his wife and hug Lonnie. He looked down at the black puppy, its tail wagging furiously. "Don't believe I know this little fellow," he said.

"I'm calling him Little Jeb," Lonnie said.

Patricia then looked into the bed of the wagon, where Clay lay. "Oh, my stars," she said, reaching across the side to touch his arm. Lonnie had already climbed into the wagon.

"I'm fine," Clay said. "Just getting lazy in my old age."

Madge assured them he was on the mend and would be okay. "I'm gonna see that he gets a visit from the doctor tomorrow," she said, "just to be sure."

Marshal Rankin tipped his hat and excused himself, saying he'd best be getting home. Before turning to leave, he looked at Clay and Jonesy. "Much as I've enjoyed knowing you boys, I hope it's a long spell before I see either of your faces again."

D OC FRANKLIN ARRIVED at the farm midmorning. Clay was sitting on the front porch, drinking coffee and enjoying the familiar sights and the smell of the new-day air.

The doctor carefully examined the injured leg, then asked Clay to stand and bend it. "This was a nasty invasion of your body," Franklin said. "Could have killed you if you had let it get infected. Appears to me you had good care at the proper time."

Clay told him about Anna Price and the lessons she'd learned from her father.

"It probably won't feel too good for a while, but my verdict is that you need to get yourself on a regular schedule of walking. I can send out a cane if you're not too proud to use it. I wouldn't try doing any chores in the near future. But all that said, you're healing nicely, thanks to that Anna woman."

He gave Clay a jar of ointment to apply daily.

"One day, when you're feeling up to it, I wouldn't mind hearing how you came to be injured," he said.

Clay didn't reply.

"And before I go, I wonder if I might see that horse I tended last time I was here. It was your brother's as I recall."

"He's over in the pasture," Clay said. "Not far."

"Then how about you walking down there with me?"

Clay grunted and got to his feet. He drained the remainder of his coffee into Madge's new flower bed. "Might take us some time."

"I'm in no hurry," the doctor said.

* * *

Being back home far outweighed the pains that still occasionally took his breath away. Returning to a normal life, viewing familiar sights, and sleeping in his own bed with Madge by his side were more comforting than he could have imagined. Even her constant fussing over him felt good. Sarge was never more than a few feet away, seeming to enjoy the return of a normal routine. He had assumed his spot at the foot of the bed in the evenings.

Occasionally, Clay's sleep was filled with restless dreams, always about his brother. But they were good, and he woke happy. In them, he and Cal were kids again, playing games, fishing, hunting, swimming, and always laughing. He came to look forward to nightfall and bedtime and the promise of visions of a glorious time in his life.

Lonnie stopped by every day after school. After he told Clay that the county fair was scheduled for the coming weekend, Clay limped to the barn and saddled his horse. With some difficulty, he put one foot into a stirrup and swung the injured leg over. For a few minutes, he rode around the yard, then up the road a short way. His smile soon became a quiet laugh.

On the porch, Madge stood, her arms folded across her chest, watching. Soon, she joined in the happy laughter.

"Lonnie says he's gonna run in the hundred-yard dash at the fair," he said. "I think we should plan to go in and see that."

Madge followed him to the barn and watched as he carefully dismounted and began removing the saddle. "I ain't exactly ready for rodeoing yet," he said, "but that felt mighty good."

* * *

CLAY AND MADGE were already at the fair, wearing their new Stetsons, when Jonesy and Patricia arrived. It was the first time they'd been together since the return. Jonesy eyed Clay's cane and laughed. "Good to see you up and about, old-timer."

Madge and Patricia hugged.

They stood in the shade of a tree, waiting for the footrace. Patricia had cut a pair of Lonnie's britches into short pants at his request. He was off somewhere preparing for the race, which he'd said would include the fastest runners in the county, men and boys.

Standing shoulder to shoulder, Clay and Jonesy said little as they watched the celebration going on around them. The wonderful smells of all kinds of food wafted through the air. "Bet there's not a single bowl of soup to be found," Jonesy said.

"Lord, I hope not."

Jonesy waited until the women left to find glasses of sweet tea before asking his friend how he was feeling. He was pleased to hear that Clay was again riding.

"Ain't nothing that'll heal things faster than being home," Jonesy said. Without even thinking, he rubbed the shoulder where he'd been shot. "Been a real strange experience," he said. "A while back, we first rode out for Tascosa, young and full of beans, planning on making everything in the world right. Now here we are finally back, two older men proud to be alive and standing under this shade tree."

Clay extended his hand. "Having a friend like you means a lot," he said. "I don't think I ever thanked you proper for all you done to help me."

Jonesy, unable to think of a response, just gripped Clay's hand. "If you're feeling all that obligated," he finally said, "maybe you could let me wear that hat sometime."

The mood had lightened by the time it was announced that contestants for the race should assemble. The men made their way toward where the judges were already in place at the finish line.

"I have to admit, I ain't been this nervous in a long time," Jonesy said.

Soon, they were cheering wildly. Without thinking, Clay tossed his new hat into the air. He raised his arms in celebration, letting his cane fall to the ground. Then he and Jonesy were hugging and jumping up and down.

Lonnie, now the fastest man or boy in the county, had won the race by two full strides.

EPILOGUE

Now only boot Hill remains, windblown and unkept, its leaning headstones the lonesome reminders of those who once called Tascosa home.

As they grew older, Clay and Madge rarely left the farm except for occasional visits to the Pate ranch. Ruben came to get them in the buggy and always delivered them back home before dark. Clay walked with a limp for the remainder of his life but did discard the cane. He died in his sleep at age eighty-eight, some say of grief rather than of poor health. Madge had passed away a year earlier when she fell from a ladder while trying to mend the roof of the henhouse.

Though they never had children of their own, they delighted in sharing Lonnie with the Pates. He was regularly invited for supper and often rode Maizy over to spend weekends doing chores Clay was no longer able to.

Clay and Madge were buried on the farm, next to Clay's parents and brother. Years earlier, when old age had finally claimed Sarge, he was afforded a resting place at the foot of Cal's grave.

Jonesy Pate lived to be almost a hundred, though his final years were spent staring out the window of an old folks' home, because he was no longer aware of what was going on in the world around him. Like Clay, he'd lost his wife several years earlier when Patricia contracted pneumonia.

Long before their deaths, they had visited an Aberdene lawyer and officially adopted Lonnie.

In time, they were all gone. Marshal Dodge Rankin, long retired, had a heart attack one evening while sitting on his back porch, smoking his beloved pipe. Doc Franklin retired after a young doctor from back East arrived in Aberdene and agreed to take up his various practices. He was later killed in a hunting accident.

Eli was shoeing a horse when it kicked him in the head. He lingered in a coma for several days, then died.

After finishing school, Lonnie married Ginger Dudley, the butcher's daughter, and together they kept the Pate ranch going. Ginger later gave birth to twins, a boy and a girl. At Lonnie's request, they were named Nester and Cora, after the Callaways, who had lovingly cared for him back when Breckenridge and Pate first traveled to Tascosa.

For a time, Lonnie studied mail-order courses in hopes of one day becoming an author. After the rejection of several short stories by a New York editor, he gave up on the idea of writing fiction and took a job as editor of the weekly *Aberdene Record*.

And for five years straight, he held the title of Fastest Man in Grayson County.

ACKNOWLEDGMENTS

Many thanks for the opportunity to Berkley editors Tom Colgan, Jennifer Snyder, and Rebecca Brewer. Having friends Jeff Guinn and James Ward Lee, and the lady of the house, Pat Stowers, read along provided much appreciated help. Encouragement and counsel from agent Jim Donovan also lit the trail.

Ready to find
your next great read?

Let us help.

Visit prh.com/nextread

Penguin
Random
House